Jett Landry: The Fuse

Volume I of the Jett Landry Saga

By Stephan Oak

Cover art by Micky Mitchell

February 2020

This is a work of fiction. Names, characters, businesses, places, events, locales, and incidents are either the products of the author's imagination or used in a fictitious manner. Any resemblance to actual persons, living or dead, or actual events is purely coincidental.

Author: Stephan Oak
Illustrator: Micky Mitchell

Acknowledgments

The author would like to thank the following people for their assistance, creativity, encouragement, time, effort, and support in the development of this project:

Micky Mitchell, Theresa Ener, Kimberly Parker, Waverly Wagstaff, Toye Babb, Shanon Chambers Shaw, Sharae Sass, Marla Singleton, and a cat named Jett. Most of all, the author would like to thank you, the person reading this book.

Table of Contents

Prologue: The Fuse

There I was, at this joint on the south side of town. It was a hot, sticky night, and all I wanted was a break from the heat... and to be left alone. The bartender just looked at me, so I said, "Give me a whiskey and Coke, hold the Coke, make it a double and keep 'em coming." I had a lot of thinking to do, and tonight wasn't the night to do it. The bartender grunted, turned around, poured whiskey in a glass, and set it in front of me. There's an art to ordering a drink; if I don't get anything else right in this life, at least I got that.

That's when she walked in. Dark hair, dark eyes, dark skin with long legs and nails. She was beautiful. I was hooked and there was no turning back. But I didn't let on. I kept my hands on my drink and my thoughts to myself. I held my breath even though her sweet, sultry scent filled my nostrils and swirled around in my brain.

The bar was empty, but she took the seat next to mine. She fumbled around in her purse, took out a cigarette, and put it between her lips. She leaned over and touched my arm. Electricity pulsed through my body and lit a fire in my gut. I turned to find her staring into my eyes. "What's a girl got to do to get a light in this place?" she asked. Without taking my eyes off her, I pulled out my lighter and flicked it alive. But I hesitated... because sometimes you're lighting a cigarette, and sometimes you're lighting a fuse.

Chapter One: Port City High

Fourteen Years Later

Mike, his girlfriend, and two other boys walked down the hall towards the small girl. Her heart sped up as they approached. As they passed, Mike sneered and knocked the books out of her hands. Her books hit the ground and scattered. She stopped to pick them up as Mike kicked one of her books out of her reach.

"Come on Jett, get the books. You're making a mess, half-breed," he said, laughing at the girl. His girlfriend, Angelique, rolled her eyes. Mike dropped one of his books on the ground. Jett looked up at him, annoyed.

"Pick it up!" Mike ordered. "Pick it up now, Balti-whore!" He called Jett 'Balti-whore' because, after her mother died, she moved to Texas from Baltimore to live with her dad. She didn't know her dad until she moved to Texas.

"I'm getting my books, Mike," Jett said. "Get your own book."

"Listen, half-breed, pick up my damn book or I swear I'll kick you in the face!"

"Mike," Angelique said, "you're being kind of a dick."

Jett grabbed his book and handed it to him. It was easier to give in than it was to argue about it.

"There, thank you. That's not so hard," Mike said to Jett. He turned to Angelique. "You gotta know how to talk to 'em. Let them know who's the boss. They'll fall in line. Half-breeds are like that."

Jett exhaled in frustration and rolled her bright, blue eyes. Years of bullying from the same kids had worn her down.

"Did you make a face at me? Bitch." Mike said. "Go ahead, make all the faces you want. Nobody likes you. You're nobody and you don't belong here. No one wants you around. So, pick up your damn books and get out of my sight."

As Jett finished picking up her books Mike knocked them out of her hands again. "Damn. You can't even get that right. Nobody cares about you!"

It was always personal with Mike. He was relentless in his bullying and because she was biracial, Jett was a target. He wasn't subtle about his racist tendencies. This had gone on since Jett first started school with these kids four years ago. They would bully her and threaten any kids who attempted to be friends with her. Jett felt isolated and spent most of her time alone.

"Dude let it go. Come on, let's get to class," one of Mike's friends said. "You've messed with her enough."

"She deserves it." Mike walked off with his friends. Jett continued down the hall, anxiously clutching her books to her chest and trying not to cry. The other kids looked at her sympathetically but said nothing.

At lunch, Jett sat by herself. This wasn't unusual for Jett. At school, all she cared about was her grades. She tried to avoid everything else.

After her last class, she put her backpack on her back and walked towards the exit where her ride would be waiting. She almost made it to the door when she felt someone grab her backpack and pull her backward.

"Whoa, almost made it, half-breed. But you dropped your stuff again," she heard a boy say as he threw her backpack on the floor. It was one of Mike's friends.

Jett felt tired and frustrated. "I'm not a half-breed. I'm black. My dad is white, and my mom is black. You can call me biracial or brown if it makes you feel better. But I'm not a half-breed. I'm not any kind of breed."

"Well you're not purebred, that's for sure," Mike said as he joined his friend. "Black, brown, biracial, whatever. Your dad's a piece of shit."

"Don't talk about my dad. He doesn't take crap off anyone."

"Well, apparently you didn't inherit that gene. Wait. Are you sure he's your dad? I've heard about your kind. Hardly ever know who your dads are. Your dad is a traitor. You're a half-breed, an animal." Mike got angrier as he spoke.

One of his friends intervened. "Come on man. Let's get to football practice." The two boys walked off. Jett noticed other kids were watching. She felt humiliated by the bullying.

Jett held back tears as she walked outside. Ashley Garcia, her dad's partner, was waiting to give her a ride to their office. She didn't want Ashley to see her cry. She took a deep breath and got in the car without saying a word.

"Hey little Chica," Ashley said. "What's wrong?" Ashley had a very slight Cuban accent. Being Afro-Latina, she was born in Miami, but her mother was Cuban. Her father was from the Dominican Republic.

Jett thought about what happened today, about how Ashley wouldn't let any boys push her around, and about how she wished she could be more like Ashley. Today would have been a good day to be more like Ashley, she thought to herself.

"Nothing."

"Okay, let me know if I need to kick someone's ass for you."

Jett was quiet as they drove to her dad's office. The office was in a five-story building on the older side of downtown. Other buildings framed their building, each with several businesses, covering several city blocks. There was a law firm, a used clothing shop, a newspaper/magazine shop, and a sandwich shop. In her dad's building, there were office suites on the first three floors. Her dad's business and a family law practice occupied the fourth floor. The fifth floor was a flat her dad rented as a residence. Jett and her dad lived in the flat.

Jett still hadn't said a word to Ashley when they arrived. She knew if she started talking, she would start crying. Jett got her backpack and rushed to the elevator. The ride up the elevator was quiet. When she stepped off the elevator, she crossed the hall to the door marked 'Investigative Associates,' and burst into the office suite, hurrying past her dad and going straight to the conference room.

Jett's dad was Markus Jackson, well known Private Investigator. Not famous or well-liked, but well known. He knew everybody's secrets, and he wasn't afraid to use them for leverage. He had a habit of going after Port City's elite, and they hated him for it.

"Hey, kid! How was your day? Hey!" her dad tried to say as she rushed by him. He set his coffee mug on the reception desk and looked at Ashley. Jett walked into the conference room, slung her backpack to the floor, and slammed the door behind her.

"She was so quiet on the way home. Something happened that upset her," Ashley said, "but she won't talk about it."

"Ok. Let me go see what's going on." He followed her into the conference room and observed her for a moment. Jett was sitting at the conference table with her head in her hands, crying. She tried to stifle the tears when she saw him, but it was too late. He walked across the room and started to put his arm around her shoulders to comfort her.

"No. I don't want a hug. If you hug me, I will start bawling again."

"Okay. I can respect that. What's wrong, kid?"

"I hate that f-; I hate that school. I f- Ugh!"

"Just say what you want to say, kid."

"Dad..." Jett said irritably.

"What's wrong, Jett?" her dad asked, concerned.

"I HATE THAT SCHOOL!!!!"

"What happened at school?"

Jett's dad sat down in the chair next to her. She turned her chair to face him. "I hate it. The kids are terrible. I'm always alone. I don't have any friends. I get picked on and bullied all the time. I'm a nobody."

Jett's dad furrowed his brow as she told him her plight. He never understood why Jett had a hard time making friends. She was friendly, polite and one of the smartest kids in school. She wasn't an ugly kid. Her skin was light brown, somewhat lighter than her mother's skin, and she inherited his bright blue eyes. Her hair was fashionable; she wore it past her shoulders, and she kept it natural and curly, like many biracial women did their hair, as far as he knew. Ashley took her to get her hair styled, and he figured she knew what she was doing in advising the kid how to wear her hair. Ashley also took her shopping for clothes, but Jett usually wore jeans, sneakers, old tee shirts, and hoodies to school. He knew nothing about teenage style, but she didn't look awkward. He figured maybe she was a loner like he was when he was a kid; except he still had friends to hang out with, smoke weed with, and do all the other things teenage boys his age did when he was young and stupid. He was glad she didn't have those kinds of friends. Jett wasn't stupid like he was, and he was grateful for this.

"Bullied? Who is bullying you?"

"A group of boys. One named Mike Krayton. He's a year older; calls me half-breed, animal, mongrel, and a lot of other ugly, racist names. He pushes me, tells me no one likes me, and knocks my books out of my arms. His friends just go along with it."

“The Krayton boy? His dad’s an asshole too. Have you talked to the teachers or principal?”

“And be a snitch? Everyone already hates me.”

“Then you got nothing to lose.”

“They act like it doesn’t happen. They try not to look.”

“The other kids don’t talk to you?”

“They try, but I’m always so nervous about what Mike will do that I don’t know how to act. And, if he sees other kids talking to me, he will threaten them too. He hates me. He’s racist.”

“How long has this been going on?” Markus, her dad, asked.

“Since Texas dad. Since Texas.”

Her dad looked at her, surprised. “This has been going on all this time and you haven’t said anything?”

“I didn’t want to look weak. I figured I could deal with it. Or it would change. Or something.”

“Look weak? If you got a problem, you solve it. If you can’t solve it, you come to me and I help you solve it. What’s this looking weak thing?”

“I guess it’s because you and Ashley always know what to do. I didn’t want to disappoint you.”

“We always know what to do? That’s crazy talk. We’re always winging it. You kept this from me?”

“Yes.” Jett started crying again.

"We're your family. You tell us everything. That's the whole point of having a family, kid."

Jett looked down a moment, and up again. "I just don't know what to do to make it stop."

"I've never had to deal with racism before. Let's get Ashley in here, I'm sure she's dealt with this. Ashley!"

Ashley walked into the room and approached Jett. "What's wrong, Chica?" she asked.

"Jett's being bullied by a group of kids and they've isolated her from the others. But the worst of it is the main kid is racist. It's Krayton's son; big surprise."

Jett started crying again and Ashley approached her and put her arms around her from behind her chair and held her a moment. "It hurts. I know. But you have to have courage and dignity."

"But how?" Jett asked. "I'm just so nervous all the time. Nothing works."

"Kid, the world is a shitty place with shitty people. It's never going to change. No matter what you do or where you go, you're going to run into this. It will be hard for you sometimes, and you're not always going to be treated fairly. That's just reality."

Jett looked up at her dad, confused. "You're not making me feel any better."

"I'm not trying to make you feel better. It's not my responsibility to make you feel better about how shitty people can be towards you. It's my responsibility to prepare you for it."

"How? They won't stop. They just keep doing it and nothing makes them stop." Jett was whining now.

"No, they won't. But you can't let that get in your way anymore. It's time for a change."

Jett looked at him. "If they won't stop, what's the point? It's hopeless."

Markus looked back at her, stood up, and said, "Stand up."

"What?"

"Stand up. Now. Do it."

Jett stood up and wiped the tears from her eyes.

"They don't like you either Dad, just so you know. He hates you because of me," Jett said.

"Good. I'm glad. If the bad guys hate you, then you're doing something right. Anyway, this guy, and his friends, they're assholes. I don't care why, or how they got that way. Not our problem. I'm not a therapist. They can figure it out for themselves."

"He's racist dad," Jett said.

"Okay, he's a racist asshole. Anyway, we don't give people like that any more time or attention than we think they deserve. If my goal is to get from point A to point B, I'm not gonna let some racist asshole distract me. My goals are a lot more important than something some racist asshole has to say. So, I'm going to stay focused on my goal. Screw that racist asshole."

"Dad! It's weird hearing you say that."

"Well, you're going to say it next. And you're going to mean it. Say 'screw those racist assholes.'"

"Dad, I don't wanna."

"SAY IT! I'm your father and I know what's best."

"Ok, s-screw those racist assholes?"

"Say it like you mean it."

"Screw those racist assholes."

Ashley interjected, "are you sure you should encourage the use of those words?"

He ignored her and said, "Say it again. With attitude."

"Screw those racist assholes."

"Hold your head up when you say it. Stand up straight. Don't act so defeated."

Jett straightened up her posture and said, with more emotion, "Screw those racist assholes!"

"Good. Now you have some attitude. You need it to deal with bullies. Give them confidence and attitude. They won't know how to react."

Ashley interjected again, "What if they react by getting violent? What if he decides he is going to put his hands on her?"

"If a boy puts his hands on you without your permission, you have MY permission to hit him in the mouth as hard as you can. I don't want you to start a fight, but you have every right to defend yourself."

Ashley interjected again, "Are you sure?"

"She's my kid. She'll know how to throw a punch. Trust me." To Jett, he said, "Don't walk around looking scared. Stand up straight, keep your head up, look people in the eyes when you talk to them. Say what you mean and mean what you say. Once you decide you need to defend yourself from some boy trying to hurt you, don't second guess yourself. Commit to it and follow through. If you're gonna do it, do it. We'll deal with the consequences later."

"How do I throw a punch? I don't think that kind of knowledge is inherited."

"Ok. Start with your feet. You need a solid foundation. Now, make a fist, and when you punch, get there by the shortest route. Now, understand, this is the last resort thing you do when someone is trying to hurt you or about to hurt you. You will not start a fight. You will only defend yourself. Understood?"

"Understood," Jett said.

Jett and her dad worked on throwing punches, with Jett punching him in the palm of his hand. As her form improved, and she punched harder, her dad reminded her of what she needed to think to herself when she comes across these guys. Jett would repeat her catchphrase and throw the punch.

“Dad,” she said between punches, “can’t you just go to school and talk to the principal?”

“I can, but it won’t help. The principal will make some excuse; talk about some stupid anti-bullying program, and those assholes will just wait until no one is looking to do something. Sooner or later you’re going to have to figure out how to deal with them.”

Jett kept punching.

“Now, here’s the deal. I don’t want you to hit anyone. I don’t even want you to talk to those kids. Just say our little catchphrase to yourself, in your mind, and keep on going to point B. Ignore those racist assholes. Ok?”

“I’ll try,” Jett said.

“No, don’t try, do it!”

“Ok,” Jett said, exasperated.

***

Later, in the evening, when Jett was in her room with her tablet, she looked up karate punches on YouTube. She found something similar to what her dad taught her. She also learned a combination of punching in the face, slamming her knee in the crotch, and using the person’s momentum to get them to the ground. Jett acted out the moves quietly in her room. She didn’t want to have to do anything, but if she had to, she decided she would be ready.

Jett practiced her moves every night until they became automatic. She did not understand how this would work in a real fight, but she finally felt a little confidence.

***

Two weeks later, Jett was at her locker, getting ready for her third-period class. She collected her books and started her walk to class. Mike passed her in the hallway and bumped her, knocking her books out of her hands as he went by.

"Asshole," muttered Jett.

The boy stopped, turned around, and said, "What did you just say, you little bitch?"

"Asshole. I said Asshole, referring to you. Because you're an asshole," Jett said back. Her heart pounded in her chest and she took a deep breath as she waited for him to respond.

"Shut up, Balti-whore," Mike turned around to walk away.

"No, you shut up, whore," Jett said to his back. It was quiet in the hall as the other kids stopped to watch.

"What did you just say, bitch?" He turned and walked back to Jett.

"I'm sorry. You really are stupid. My mistake. First, I called you an asshole and I told YOU off. And I called you a whore. Any questions?"

"I don't think you know what you're saying. I should just kick your ass. And I don't care if you're a girl. No one, especially a little bitch like you, talks to me like that. No one. Got it, half-breed?"

"I'm not scared of you," Jett said without reservation.

"What?"

"I'm not scared of you. All these kids here, they're scared of you. Me, I'm not. You don't scare me. You're stupid and weak."

"I suppose you can back that up."

"Why?"

"Because I'm gonna kick your ass if you don't shut up."

"Kick my ass? Didn't you get your ass kicked enough already, Friday night, at the game?" The other kids chuckled at her response, which only made Mike angrier. Mike was the quarterback of the football team. The team had been winless for two seasons.

"Look, Jett," another boy walked up beside her. "Don't start this. He'll fight you, and it'll be bad for you if he does. Just, back off. Walk away."

Jett ignored the interloper and looked directly at Mike. "I'm not scared of you. You're stupid and weak. You're all talk. You're nothing to fear."

Mike stood there, confused. First off, no kid talked to him like this; second, this was a girl talking to him like this. He had to do something.

"Shut the hell up," was all he could muster.

"I'm not scared of you. Or your friends. And I'm tired of you messing with me."

"Shut up!" he said louder.

"I'm not scared of you," she said.

"SHUT THE HELL UP!"

"I'm not scared of you."

Mike moved even closer to Jett, chest out, face red, doing his best to intimidate the girl. "SHUT UP OR GET YOUR ASS KICKED!"

She calmly stared him down. "I'm not scared of you."

Mike put his hand on her chest and started to push her backward. She stood her ground and leaned forward, with her legs set. "Get your hands off of me now."

"SHUT UP," the boy said.

"If you don't get your hands off of me by the time I count to three-"

"Or what?" the boy challenged her.

"One," she said, and punched him hard in the mouth, putting all her weight and momentum into it. Before he could react, she kneed him hard in the crotch. The boy lurched forward in pain. She grabbed his shirt and used his momentum to sling him to the ground. When he hit the ground, the other boy jumped in, to defend his friend. She turned and punched him in the mouth. He fell backward, in shock, and landed against the lockers. A random locker door swung open and hit him in the face as he stood there, stunned.

She jumped on Mike, who was still on the ground. She hit him in the face and chest as the other kids looked on, surprised, "Listen up assholes," she said to Mike's friends, who were in shock, seeing the small girl beat up their friend, "the next time one of you assholes thinks about messing with me, remember what I did to your little friend's face here. And that goes for messing with any of the kids in this school that you've been messing with."

She stood up as school security arrived, shocked at what they were seeing.

"Did you do this?" one of the security officers asked her.

"He started it," Jett said, as they escorted her to the principal's office.

***

"Why are we here?" Markus Jackson asked as they sat in thc principal's office, waiting for their meeting.

"You told me I can defend myself if someone else starts it. He started it, I defended myself. Simple."

"I didn't tell you to get in a fight. I told you to have a little attitude."

"I did. But that led to me getting in a fight. I just told him I wasn't scared of him."

"And how did that lead to getting into a fight?"

Mr. Preston, the principal, walked into the office, looked at Jett, shook his head, and sat down. Before he could start, Markus spoke up. “I know we’re here because my daughter got into a fight, but we both know she isn’t the one that started it. She gets picked on all the time, and it’s always the same kids doing the bullying. At least my kid has the guts to stand up to them. Why is she the one having to get punished?”

Jett smiled at her dad and looked at the principal. He was a tall, stocky man with a bald head and a mustache. Without saying a word, he handed her dad a printout of an email. It was from Jett’s third-period math teacher, who saw the fight and called security. Her dad read it and looked back at the principal.

“So, this other kid; is he okay?”

The principal handed him another printout. “This one is from the nurse.”

***

They suspended Jett for three days for fighting.

“I don’t understand why I’m punished. HE started it. HE put his hands on me. YOU told me no boy can touch me without my permission. HE didn’t have permission. HE pushed me. Why am I punished?” Jett said as her dad drove her to his office.

“You’re right. No boy should touch you without permission. You can defend yourself. That’s not the problem.”

“What did I do wrong? He pushed me, and I kicked his ass.”

"It's because you didn't know when to quit. You defended yourself, you held your own. But you kept going. You need to stop when you're ahead."

"Stop? I want them to stop picking on me. I just want them to leave me alone. And leave the other kids alone. It's not too much to ask."

"Well, you need to learn when to stop. You went too far."

"How did I go too far?"

"You just did. Once you had him on the ground, you should have stopped. Look. I'm sorry. Yes, I hate that those kids pick on you. But you're going to get expelled if you keep doing this."

"I don't know. They have to stop picking on me. I'm not going to let them push me around anymore. It's not fair and I'm literally the ONLY person willing to do something about it. They think because they are on the football team, they can do what they want. And the school lets them. All the time. They are older than me and the kids they pick on. It's not right."

"I get it, Jett. I know. Where did you learn to fight like that? I only taught you how to throw a punch. Where did you learn the rest?"

"The internet, where I learn everything else. I just looked up karate moves and practiced them until I got them down. I decided to use the first three moves I knew before he had a chance to make a move. It wasn't hard at all."

"Do you need more to do? Do you want to try a sport or something?"

"Sports? No. That means I have to be on a team... with... people... no way. It's not my thing. I don't like people."

"You're a people too. It worries me that you don't have friends. Maybe joining a team would be a good way to make more friends?"

"NO. Out of the question. I have no friends because I don't need to be popular. People who are nice to me, I can be friends with them. But I can be by myself too. It doesn't bother me."

"What am I gonna do with you, kid? Three days' suspension. I have to work. What are we going to do?"

"I don't know. I can stay at home while you're at work."

"No."

"Then what?"

"You're coming to work with me, like during summer break."

***

When they got to the office, Jett ran ahead to greet Ashley.

"Hey, Chica! What are you doing here? Give me a hug." Ashely opened her arms.

"You know I don't like hugging," Jett said.

"Shush, you like hugging me." Ashley put her arm around the girl's shoulder, as a compromise. Jett responded by putting her arm around her waist. “Now, what are you doing here on a school day?”

“I got in trouble for fighting. Three days' suspension.”

“Those boys pushing you around still?”

“Not anymore,” Jett shrugged.

“That’s my girl. Don’t let those boys push you around.”

“Show her the email from your teacher. You need to see what ‘your girl’ did today,” her dad said.

Jett handed her the printout of the email.

Ashley took the email and read it to herself, making faces of approval and disapproval as she read.

“You said all that to those boys? And you beat one of them up?” she asked.

“Yes,” Jett replied. Her dad finished pouring a cup of coffee and waited to see how Ashley would respond.

“Hmm, you are definitely your dad’s child.” Ashley raised her eyebrows as she spoke.

“Alright, that’s enough of this talk. Right now, I have to get to work. Could you put her to work while she’s here? No goofing off.”

“I have an idea. Since your daughter is getting picked on by those kids, and she seems to be pretty good in a fight, why don’t you enroll her in karate or something?”

“Yes!!!! Please!!!!!!” Jett said, excited.

"Karate? I think she knows how to fight. Do you really think she needs to get better at it?"

"Well, it's a sport, and they have tournaments. She'll learn some discipline; I think they teach self-control too."

"Please???? You asked if I wanted to do sports. It's a sport, I would love to learn how to do karate."

"Come on. I'll even bring her to the lessons. It'll be fun," Ashley said.

"I swear, you two plan this stuff. Ok, on one condition. You work hard, and practice and you DO NOT use this at school unless you have to. You got some respect today, no doubt. But don't press it. From now on, stay away from and ignore those kids who push you around. No matter what they say, you just walk away. You made your point, and you don't have anything to prove now. They know what you can do. If you can do that, I'll let you do karate. If you start picking fights with these guys, then no more karate. Got it, kid?"

"Yes, sir. Thanks! What if they try to hit me first?"

"You hit them back. Hard. But otherwise, don't start trouble you don't need."

"You can use my tablet to look up karate schools. We'll find a really good one for you," Ashley said.

"Work, she's supposed to work today."

"Whatever. You have a job waiting for you in the field. You may want to get going before you lose your window. We'll be fine." She looked at Jett and winked.

Chapter Two: Everyone Hates A Bully

Jett sat in the cafeteria eating her lunch. It had been four weeks since the fight with Mike. Across from her was another kid, a girl she talked to sometimes. Jett had just taken a bite of her sandwich when she felt an arm around her throat, pulling her backward. Thinking quickly, she spat the bread out as she was pulled violently to the ground. Her assailant dragged her across the floor by her neck. Kids scattered as they careened into tables and knocked over chairs. In a panic, Jett tried to grab anything she could, but she wasn't successful. She had just started karate lessons, but all she had been working on so far was breathing and stretching.

"Choke her out, Billy! Do it! Make her pass out!" she heard another kid yell. The boy, Billy, stopped dragging her and put even more pressure on her throat. In a moment of clarity, Jett stopped panicking and went limp, pretending to pass out. The boy relaxed his arm-lock on her neck. Jett took a deep breath and stomped on his foot with her heel as she exhaled. She grabbed his arm and, while bending forward, pulled it down. The momentum shift caused both kids to fall forward and to the floor. Billy let go of her neck as they hit the floor and Jett started to get up as Mike jumped on her and pushed her back down.

"Kick her in the face, Billy! Kick her!" the boy yelled, pinning her arms behind her as Billy started getting back to his feet. Kids crowded around to watch the fight. Amidst all the confusion, no one saw the chair slide a few feet and hit Billy on his head and shoulder. The chair slid the opposite way, barely missing Jett and hitting Mike in the face. He yelled, releasing his grip on Jett as she scrambled forward, grabbed the chair, and struggled to her feet. Jett stood up with the chair in her hands, confronting the two boys who were still on the ground. Jett's heart was pounding, and she was gasping for oxygen, unsure of what happened.

Security staff and a teacher, Ms. Henderson, rushed to the scene. Jett screamed

"SHIT!!!!" in fear and anger.

"Step away from the chair, NOW," the first security officer said to Jett. She dropped the chair, put her hands up, and stepped away. The officer moved towards her, but Ms. Henderson intervened, purposefully positioning herself between Jett and the security officer. Ms. Henderson was a younger teacher who often looked out for Jett. With her long red hair and slim build, she was very attractive. She was also tough.

"Leave her alone!" she said through gritted teeth to the security officer who approached Jett with handcuffs. "You will not treat this child like a criminal."

"She attacked those boys with a chair," the first officer said, as the other officer kneeled to inspect the boys' wounds.

Jett, still breathing hard, started to cry. She sobbed out loud and buried her face in her hands, shaking from the trauma of the assault. Ms. Henderson hugged her and said, "I know, honey. I know."

"We're going to take her to the office and decide if we're calling the police or not. There was no reason to hit those boys with a chair," the security officer said.

Jett's crying escalated, and she began to shake all over. She was overwhelmed with rage, anxiety, and fear.

"I'll take her to the office and call her parents. I saw what happened. This one attacked her from behind and that one tackled her and yelled for the first one, Billy, to kick her in the face while he restrained her." Ms. Henderson said.

Billy was stunned. Truthfully, he didn't know how Jett could have thrown the chair; Mike had her arms pinned behind her and he never saw her get free of the restraint. He didn't know what to say, so he opted to say nothing. Mike also didn't know how she could have thrown the chair, but he saw an opportunity. "I want to press charges for assault, with a weapon. My dad's a lawyer. I know my rights."

The security guard looked at both Ms. Henderson and the boy. "Ok. Get her to the office, and let's figure out where we're going next."

Ms. Henderson ignored the security officer and said to Jett, "Let's go to the office and call your dad so we can get this sorted out, ok?"

Jett, face streaked with tears, nodded and wiped her eyes with her hand. "Okay," and I didn't throw the chair. I don't know what happened."

***

Markus and Ashley were directed to the conference room as soon as they arrived. Jett was already in the room with Ms. Henderson, the security officer, and another student. The security officer was interrupting the other student by asking her if she saw Jett with the chair, while she tried to explain what she saw.

Ashley rushed over to Jett and put her arms around her and held her close. Jett started crying all over again, sobbing into Ashley's neck. Her dad put his hand on her shoulder and said, "Are you ok?" Jett nodded and released herself from Ashley to hug her dad. He put his arms around her and said nothing. When Jett pulled away, he looked at her and said, "What happened? Did they hurt you?"

"They want to call the police on me. But I didn't star-"

"She attacked two boys with a chair, sir," the security officer interrupted.

The other girl said, with urgency, "That's not what happened at all!"

"You saw her with the chair," the guard said.

"Who the hell are you and why were you berating this kid?" Markus said to the officer, referring to the other student in the room. He figured Ms. Henderson could stand up for herself. He wasn't wrong.

"I'm the security officer who intervened when the fight started. And I..."

"Okay. I want to know what Jett has to say; what this girl here, what's your name?"

"Melinda, sir," the girl said.

"And what Melinda has to say, and what Ms. Henderson has to say about what happened; without you interrupting to tell people what you want them to say. Got it, security officer?"

"Yes sir, but I know what happened."

"Fine, you can wait, though. Jett, what happened?"

Ashley prompted Jett to sit down and took the girl's hand to steady it. "I've never seen her like this before. She's trembling."

"What happened kid?" he said, his tone softer.

"I was eating lunch and this kid, Billy, grabbed me from behind. He pulled me out of my chair by my neck. I couldn't breathe, and everyone was yelling, and someone was yelling at him to choke me and I panicked. I guess I flipped him. But Mike tackled me and pinned my arms behind me while I was on the ground. He was yelling at Billy to kick me in the face. I couldn't have grabbed the chair because he had my arms. I don't know what happened, but suddenly Billy got hit with the chair, then someone threw the chair over my shoulder and it hit Mike. He let go, so I got up, grabbed the chair, and was just holding it when Ms. Henderson and School Security got there." Jett started breathing fast and crying again as she finished her account of what happened.

"And you?" her dad said to the girl, Melinda.

"That's what happened. I was sitting at the table when Billy attacked her, just like she said. She didn't throw the chair. She couldn't have because Mike had her arms behind her."

"Who threw the chair?"

"I don't know. It happened fast. One moment Mike had her arms and was yelling at Billy to kick her in the face. I closed my eyes because I didn't want to see it and next thing, I opened them, and the chair was flying at Billy, while Mike was still holding her arms. I don't know."

"Ms. Henderson. What did you see?"

"I saw the same thing. The first boy grabbed her from behind, she struggled with him while the other boy egged him on. I called for security. At that point, I saw the other boy having her pinned right as the chair hit the first one."

"My point, SIR," the security officer said, annoyed with the accounts he was hearing, "is that she could have gotten loose when they weren't looking and thrown the chair at the first kid right as the other kid grabbed her again. They wouldn't know because they didn't see that part of the fight."

"Did you see that part of the fight?" Markus asked.

"No. But I saw her threatening those boys with a chair when I got there."

"So, you didn't see her throw the chair. And you didn't see her throw it when you got there?"

Melinda stood up. "She put it down as soon as they got there. She was never going to throw it."

"Ok, so what we have is two people who saw this boy, Billy, attack my daughter from behind, and another boy tackled her and attempted to hold her, so the first boy could hit her when she was defenseless. No one saw her throw the chair, and she put it down as soon as you got there. And you're going to call the police on her? I bet there are a lot of kids watching the fight who can corroborate what we've heard so far. Did you interview all of them too? Or are you going to keep going on about what they didn't see instead of what they did? I want to talk to this Billy kid now. Where is he?"

"He's with his dad in an office across the hall," Melinda said.

"His dad is there, good. I think he needs to hear what happened. Jett, come on, let's get this worked out."

"I don't want to see him. I don't want to see either one of them." Jett said, shaking.

"I don't want to see them either, but what we want and what we need are two different things. Let's go."

"Okay, but..." Jett started to say something else but changed her mind.

"Let's get you cleaned up first, and we'll meet them in the room," Ashley said.

"Sir," Melinda raised her hand.

"Yea, kid?" he said.

"There's more. Another kid said she overheard Mike offering Billy one hundred dollars to put Jett in a chokehold until she passed out. I believe it. I hate those guys."

"Really? Thanks for the info. Did you get that Security Officer? Interesting case you have here. Sorry, it takes me to work it for you."

Without waiting for a response, he turned, left the room, and went across the hall.

Billy's dad was not pleased. Billy was a short, stocky boy who looked like he could hold his own in a fight. Both he and his dad dressed in jeans, boots, and flannel shirts. As soon as he walked in, Billy's dad rose and approached him, with his hand out and a look of concern on his face.

"Sir, are you the father of the young lady my boy attacked? I sincerely apologize for the behavior of my son. I promise you we did not raise him to attack girls or treat girls with any kind of disrespect. I feel downright sick about what happened. Is your girl okay?"

"She's shaken up, but she's fine. I appreciate your apology," Markus said.

"It's the least I can do. If you want to whoop my boy, I'll stand aside and let you have at it. He'll get another one from me when we get home. Again, I'm sick about this. I never thought any of my boys would ever act this way. I don't blame your girl for hitting him with a chair. Like I told him, she has a right to defend herself, and having two boys attack a girl she needs to just do what she needs to do."

"Oh, I'm not gonna whoop anyone, but I trust you'll handle it. Billy, what happened? Why did you do it?"

"Sit up, look him in the eyes and answer him, boy," Billy's dad said.

"I'm sorry, sir. It was a mistake," Billy said, sounding frightened.

“Answer his question. Why did you do this, boy?” his dad said, getting louder as he spoke.

“I know why he did it,” Jett said as she walked into the room. This time she was with Melinda. Ashley walked in behind the girls. “If you check his pockets, Billy has one hundred dollars on him. Maybe he can explain where he got the hundred dollars.”

“Boy, why in the hell do you have a hundred dollars?”

“Mike offered him one hundred dollars to choke Jett,” Melinda said. “Another girl heard it. Ms. Henderson is going to get her right now to tell us about it.”

“Empty your pockets boy,” his dad said, with an angry snarl.

Billy started to refuse, but he thought better of it and took five twenty-dollar bills out of his pocket and showed them to his dad.

“To choke a girl? Boy, are you out of your damn mind?”

“Yes, sir. It was stupid. Mike kind of talked me into it. Just until she passed out. Said it wasn’t a big deal.”

“Are you that dense? Not a big deal? Boy. You are asking for the biggest ass-whoopin' of all time. I’m gonna take all day with this one. I’m gonna take a day off work for this.”

Ashley gasped. “These kids are just awful.”

After a long, quiet pause, Billy’s dad spoke up. “Give the girl the one hundred dollars and tell her you’re sorry. And tell her that you’re gonna work all summer and every dollar you make is going to her to pay for any doctor appointments, or anything else, like counseling or even shopping, or whatever she needs to get over what you and this other boy did today."

"Yes sir," the boy reluctantly stood up and approached Jett. "Here's the money. I'm sorry I tried to choke you. It was wrong."

Jett put her hand out to take the money. "Thanks for the money."

"Okay," Markus said. "Now I want to talk to this other boy. Where is he?"

***

Mike and his dad were sitting in yet another room, but Mike's dad wasn't as conciliatory as Billy's dad.

"Is this the girl who assaulted you with a chair? Is this her?" his dad said as Jett, her dad and Ashley entered the room.

"I didn't hit him with the chair. He's lying."

Markus Jackson stopped and eyed Mike's dad. Michael Krayton Sr. The two stared each other down. They were already adversaries, but now their kids were getting in on the conflict.

"It's your word against his. You were fighting. You hit him with a chair, and when security arrived you were holding the chair like you were gonna throw it. I want the police here immediately. The police chief is a good friend of mine."

"My dad is good friends with Diana Jones, the attorney. He does work for her sometimes. So, you can take your police chief friend and-" Jett said.

Her dad put his hand on her shoulder and said, "Jett, quiet."

"Yea. Shut your little animal up. I'm tired of my boy coming home all beat up because of her."

Markus cringed at the 'animal' comment but motioned for Jett to sit down. He needed to keep a cool head to handle this situation, and he figured Krayton was trying to affect his composure.

Ashley sat down next to Jett and held her hand. Her dad sat on the edge of a desk in the office, as there weren't enough chairs for everyone. He looked Krayton in the eye for a moment before he addressed Mike Jr.

"Michael, right?"

"Yea," the boy said, defiant.

"You paid Billy one hundred dollars to put my daughter in a chokehold. You were overheard saying it and Billy admitted to it. Then, when she got out of the chokehold, you grabbed her and held her arms and yelled at Billy to kick her in the face. Again, the other kids saw and heard the whole thing. I'm right, aren't I?"

"You don't have proof of anything, and you don't talk to my son that way."

Mr. Preston, the principal, abruptly entered the room as the two men stared each other down again.

"I didn't approve of this meeting," Mr. Preston said. "You really shouldn't be in here talking to each other until I have a chance to talk to each of you. Either way, after reviewing all of what happened and talking to the security officers about what they observed, I have decided how this will be handled: Billy attacked Jett during lunch. Jett wrestled him to the ground and attempted to throw a chair at him. Michael, in an attempt to break up the fight, tried to restrain Jett from throwing the chair. Unfortunately, he was not successful, and Jett was able to hit both Billy and Michael with the chair. She got up with the chair and was threatening to attack them again when our security officers arrived. So, Billy will be suspended for one week for attacking Jett, Jett will be suspended for one week for using a weapon to attack Billy and Mike. Mike, we won't suspend you, but we will caution you to refrain from attempting to break up fights. Jett, we aren't going to call the police on you. But we're going to recommend to your dad you work on your anger. If you don't learn to calm yourself, I'm afraid you are going to keep getting in more and more trouble in life."

"Oh my gosh," Ashley said. "You cannot be serious."

"That's not acceptable. I want the police called on this girl or I want her expelled," Krayton said.

"About what I expected," Markus said. "Is this what's going in your official report for her file?"

"We're going to keep this one off the books and just handle it like this. She is a bright young lady who works hard and makes good grades, so I don't want to keep her from getting into a good college. She just needs to learn how to get along with the other kids."

"Actually, you don't want to have this in her file because you know I'll call an attorney and the truth about what happened will come out. Come on Jett, let's go. You can work in the office this week."

"I've asked your teachers to list your assignments for you, so you can keep up while you're out. We don't want this to affect you academically. But you need to learn how to fit in and get along."

"We're not the fit in and get along kind of people," Markus retorted.

As they turned to leave, Jett stopped and approached Mike. "Mike," she said, taking the five twenty-dollar bills out of her pocket, "Billy wanted me to return the money you paid him to beat me up. Apparently, he wasn't able to provide the service you contracted with him for so he's giving you a refund. I'm deducting my twenty-dollar fee for delivering the message. Here's your eighty dollars. See you in a week." She turned and followed her dad and Ashley out the door.

Her dad gave her a look as they walked out. He put his arm around her shoulders. "Keep your head up, kid."

Chapter Three: Frankie Makes a Deal

Ashley was already at the office, making coffee and getting organized when Jett and her dad arrived. Jett walked in and hugged her, on her own this time. Her dad did what he always does when he arrives at the office: grab a mug and pour some coffee. "What do we have today?" he asked Ashley.

"We have a few things to look at this morning. I think we need to review our material for the hearing on Friday. There is some fieldwork to do. I also need to get some information on the case Diana has me working on. Jett, could you look stuff up on the internet for me?"

"Yes, she can," her dad answered before Jett could speak up.

Suddenly a man opened the door and, followed by two other men, entered the office. The first man was obviously in charge. He was short but muscular, with short hair and a red face. He wore khaki pants and a polo shirt which seemed to be a size too small. The second man was taller, muscular, and wore a pair of slacks and a sport coat over a gray tee shirt. The third man wore olive-colored khaki pants and a black shirt. He was short, obese, and menacing. Markus recognized the first guy. He was a jerk, and he tended to work for other jerks who often paid him to act like a jerk.

"I'm sorry, but you don't have an appointment," Ashley said.

"Work us in," the first guy said, "and work us in for a date later tonight, sweetie." Ashley put her arm around Jett, pulling her close.

“The liquor store is two floors down, but they don’t open until noon,” Markus said, looking at the first man. “Frankie, what are you doing here?”

“We need to talk, that’s all. Me and the boys here. We need to talk.”

“Ok. Ashley, set up an invoice for these guys. Frankie, I’ll talk but I’m gonna bill you for it. My time isn’t free. Got it?”

“Yea, whatever; we gonna talk in here or you going to invite me into your office?”

“Sure. After you. Ashley, Jett. I want you both to join us.”

“Yea and I’ll bring my boys too. It’ll be a party,” Frankie said.

Markus sat behind his desk. Jett sat in a chair near the window and Ashley, who brought her tablet, sat on the right side of the desk. She activated the recorder on the tablet. Frankie sat down across from Markus. His two associates stood on either side of the door.

“Who’s the kid?” Frankie pointed at Jett.

“My daughter.”

“I’m Jett,” Jett said innocently.

“You have a freaking kid?”

“I said I did, didn’t I?”

“Anyway, I’m here to talk about a case you’re working for that hot lawyer chick.”

"What about it, Frankie?"

"I want you to drop it. You don't have a case. It's time to let it go."

"If we don't have a case, why not let it play out?"

"Because it's getting close to the election, and no one needs the stress."

"So, you show up in my office with your thugs telling me to drop a case. Are you going to beat me up if I don't?"

"Not with your kid here. But you need to drop the case."

"I tell you what Frankie, I'll send the kid out of the room and call your bluff. I'm not giving up the case. Maybe your client needs to settle this instead."

"Look, I'll be reasonable. We'll pay you triple what your lady friend is paying you, to do nothing. You make money from us while working on other cases. It's business. Take the best deal."

"Not happening Frankie."

"What the hell is wrong with you?" Frankie was agitated.

"Is this what you're reduced to Frankie? Intimidating people, trying to get them to drop cases against your client? You could do so much more, but you just chase money. One day you're gonna chase that money right off a cliff and end up in a place that you don't want to be. No, if Diana takes it to court, we're going to court. You could bring a whole army of stupid thugs to try to intimidate me, but nothing changes. Now, Ashley is getting your bill ready. Be sure to pay on time. I'd hate to have to send collections after you."

Ashley looked at Frankie and smiled. "You have ten days to pay, sir."

Frankie looked at Jett. "So, Jett... you're the kid that beat the shit out of Krayton's boy, Mike. Attacked his ass with a chair. Amazing. Was it really you?"

"Frankie, leave my daughter out of-"

"Yea, it's me. I never attacked him with a chair though, he's lying. But Mike started it. He's an asshole."

"I agree with you on that kid," Frankie said with a laugh. "Mikey's an asshole. Go look out the window, I want you to see something."

"Okay," Jett said, hesitantly. "What am I looking for?" She looked out the window.

"See the BMW parked on the street? The black one? See... Little Mikey's an asshole. You're right. His dad is an asshole too. But his dad is a rich asshole, and Mikey will also be a rich asshole one day. You may not like Mikey, I don't like his dad, but I work for him. He pays me a lot of money to do stuff like I'm doing now so I can afford to drive the nice, beautiful BMW down there. I kiss his ass and he pays me to do it. Now, there's a life lesson your dad won't teach you. You want Mikey to stop being an asshole to you? Kiss his ass. Tell him what he wants to hear. Start acting like the other kids. Stop being friends with the nerd kids and bully them like Mikey does. That way, you'll be popular, and Mikey will look out for you. It's simple. Your dad, I'm sure he's a great guy and all, a great dad even, but there is a reason he's holed up in this crappy little office in this old building not driving a BMW. He's always on the wrong side of the rich assholes and he doesn't make the money. Understand?"

"Yes, but you parked in a handicapped spot. That's wrong."

"I work for rich assholes, kid. No one cares about what I do."

"I think the tow truck driver towing your car cares. Bye-bye beamer," Jett said as she turned around.

Ashley walked in with the invoice. "The tow truck driver. He's a good friend of ours. Maybe we're his rich assholes. I saw where you parked on the security cam and texted him. Sorry, Frankie. Be sure to pay your bill. And next time, make an appointment."

Markus looked at Frankie. "You better go see about getting your car out of the slammer, Frankie; and tell your client we'll work this all out in court."

***

"Jett?" Denise Williams, Jett's karate teacher, said as she was going through breathing. It was the afternoon after the encounter with Frankie. "Ms. Garcia said you're suspended from school for fighting. Would you like to tell me what happened?"

Jett was in her karate class. After working on breathing and stretching, they would work on simple techniques. But class always started with breathing and stretching. At this moment they were finished stretching, and they were breathing.

"I did."

"Keep breathing as you tell me. Breathe, then talk. What happened?"

"Two boys attacked me. One at first. He grabbed me around the neck and tried to choke me while I was eating. The other boy was yelling at him to choke me out. It was scary."

"Take another breath and tell me what you did."

"I was able to calm myself and think for just a second. I went limp, and he started to let go. I took a deep breath, stomped on his feet, and leaned forward and he fell over my shoulder."

"Breathe, then answer; is that all?"

"Another kid tackled me and held my arms while yelling at this kid to kick me in the face. We were on the ground."

"You don't look like you've been kicked in the face. Breathe."

Jett took a deep breath and continued. "He didn't. A chai-"

"I asked you to breathe, not talk. Focus Jett."

Jett went silent a moment. Denise said, "Now, breathe and tell me about the chair."

"Someone threw a chair, and it hit the boy trying to kick me and the boy holding me."

She stood over the girl, thinking for a moment. "Jett, stand up."

Jett stood up slowly and faced her teacher. Denise was a petite woman; about five foot two and thin. She had straight brown hair, which was usually in a ponytail, high on the back of her head. Her skin was pale with a few freckles. Jett figured she was about thirty-five years old. Her demeanor was positive, and she was always calm and controlled around her students.

"What is our rule about fighting?"

"We're supposed to avoid fighting unless it is the absolute last resort."

"Yes, and was it?"

"I... I think so?"

"You said he started to let you go when you went limp. So, did you have another option than stomping on his feet?"

Jett looked down, embarrassed. "I wasn't sure if he was going to let me go."

"Did you have to stomp his feet to get him off balance?"

Jett thought about this for a moment. She looked at her teacher and said, "I guess so. I can't think of what else to do. He was much bigger than me." She didn't sound so sure of herself.

"In a self-defense situation, what is your objective?"

"To defend myself?"

"Yes. In the most efficient manner possible. Is it your objective to get revenge or punish your attacker?"

"No."

The teacher regarded her a moment longer. "Jett, put me in the hold this boy put you in. I'm going to teach you something."

She walked around to the back of her teacher and put her forearm around her neck as the teacher instructed. Because her teacher was short, Jett was able to get her arms around her neck.

"Now Jett, I want you to pay attention to what I'm about to do. First, I'm going to place both hands on your wrists, where they meet. Instead of pulling down, like what seems natural, I'm just going to hold on to your wrists. Watch what I do next."

Her teacher stomped her feet on the mat, in front of Jett's feet. Jett reacted by shifting her balance to avoid getting her feet stomped. Her teacher pulled Jett's hands down, pushed them into her chest, leaned forward and Jett went flying over her shoulder and landed on the mat.

"Stand up," her teacher said. Jett stood up.

"I got the same effect by stomping the mat that you got by stomping on the boy's feet. Your assailant won't know the difference. He will just react by getting off balance. You use this reaction to either secure his hands against your chest, so you can breathe or, in a more dangerous situation, leaning forward as I did and releasing yourself from the chokehold. Do you understand?"

"Yes, ma'am."

"If you stomp his feet, you risk angering him further. He may get an adrenaline rush from the pain. This may cause him to react more aggressively and less predictably. This puts you in more danger, not less. Therefore, stomping the ground is more efficient than stomping his feet. Do you understand?"

"Yes ma'am."

"You may want to inflict pain because his attack was a threat to your pride, and you want revenge. But we are learning that pride is not what we defend. Pride is self-destructive. We make poor decisions because of it. We must deny our pride and focus on the needs of the moment. But we must always be focused. Anger, pride, fear will cause us to lose focus. We must focus on the moment, not on our emotions. Now, I am going to put you in the same hold and each of you will practice getting out of the hold."

Jett stood in front of her teacher and waited. Her heart started racing as Denise reached around her to put her in the hold. Jett started to sweat. She started to move out of the way; she started to panic.

"Okay Jett, you are now serving your fear. This will only make it more difficult for you to focus on the moment. Just breathe and focus."

Jett nodded, her face shiny from sweat, and swallowed hard as her teacher put her in the hold.

"Breathe Jett. Just take a moment to breathe. In time you won't need a moment to get focused. But we have to start here."

Jett took a deep breath as she secured her teacher's wrists. As she took another breath, she could feel her heart slow down just a little, then a little more. She was becoming more focused on the moment, less fearful.

"Good, Jett. I can tell you're getting more focused now. Stay with that. If you can breathe, you can talk to your assailant first about releasing you. If I am not going to release you, show me what you do next."

Jett took another deep breath and, as she exhaled, she stomped the floor twice with her right foot. Her instructor reacted by stepping backward and Jett popped her shoulder up while she pulled her arms down, into her chest, and leaned forward. While her teacher did not go to the mat, Jett was able to keep her teacher's arm off her neck, so she could breathe without fear of being choked. She was now in control, even though she had not secured her release.

"Good. I see you stopped at the point where you could breathe and did not try to release yourself. And you are in control. Now you are learning to defend yourself and use self-restraint. Now, if I continue to attempt to choke you, even pull you back upright, show me what to do, and don't worry about flipping me."

Jett stomped again and quickly leaned forward while pulling her teacher's arms down with much more force. Her teacher fell onto the mat. Jett stood there in disbelief.

Her teacher stood up and bowed to Jett. Jett bowed back.

"Good, Jett. Now you are learning. Good technique, but, more importantly, you were calm and focused."

The girls paired up and practiced. Jett stayed focused on her breathing and her technique.

Chapter Four: The Shakedown

Jett enjoyed the freedom of riding her bike in the summer. On this day, about midsummer after her freshman year, she was riding her bike to her karate lesson. She planned to take her lesson and stay late to spar with her teacher, so she could get more practice. After her lesson, she would ride back to her dad's office and watch YouTube videos about karate. Tomorrow, like most Tuesdays, Jett would ride her bike to the Recreation Center, lift weights, and do some running on the indoor track before riding to the karate studio.

Jett arrived at the studio and took her lesson, sparred with Denise and one of the other teachers, and got on her bike to ride to the office.

On her way to the office, she passed a group of kids hanging out at a park. She recognized them as Mike and his friends. She crossed to the other side of the street, far from the park, and ignored the kids. One of the boys yelled at her, calling her something she didn't understand, but she continued to ride. She made a note to herself to figure out a new route.

The next day Jett rode the new route, but this time she saw several kids at a convenience store where they played arcade games. She realized they knew she was coming from the karate studio and going to her dad's office. She again ignored the boys as they yelled at her. This time Mike was glaring at her as she rode by. Jett's heart raced, but she was able to hide her anxiety from the other kids.

A few days later, Jett was riding her bike to her dad's office again. Out of the corner of her eye, she saw a kid watching her. She saw others approach. No problem, she thought, she just made a left and cut through an alley between the two buildings near the corner. This would take her to a road near a small field in a recess flanked by the walls of two empty buildings. She would ride past the buildings, over the tracks, take a hard left, and would be three blocks from her dad's office. If the kids were hanging out at the park, they wouldn't have time to catch up.

As Jett made her turn, another kid was there, behind the building. He threw a huge rock at the back wheel of her bike. Jett had no chance to dodge the rock, and she lost control of her bike and began to slide just as a car passed in front of her. She jerked her bike to the side, went off the sidewalk, and skidded to a stop on the edge of the field. Jett flew off the bike and landed in the grass as several kids approached her.

"Damn! That was easy. Bitch went flying too. Didn't expect that," one boy said, laughing.

Jett got to her feet and checked her bike as several kids approached her. The rim of her back wheel was bent. Her heart sank. She'd have to walk home now. Her ankle hurt and she landed on her left knee.

Mike got to her first. Most of the kids were his friends, but Angelique, his girlfriend, and one of her friends, whose name was Becky, were also there. The boys blocked her exit from the field. She had walls behind her and on either side. She also noticed the boys looked different. They looked like they had gained muscle mass since the last time she saw them. Mike had an angry look on his face.

"You. I'm so sick of you. You throw a cheap shot at me, you throw a chair at me, and now, you and your dad and that bitch lawyer defending that whore are going to cost my dad a shit ton of money. Your bullshit ends today."

"That's between our parents, Mike. I don't even know about any of it," Jett said, somewhat shaky because of the intensity of Mike's anger.

"No. You know."

"I don't know, Mike." Jett attempted to stay calm.

"No. You little bitch. It's time we settled this shit. You need to learn to keep your mouth shut and stay out of our way."

Angelique appeared uncomfortable with Mike's anger. He was escalating. She folded her arms and, in a shaky voice, said, "Ok Mike. Let's go. That's enough."

"Oh, it's not enough. She's gonna pay for this past year."

"You said we were only going to scare her Mike. Look, she's hurt, and her bike is messed up. Let's go now. Come on."

"No. No. We're just getting started. She has got to pay for what she's done."

"Mike, I'm not going to fight you," Jett said.

"You're scared?"

"No Mike, I just don't need to. I'm just going to leave now," she said, leaving her bike behind, as she started walking towards the kids, attempting to leave the field. Mike's friend, a rather large boy named Ray, stepped in front of her and stared at her.

"Please move," Jett said and waited a moment. "I guess you're not going to move, are you?"

Jett started to get nervous. She reminded herself to breathe.

"She's getting scared now. She realizes she's not getting out of this one," one of the other boys said, snickering. To Jett, all these boys looked about the same: tall, muscular, and angry. Some boys were larger than the others; they were more obese. Jett figured they were on the offensive line in football or something. Mike, unlike the others, was blond and had longer hair. He had green eyes, and he appeared to be the angriest. Even his friends, who were no saints, would get anxious about how he would escalate when it came to Jett.

"Kick her ass, Mike. Just do it. She's not like a girl. She wanted to fight you so she's fair game," one of the boys said, while others laughed. Mike stared at her, saying nothing.

"Mike, stop." Angelique was worried about where this may lead.

Jett decided to walk past the kids. She started walking towards Angelique, thinking she was the one kid who would let her pass. She planned to run to get away from the boys. She figured with all the running she'd been doing she could hold them off until she got to a store or a public place. There was a pharmacy a block away. If she could make it there, she could call her dad from inside the building.

Ray blocked her path again. As she got to the edge of the crowd, Ray grabbed her and picked her up. Legs flailing, she struggled against his grasp with no success. Ray carried her back to the field, laughing as she struggled. Jett was near panic now, as she didn't know what these boys had in mind. The other boys began yelling at Ray to throw her down hard. Jett heard Angelique yelling at Mike to make them stop. Ray obliged his friends by throwing her to the ground. Jett tried to get up, but another boy shoved her back to the ground while Ray grabbed her legs and held them. The second boy jumped on top of her, yelling obscenities at her, and grabbed her arms as a third boy began hitting her in the face and head. Jett got one arm free and covered her face, but not before taking several blows to her cheek and forehead. The boy who pushed her down began throwing punches at her body as Mike attempted to kick her in the face; he kicked her forearm instead. Jett was in a panic as she realized how hard these boys were trying to punch and kick her. She was buried, as the three large boys were on top of her, swinging at her head.

Angelique began screaming and grabbed Mike and pulled him away from the pile. "STOP IT!! YOU'RE GOING TOO FAR!!!" She started grabbing the other boys trying to get them to stop. The other girl, her friend, joined in and started trying to pull the guys off the pile. One by one each boy stopped and got up as Jett rolled over and sat up, stunned. The boys backed away but were still facing Jett, fists clenched. The two girls stared in shock at what the boys had done.

Angelique was near tears. "I can't do this, Mike. This is too much. You could have killed her!"

"I know what I'm doing," Mike said.

"No, you don't," she replied. "It's too much!"

Jett was still sitting on the ground trying to pull herself together.

"I'm finished with this," Angelique was now crying. "I'm done. We're over. You'll do that to me one day too. I just know it."

"I'll decide when we're over. You don't decide shit," Mike said. He seemed to be escalating again.

"Mike. Just leave me alone. I'm going home," Angelique said.

"No, you're not. I'll bring you home when we're finished."

"You're not finished yet?" she said, surprised. "Seriously? You haven't made your point?"

"No. I'm not," Mike barely contained his rage. He glared at Jett. "I'm not. I'm sick of her."

Angelique's face turned red. "Well, I'm going home. I'm going to call my dad. This has to stop."

Mike slapped the phone out of her hand, grabbed her wrist, and pulled her closer to him. "You want to test me? You want to test me? We're not breaking up, you're not going home, and we're," he gestured at the guys with his free hand, "not finished yet." The other boys looked uncomfortable. Mike had gone too far for some of them too.

"Hey bro. She's right. We're done here. You made your point. Let's just go, grab a few beers from your dad's fridge or something," one of the boys said.

Mike continued to squeeze Angelique's wrist and stared at her. "Go ahead, test me. Try to leave."

Behind him, he heard a rustle as Jett got up from the ground. "Mike," she said, calm but angry. "Leave her alone. If you want to fight a girl, fight me. One on one. Your friends can watch."

Mike let go of her wrist and slowly turned around to see Jett, bleeding from a cut on her cheek, facing him.

"You want to fight?"

"One on one, Mike. Leave your friends out of it and let her go. I'm not scared of you."

"You want to fight me?" Mike was stalling. "One on one? Without my friends?"

"Yes, Mike, but leave her alone. You don't need to hurt her. I'm right here. I'm the person you want to hurt."

Mike stared at Jett.

Jett looked at Angelique and asked, "Are you okay?"

"Don't Mike. Let's just talk about this," Angelique said. The other boys, however, started egging Mike on. "Come on, bro. Take care of business," one of them said. "She's giving you a chance, take it," another guy said.

"Okay, you just got yourself an ass beating, bitch." Mike took off his shirt and threw it down, flexing as he did.

"Just so you know, I'm keeping my shirt on," Jett said, sarcastic. She assumed a fighting position. She took deep breaths, cleared her mind of any expectations, and focused on Mike. Mike circled her, made movements as if to hit her, laughed, and backed off.

The kids were startled to hear a loud voice from across the street. "Hey! Knock it off, you dumbasses!"

It was coming from the inside of a car parked on the road. "What tha hell you little shits doin' on my property? Get outta here." It was Vinnie Donelli.

The boys froze.

"Hey! You okay, kid? Those boys bothering you? You need me to come over there and handle business?"

"I'm okay, Mr. Donelli. Thanks!" Jett replied.

The Donelli family owned and leased most of the property in downtown Port City. They were also friends with Markus Jackson.

Jett breathed a sigh of relief and walked to her bike, but when she put pressure on her leg, her knee gave. She also realized she had a massive headache from some of the punches she took. She picked up her bike, but it was too damaged to ride. Angelique looked at her. "Are you ok? Seriously?"

"Are you?" Jett said.

"I'm fine. But you need help. Where are you going?"

"My dad's office, three blocks that way." Jett pointed down North Street.

"Ok. Let's go. I'll walk you there. Becky, can you get her bike? She's hurt."

"Yea, sure," the other girl whispered, as she picked up the bike and started rolling it towards the road. She walked behind Jett. Angelique put her arm around Jett's waist and supported her as they walked down the street. The boys just stood there, confused, as the girls walked away. Vinnie Donelli eased the car back onto the road and drove west, watching the kids in his rear-view mirror until he was satisfied the boys were going in the opposite direction than the girls. He also had some insurance keeping an eye on things, just in case they get stupid again.

"You're Angelique, right?" Jett said to the girl helping her.

"Yes. You're Jett. Cool name."

"Thanks," Jett said, "and thanks for helping me get home."

"Thanks for standing up for me. I was scared shitless, and I really thought he would hit me. Seriously Jett, thanks for standing up to him."

When the girls arrived at the building, Jett locked her bike up and the two girls supported her as they rode up the elevator. Ashely greeted them as they entered the office.

"Oh no!" Ashley exclaimed, "Sit her down here," she said, gesturing at the couch in the waiting area. She sat down next to Jett and put her arm around the girl.

“What happened?” she asked the girls.

“Are you Jett’s mom?” Becky asked.

“Might as well be,” Jett said.

“Are you okay?” Ashley asked the girls, “Are you hurt too?”

“No. Just freaked out, but she needs to see a doctor or something,” Angelique said.

“What happened? Sweetie, can you go to the room over there and get some ice out of the freezer?” Ashley asked while gesturing for Becky to go to the kitchen area. Becky turned and rushed into the kitchen and came back with a bag of ice. Angelique started talking as Becky left.

“It was Mike and his friends. They followed her on her bike and threw a rock at her. They all got into a fight and they all beat up on her. I made them stop, Mike started to hit me, and Jett stopped him. But some guy started yelling at the boys to leave her alone.”

“Mike tried to hit you? What’s your name, sweetie?” Ashley said as Becky brought the ice.

“Becky, and she’s Angelique,” Becky said.

Ashley placed the ice on Jett’s cheek and told her to hold it.

“Mike’s my ex-boyfriend and I freaked out on him to get him to stop and leave her alone. He and his friends were just crazy. I’ve never seen them like this. They’ve been getting meaner and meaner since they started bulking up.”

Ashley looked at Angelique, concerned. “Do you mean steroids? Are they doing steroids?”

Angelique just stared at Ashley. She was afraid to answer the question.

“I understand,” Ashley said, “You don’t have to say anything. You did good to break up with him and I appreciate both of you helping Jett. Stay away from those boys from now on. It’ll only get worse.”

“What does your dad do, Jett?” Becky asked.

“He’s a private investigator. Ashley is too. They’re partners.”

“Cool. My dad runs a bank,” Becky said. “Your dad has a cooler job.”

“Jett, I’m going to take you to the ER as soon as I call your dad. He’s meeting with a client right now, but he’ll meet us at the hospital, ok?”

“I don’t need to go to the hospital,” Jett was irritated. “I’m fine. Can’t I just go to the doctor tomorrow instead?”

“No. You need to get your head examined. And your leg too. You’re limping. We can’t wait. We need to get you started healing, so you’ll be ready for the tournament this fall. Look at it that way.”

Ashley looked at the girls, “If you can help me get Jett to the car, I can drop you off at home on the way to the hospital. Do you mind? I don’t want you walking home with those crazy boys out there. They may want to get even.”

Angelique looked at Becky. "That's fine." Becky nodded. Jett struggled to her feet with Ashley's help. Ashley took her phone and purse from her desk and walked the three girls out of the office.

***

The next day Ashley called Angelique's mother. What sounded like a tired, middle-aged woman answered. Ashley identified herself and explained what happened.

Angelique's mother responded. "This child, Jett? Is that her name? Yes, Jett, needs to stay away from my daughter. Apparently, this all started when she tried to attack my daughter when all those kids wanted to do was help her after she fell off her bike. She needs to go to a home or something. Are you her mother?"

"I'm... I... work with her dad but we are very close. Your daughter told me a completely different story yesterday."

"Yes, my daughter. Well, her boyfriend and his dad came by later and told me the truth. They said my daughter didn't want to get that poor girl in trouble because she is already a very troubled child, so she just went along with her story. Her friend Becky, too. Her mother called me last night and told me the same. Did you take them both in your vehicle? Without my permission? I don't know you and you drove my child in your car?"

"Ma'am, she told me her boyfriend tried to hit her. I asked her if she wanted to come along so she wouldn't have to walk home and see her boyfriend again; in case he tried this again. I dropped the two girls off at home on the way, so they'd be safe."

“No,” the woman said. “Michael did not hit her. That’s just something this Jett child made up to justify picking a fight with these kids. She doesn’t belong with these kids. No offense, but these are good kids, and this Jett is just causing them all kinds of problems. I will not tolerate her in my daughter’s presence again. And I appreciate your concern for my daughter, but she was safe with Mike. It’s your problem child I’m more worried about.”

Ashley felt the frustration welling up in her. She tried to speak, but the woman continued.

“We all got together, all the parents from yesterday, and agreed we would not press charges for assault, even though it’s well within our rights, but we expect you, or this child’s parents, or whatever arrangements you people have for this girl, to control her from now on and keep her from harassing our children. They work too hard and they are good kids and don’t need the problems. Just control her. Keep her away from our kids. This is our expectation. Some of the fathers are going to talk to her dad today. My husband will be there to explain in no uncertain terms about this, so he will get the message. And frankly, I wouldn’t dare cross my husband. He’s not to be trifled with. He’s very impressive. You tell her father this. We have our expectations and we expect you to meet them. Do you understand, Miss, or is it Mrs. Garcia?”

Ashley resisted the impulse to tell this arrogant woman off. She paused a moment and replied, “It’s Miss. I’m not married. But I am a big part of Jett’s life and I appreciate your daughter showing some compassion to Jett yesterday and helping her home, and for trying to stop those boys when they were beating her up. And, I will also tell you that *your daughter* said it was Jett that took up for her, after those boys beat her; when Mike threatened to hit *your daughter* for getting in his way. Your standing in polite society is much more important to you than your daughter's safety, but I guess I can't judge. I've never had what you have, but I've never wanted it either. So please, send over your 'quite impressive' husband that we 'wouldn't dare cross' and we'll take it from there. Thank you, have a good day, and tell your daughter I said hello and thank her again for what she did yesterday on my behalf." Ashley hung up the phone with a thump.

Markus walked out of his office. "What was that all about?"

"I called one of those girls' moms to talk to her and she just went on and on about how her kids were victimized and she has 'expectations' about how we will 'control' Jett from now on. They are sending some of their fathers to talk to you about her. Being a parent is so hard."

He looked at her a moment after the last sentence.

"I know. Sorry. I should have let you handle it. I just meant it must be hard for you."

"They are sending a guy over to talk to us? Everybody's got a guy."

"I'm guessing he's intimidating or something. I'm sure he's just another sanctimonious prick."

"I'll take care of the guys. If they bring those boys along, you take care of them."

"Gladly," Ashley said.

***

At five o'clock in the afternoon, the group arrived at the office. Four men, including Michael Krayton Sr., were present. Three of the men brought their sons. Ashley came out to greet them with a smile, shook each man's hand and introduced herself. She smiled at the boys but didn't offer a handshake. She was wearing a dark blue skirt which stopped at her knees with a matching blazer and a burgundy blouse, unbuttoned to the third button. Three-inch black heels completed the ensemble. She wore her thick, black hair down with several strands flowing over the right side of her face. To Jett, she was the picture of class and beauty. Jett was wearing a pair of jeans and a blue hoodie. She looked at Ashley, hoping she would be just as beautiful and confident when she grew up. Today, though, she feared this meeting would go wrong, and these men would put her in jail.

Jett's dad entered the lobby with his coffee cup in his right hand. Markus Jackson wasn't a large man; he weighed one hundred and eighty-five pounds. He was slender and had the look of someone who was athletic in his younger days but only works out casually now. His thick brown hair had grown lighter and had been graying during the last four years. He wasn't outgoing or arrogant; nevertheless, he carried himself with a subtle swagger. He wasn't the type to get in a man's face or stare someone down. His confidence was quiet, introspective, and deliberate. He dressed well at work. Today he wore a pair of gray slacks, a shiny white dress shirt with the sleeves rolled up to his elbows, with a black belt and dress shoes. He had the same blue eyes as Jett.

"Gentlemen, nice to meet you. Hello Mr. Krayton," he said. "Welcome to my office. You've met Ashley Garcia, my partner, and this is my daughter, Jett. Before we get started, would you like some coffee?"

He walked over and started pouring some coffee into his mug. One of the men asked if they had any cups. Markus responded by handing him a ceramic mug with the company's logo, "Here. Coffee tastes much better in ceramic than Styrofoam." He poured the coffee into the mug and asked him if he wanted anything in it.

The significantly larger man shook his head. "I like mine black too," he said. One of the other men snickered and started to say something.

Markus looked at him. "I get your joke. It's good to have a sense of humor. Step into my office and let's get started. The boys can stay in the lobby with Jett. Ms. Garcia will look after them."

***

Two of the boys sat on the couch while the third sat on a chair. Jett sat on the other chair. Ashley leaned up against the desk facing the kids in the room. She brushed her blazer back just enough for her sidearm to be visible. Her sidearm was a Sig Saur P320. Sexy, sleek, and powerful, it was an appropriate weapon for a woman like Ashley Garcia.

"I can't believe we have to sit here and wait with you," Mike said. "I really want to see my dad put your dad in his place."

Jett felt anxious and didn't know what to say. Ashley folded her arms and addressed the boy. "Can I get you something from the refrigerator to make your wait more comfortable, some bottled water, a soda?"

"I'll take a soda," the larger boy said. It was Ray, the same boy who picked Jett up and threw her down. Ashley gave Jett a look, indicating she wanted her to get drinks for the boy. Jett got up and went to the refrigerator.

"Anyone else?" Jett asked when she opened the door.

"Water please," the other boy said, and laughed. "She's our servant now; waiting on us."

"She's just being polite and hospitable," Ashley responded, unfolding her arms again.

The boy saw Ashley's gun just as Jett handed him the water. "Is that your gun? Cool," he said. "Does your dad carry a gun too, Jett?"

"My dad carries a Glock. He ends up in some scary situations with his work," Jett responded.

"Why do you have a gun?" the boy asked Ashley.

"Sometimes people don't like what we do, and they show up starting trouble. I need to protect myself and Jett when we're here, and myself when I'm out there, on the job. Don't worry though, I'm licensed to carry." She winked and smiled at the boy. The boy blushed.

The larger boy looked at the gun. "That's so cool."

Mike didn't say a word. He was fuming; his friends seemed to like Ashley.

"Let me ask a question," Ashley sensed an opportunity. "What's this thing with Jett here? Why are you always fighting?"

It was Mike who spoke up. "Because she's fu... she's crazy. That's why I don't like her. The other kids know how to act," he pointed at Jett. "She's just weird. She doesn't know how to act." Mike realized he wasn't making sense, so he let it trail off.

"Jett says you call her terrible names. You have since she started school here. And you say ugly things to her. Why Michael?"

"I don't. I don't pick on her at all. She picks on me."

"Half-breed, mongrel, just pick a race and go with it," Jett said, mocking Mike.

"Shut up." Mike was irritated. He was doing his best to keep his composure.

"It's true," Ray said, almost whispering. "Mike gives her a hard time. I'm surprised she didn't snap before. Since the fifth grade."

Mike shot the boy a dirty look.

"Why would you do this, Michael? Is it a racial thing for you?"

"I don't know. She's not black. She's not white. She's not anything. My dad says... he says he doesn't hate anyone, but he thinks people should stick to their own race, especially with sex and all. He says if people are going to have kids like Jett, they are just asking for it."

"Do you think Jett is asking for you to ridicule and threaten her all the time?"

Jett was uncomfortable, but she wanted to know what these boys think. Ashley is amazing, she thought to herself.

"I don't know. Why is she in our school? Isn't there another school where she would fit in?"

"Do you think it's okay to call her those names just because she's different? Does your dad believe this?"

"It's not that bad. I don't call her the N-word or anything."

"Ok Mike, so you can rob me, but as long as you don't kill me, robbing me is just fine?" Jett said, exhaling in frustration.

Ashley gave Jett a look. She needed Jett to be graceful under pressure. They talked about this earlier in the day.

"Bullshit Mike," Ray said. "You call her the N-word all the time behind her back. Remember when you said she was like a dollar store N-word: fifty percent off."

"What's your name again?" Ashley asked the larger boy.

"Ray. And Mike's an asshole." the boy's face flushed, turning red. "Mike pushes people to do things. I don't know why I even hang out with him. Gawd, it felt good to say that."

"Shut up, fat-ass. It's not true and you know it. You're just letting this piece of ass get to you because she's hot. You'll say anything to kiss her ass."

"Michael! So disrespectful to everyone. I'm not sure what to make of your compliment? I guess you're saying I'm attractive. I can assure you I am much more than 'a piece of ass' though. You should learn the proper way to speak to a lady. And you shouldn't call your friend such an ugly name. You need to learn some manners."

Ray continued, feeling empowered. "I tried to tell my dad, but he had already heard what Mike said happened and he didn't want to hear it. He just kept cutting me off and telling me what Mike's dad said. He's a lawyer so I guess they were trying to defend themselves. What happened, was that we were being assholes, and it went too far. Way too far."

"Drama queen. Rookie PI uses her bullshit mind games on us and Ray breaks in ten minutes and confesses to a bunch of stuff we didn't do. Dumbass."

Ashley ignored the other two boys.

"It's like a freaking after school special in here," the third boy said, laughing. Mike laughed too.

"Jett, can you come in here, please?" her dad asked as he stuck his head out of his office door.

She approached her dad in the office. Ashley followed to confer with Markus.

"You were at the ER because you were trying to cover what your kid did by claiming injuries," the larger man, Ray's dad, was saying.

"How's it going?" Markus asked Ashley.

“Well, so far I’ve been called a ‘hot piece of ass’ by Michael and we’ve learned a lot about what’s been going on with these kids. I told you they weren’t all bad kids. Just misguided. They get so much peer pressure, not just from Michael, but from their own parents,” Ashley whispered.

“I stand corrected. Jett, come here.”

Jett walked over to the desk.

“You see how she’s walking funny? That’s from injuries caused by one of these kids throwing a rock at her bike and causing her to fall. She almost got hit by a car. Next, look at her face. See the bruise? That’s from getting hit in the face and head. We were at the ER because we were concerned about head injuries.” He said to Jett, “Thanks, kid. Can you wait outside again and keep an eye on those boys?”

“Yes sir,” Jett said. Ashley had already returned to the lobby.

***

One hour later the door opened again, and the men came out.

“If you think this is over, it’s not, Jackson. The footage was edited, and I’m not intimidated by some wannabe gangster making veiled threats against my boy,” Krayton said.

“Well, I didn’t ask you to like it, just accept it. From here on out I want you to talk to your boys about leaving my girl alone. That’s all I’m asking.”

Ray's dad looked disturbed. "Come on, Ray, let's go." The other man followed them out with his son. The two Mike's lingered a moment.

"Mike, leave this kid alone from now on. She's not worth the trouble. Just, find something else to do, okay?"

"But dad, you sa-"

"I don't care what I said. What I'm saying now is that you will leave her alone. Hey, look, if she starts it, fine. Do what you want. But don't be the one to start it. I really don't want to have to deal with all this anymore. We have more important things to think about right now." He looked at Markus. "Damn it, Jackson, you haven't heard the last of this." He left the office.

"So, it went well?" Ashley asked.

"Yea. Apparently, Vinnie Donelli paid Krayton a visit at his office yesterday afternoon and had a little talk with him about these boys messing around downtown and harassing a local girl. I guess I have 'a guy' too, right?"

"Vinnie. I love the way he looks out for Jett."

"Vinnie broke up the fight dad. He yelled at those guys and made them leave."

"That's not all he did, kid. He also sent me cell phone footage of the whole thing. Somehow, he got the security footage from the school. So, I showed them how their little assholes were starting all the trouble. They aren't remorseful, but they realize they don't have a tenable position right now. So, they had to drop it."

"So, they'll leave me alone now?"

"I hope, but don't count on it. I don't think those boys are smart enough to just drop it. But hopefully, I'm wrong." He looked at Ashley. "As far as what you said about the peer pressure coming not just from kids like Mike, but their own parents: this is how they indoctrinate them. After a while, it gets easier just to go along with it and make everyone happy. Some of those kids don't stand a chance of ever thinking for themselves."

***

Chapter Five: Pulp Fiction

"They didn't have a brave leader to show them the path to glory; they had Bob. Bob wasn't the strongest guy. He wasn't the fastest guy. He wasn't the smartest guy. He wasn't the anything-est guy. He could throw a ball far, all kinds of balls, and apparently, that earns a boy some status in this town. He could throw it far, but he wasn't very good at getting it exactly where it was supposed to go. But the bar was low in this town and Bob's ability to throw a ball, combined with his dad's bloated bank account, apparently buys a football team a quarterback, or a baseball team a pitcher. I'm not sure what the going rate was for a quarterback, but there wasn't much of a market by my estimate. Zero wins and ten losses last year. Pep rallies were more like group therapy and cheerleaders were pleading instead of cheering."

Jett finished reading her story to the class and was surprised at the laughter from her classmates.

"I love your story, Jett. It's funny and makes a statement about bullying. Do you guys have questions for Jett about her story?" Miss Stark said.

"Yes," Melinda raised her hand to ask a question. "Did this really happen?"

"Yea, but not exactly like that. I changed it to write a story about it. But they chased me around all summer and finally caught me one day."

"The same guys that. . ." Melinda's voice trailed off as she looked at her teacher.

"Yea. Same guys," Jett said.

“This is based on a true story, Jett?” Miss Stark was concerned.

“Yes, ma’am. My dad took care of it though. He met with the dads of the guys and they had a big talk about it in his office. They all agreed it would stop.”

“Thank God,” one of the other kids, a girl, said. “Can he talk to them for everyone else too?”

“I don’t know. I may ask him.”

“Last year sucked,” another kid, a boy named Greg, said. “They were so mean to you. I saw what happened at lunch. I was so freaked out, and angry, at what they did.”

“If you’re having a problem with bullying, you all know you can talk to me anytime about it, okay?” Miss Stark said.

The class was quiet for a few seconds.

“Thank you, Jett. Your story got us talking about bullying. A good story is supposed to get people talking about important things, so you nailed it.”

Jett returned to her seat as a few of the kids held up their hands for high fives as she passed.

***

Later in the week, Jett was sitting on the floor by her locker looking at a book she had been reading when Mike approached her, angry.

“Mike, No. Stop,” Angelique was saying to Mike. His face was red, his muscles bulging, and he had an intense look on his face. "You said you weren't going to do this, not this year. Not again."

Jett hurried to her feet, but another kid stepped in front of Mike first. It was Greg, from her class. Jett rushed to him, but she was too late. Mike was in his face.

"Leave her alone, asshole," Greg said. "It was just a story."

"Yea. What was in the story, Greg? You little bitch. Tell me what she said."

"Greg, it's okay. I'll handle it. But thanks," Jett said, admiring the boy's courage while questioning his judgment.

"No. Let little bitch Gregory here tell me what was in the story." The veins in Mike's neck bulged.

"Stop it, Mike," Angelique pleaded with him. Mike didn't respond. He kept staring at Greg, whose resolve was starting to give.

"And Jett, don't think I'm protecting you. I just don't want my BOYFRIEND to get in any trouble this year. Not with football season and all." Angelique added, "I couldn't care less about you."

"Noted, Angelique, and it's good to talk to you too," Jett responded with sarcasm. Angelique rolled her eyes and shook her head while Greg tried to figure out an endgame to this confrontation that didn't involve getting killed.

"Ok. Everyone calm down," he said. "It was just a story. No big deal."

Jett moved him out of the way and stood between him and Mike. Greg didn't resist this time.

"I'm not looking for trouble, Mike. I wrote a story for a class; I didn't use anyone's names. If you want to get mad about it, that's up to you."

Mike looked at her, confused, and pointed his finger at her. "Give me one reason, Jett. One reason. I will go off and destroy you. I won't stop this time. I will own you. Just give me one reason."

Jett didn't respond. She looked at Mike, waiting for him to walk away. When Mike stood there awkwardly, she addressed Angelique. "I know you act like you hate me and all, but I did want to thank you for walking me to my dad's office last summer. You and Becky. Anyway, you can get back to hating me now. I just wanted to say thanks."

Angelique cut Jett a look and walked away, pulling Mike with her. Mike went along, but he stared at Jett over his shoulder. Jett turned around and saw several kids from her Literature class standing behind her.

"Are you okay?" Melinda asked. "That was intense."

"I'm fine. That was an easy one. At least he didn't try to fight me this time," Jett responded. "Thanks for helping me, Greg."

"I didn't do much. I was scared shitless." Greg was embarrassed.

"That's what makes you brave," Jett said.

"How do you stay so calm with those guys," another girl asked.

"I know I can defend myself. I just don't really want to. But those guys are getting bigger and angrier, so I could be in trouble this year. I need to keep it cool." *Kind of late for that,* she thought.

"Maybe they'll win a game this year and won't be so mad at the world," Melinda said, and immediately started laughing. "I almost said that with a straight face. Pep rallies are group therapy and cheerleaders are just pleading now." All the kids, Jett included, started laughing. Jett, though, felt uncomfortable as this could provoke another confrontation.

"Come on, let's get to class," she whispered, "before they come back and start up again." The kids obliged and began walking down the hall.

Greg, spoke in a fake English accent. "The football players are easily startled but will soon return in larger numbers."

"Okay Obi," Melinda said, "let's go."

The small group of kids laughed as they continued to their next class.

***

After Thanksgiving Break Jett was excited to return to school. She felt like she was finally making a few friends and was getting over her social anxiety. But when she got to her first class, her heart sank when her teacher told her to report to Mr. Preston's office.

"Mr. Preston, I didn't do anything. Why am I here?" she asked when she walked into his office. Mr. Preston had a copy of her story sitting on his desk. He looked up at her and pointed at the chair across from his desk.

"I got a complaint from a parent that you wrote a story in which you ridiculed members of the football and cheerleading teams and now other kids are laughing at them. Care to explain?"

"I wrote a story for my class. She gave us an assignment, and I completed it. I got an A on the assignment. I didn't use any names of people I know, and I didn't say it was about this school."

Mr. Preston stared at her a moment and sighed. "Miss Landry, you wrote the story in the first person. If it was about yourself, we'd obviously know what school and team you're talking about."

"I wrote it in the first person because that was the style of literature for the assignment. I wrote it in the noir/pulp style, which is often in the first person. Like Raymond Chandler. The Phillip Marlow stories, you know? It was my influence."

"I'm familiar with Raymond Chandler. I'm not buying that it's not about this school though."

"The narrator of the story is a character. They aren't telling the story as the author, but as a character who is telling the story within the story. The author is separate from the narrator. Just like Raymond Chandler wrote his novels in the first person, but he was telling the story as Phillip Marlow, who is a character in the story."

"But your story is set in a school like this one, with a football team like this one."

"Write what you know. I don't know what it's like to be in another school. I only had a week to write a story."

"Nonetheless, you've caused a lot of stress for a certain group of kids at the school. Now kids are quoting your story when they talk about the football team and the cheerleaders. They feel like they are being teased."

Jett's face got hot when he said the football players felt like they were being teased. She tried to hide being angry, but her voice shook. "You'll excuse me if I don't feel bad for them. As long as I've gone to school with those kids they have teased, picked on, humiliated, intimidated, and bullied the other kids. Every single day. They think because they're bigger and stronger than everyone, they're somehow superior. Now, a bunch of kids realized being smarter gives them some power too. At least it helps people feel less bad about being bullied and beat up all the time. If they think my story was about them, it's because they recognized something about themselves in it, not because I wrote it about them. You can't prove what I wrote it about. I did my assignment the way they told me to do it and I got a good grade. I also got a bunch of kids talking about what it's like to be bullied."

"Jeticia, stop," Mr. Preston said.

"My teacher said good literature, a good story, tells a truth that some people identify with, and that makes others uncomfortable. If some kids identified with it, and some other kids were uncomfortable, what I wrote was a good story."

"Jeticia! I said to stop."

Jett was too far gone to stop. Her frustration escalated, and she started tearing up. A lone tear rolled down her cheek as she continued. "If we have to put up with being attacked, threatened, pushed and picked on all the time, they can put up with whatever stories we write. And since you're not going to do anything about it, we may as well defend ourselves in writing. But no one cares about us. Only your football players. The smart kids, the ones who make this school look good academically, where it's supposed to count, go unnoticed and unheard while you all suck up to the parents of the rich kids, none of which are half as smart as the kids in my classes and couldn't hang with us academically. I make straight A's and you don't care. You only want me to go back to being quiet and allowing the other kids to walk all over me. Just because I'm black doesn't mean I have to put up with their racist crap. I'm-"

"You will be suspended if you don't stop. I have repeatedly told you to stop. I'm sorry if your experience here isn't up to your standards and we don't publicly thank you enough for doing what it is you are supposed to do here, but I will not stand for you to make baseless, insulting comments about other students."

"You allow them to make baseless, insulting comments about us. All the time. Racist comments too. You allow it. They have called me a half-breed since I was ten years old and you don't care."

"Stop it, Jeticia. Just stop before you talk yourself into more trouble."

“I’m going to graduate from this school and I’m going to be number one in my class despite all of them. All the Krayton’s and the other parents who want me gone. Because I know they would hate it more than anything. I’m going to succeed because they want me to fail. Could you please call my dad?” Jett finally burst into tears as she finished. “It’s not fair. This whole school isn’t fair. It sucks, and I hate it,” she said with her face in her hands.

“I’m sure he’s on his way. I had my assistant call him before you got here.”

Markus walked into the room, followed by Mr. Preston’s assistant. She looked sympathetically at Jett and cut Mr. Preston a dirty look before she turned and walked back out.

“What the hell is going on here?” her dad demanded of the principal. “Hey kid, you ok? Come here.” He put his arms around the girl and hugged her. She buried her face in his chest and started sobbing louder, shaking as she did. “What did the bad man do this time?” Jett stopped crying a moment, laughed, and started crying again.

“You’d better have a damn good explanation for why my daughter is sitting in your office, alone with you and crying.”

“I’m sure you’ve read this, but I’ll let you read it again. It’s a story your daughter wrote about the boys on the football team.”

“I told you I didn’t use their names. If you think it’s about them, it’s because you recognize the behavior of the characters in the story. It shows that you understand how awful those guys are,” Jett said, through tears.

"The kid's got a point," he sat down and returned his daughter to her chair.

"I'm in trouble again, dad," Jett said, calm now, while wiping tears away with her hand. Her father reached into his blazer pocket and pulled out a handkerchief. She took it and started wiping her face. "For the paper. I'm suspended for writing my story. It hurt their feelings and their parents complained because other kids were making jokes about the football team, gag, and they are now the victims of the mean nerd bullies. So, the smart black kid must be suspended so the football players and their moms can feel better about putting me in my place. Again. It's just not fair, and it sucks."

"I know, kid. It's not fair. It's not going to ever really be fair here, it seems."

"I'm suspended."

"Mr. Preston, I expect better than this. I hope you understand that. You have no idea how much the bullying, and the racism, hurts her. She tries to be tough and act like it doesn't bother her, but I'm her dad. I know it's pulling her apart at times. You need to stick up for these kids. All of them, not just the kids whose parents have the most money or influence. I thought, maybe things would be different this year. I'm very disappointed that you would have my daughter in this condition. And suspending her over an assignment?"

"Oh, it's not the assignment alone. It's also for the way she was talking to me just now."

“No matter how angry she gets, she’ll tell you the truth. It’s not in her to lie. If it made you angry, it’s because you know it’s true.”

Jett looked at her dad and, through tears, smiled, and started crying again.

Mr. Preston looked at her dad for about five seconds before he said, “Ok. Here is what I’ll do. I will retract the suspension if she writes an apology to the students offended by her story. And Jett, would it kill you to support your school at a football game? Maybe if you saw them play, you’d have a different attitude.”

“Would it kill them to watch the chess club play at a tournament or to support honor roll kids at academic competitions? No, but they’ll never do it. So why do I care about football? And how come you never go to those events? Those kids are representing your school too. Just because we all get out of class and are forced to go to a stupid pep rally and worship all those entitled brats and make them feel superior to the rest of us doesn’t mean the rest of us don’t matter.”

“You’re not helping your case, kid.”

“My compromise stands. No suspension if she writes an apology. No apology, three days' suspension.”

“It’s up to you Jett. You’re old enough to make this decision on your own.”

“Suspension will hurt my grades but apologizing to those guys will hurt every other kid at this school that’s bullied or teased by them. It’s not right. It’s a terrible choice to make.”

“What’s it going to be?” Mr. Preston asked.

“No apology. I won’t do it,” Jett said, after a long pause. “I won’t apologize. Mike already said he would destroy me and that he would own me. I won’t apologize to someone who says those things to me. It wouldn’t be fair to the other kids who would be punished even worse by those guys once they realize they can force us to apologize to them. It’s wrong.”

“It could hurt your chances of graduating first in your class, as you said you would do to spite everyone,” Mr. Preston said.

“I’ll study extra hard. I’ll find a way. I finally made some friends in this school and I will not let them down. What you could do to me isn’t as bad as how I’d feel about myself if I gave in,” Jett said. She knew she was being dramatic, but she was determined not to apologize to the kids that have bullied her since she was ten years old.

“Okay. It’s settled,” Mr. Preston said. “Three days' suspension. We’ll see you on Thursday.”

As they left the office and passed Mr. Preston’s assistant, she stood up and approached the girl. “Oh Jett, I’m so sorry. Come here,” she said as she hugged her. Jett halfheartedly returned the hug. She was ready to go.

***

Melinda texted Jett at lunch:

Melinda: *wya J? It’s lunch.*

Jett: *My dad’s office. Suspended.*

Melinda: *What?? For what???*

Jett: *Preston was mad about my story. I went off on him.*

Melinda: *What??? Why was he mad?*

Jett: *Parents got mad. Felt my story ridiculed their kids. They felt bullied.*

Melinda: *Bullied? They're a bunch of dicks. They don't know what it means to feel bullied.*

Jett: *That's what I said. Except the part about them being a bunch of dicks. But they are.*

Melinda: *Yes, they are a bunch of dicks. He suspended you?*

Jett: *Told him it was a racial thing with 0-10 and he doesn't do anything about it.*

Melinda: *Damn. . . It's true. 0-10 are so racist.*

Jett: *I know. But I got suspended. Sucks.*

Jett: *Preston told me I could write an apology to 0-10 and I would not be suspended.*

Jett: *I was like "nope." 0-10 owes everyone apologies. So Preston suspended me.*

Melinda: *How long?*

Jett: *Til Thursday.*

Melinda: *Damn girl. Your grades. We have exams in three classes you'll miss.*

Jett: *I know. I'm fuming. Preston can't break me down though.*

Melinda: *I'm gonna tell Miss Stark. Maybe she can do something.*

Jett: *Thanks! I doubt they will let her though.*

Melinda: *She loved your story, and she's such a crazy hippie. She needs a protest. LOL*

Jett: *LOL Maybe.*

Melinda: *LOL I like her. Wyd at your dad's office?*

Jett: *Work. I'm doing the front desk. He pays me $$ to help out.*

Melinda: *Are you grounded though?*

Jett: *No, my dad was there, and he was angry at the principal. He told me I made the right decision to not back down.*

Melinda: *Wow! My dad would kill me, even if I was in the right.*

Jett: *I bet your dad would be high fiving you and stuff.*

Melinda: *Maybe. LOL. He's a big nerd. I'm gonna go tell Miss Stark now. Later!*

Later, Melinda texted Jett again.

Melinda: *OMG J. You're not gonna believe this stuff.*

Jett: *What stuff M?*

Melinda: *I told Miss Stark what happened, and she was upset for you but didn't say anything at first.*

Jett: *K, I believe that.*

Melinda: *Here's the cool part. She made this announcement that she wouldn't have the exams ready on Wednesday because of problems with the printer, network, or something She put them off for Friday.*

Jett: *Awesome!*

Melinda: *But wait, there's more.*

Melinda: *That exam in Mrs. Henderson's class? Friday. Same excuse about the printer/network.*

Jett: ?

Melinda: *And Mr. Jack assigned a paper that is due Thursday.*

Jett :?

Melinda: *But then he said this: "If you know of anyone who may be suspended, don't tell them about the assignment. Preston wouldn't think it would be appropriate for suspended students to find out about assignments, even though if they turn them in the day they return, we have to take them and grade them. So (he looked right at me and said) DO NOT TELL SUSPENDED STUDENTS ABOUT THE ASSIGNMENT BECAUSE IF THEY SOMEHOW FIND OUT AND DO THE PAPER AND HAVE IT THURSDAY, I HAVE TO GIVE THEM CREDIT FOR IT. SO, DO NOT TAKE A PICTURE OF THE ASSIGNMENT INSTRUCTIONS AND EMAIL OR TEXT IT TO*

THEM. DO NOT EMAIL OR TEXT IT TO THEM OR THEY WILL TURN IT IN AND GET FULL CREDIT EVEN THOUGH THEY ARE SUSPENDED FOR A REALLY BOGUS REASON."

Jett: *That. Is. So. Awesome!*

Melinda: *Check your email. I "didn't" email you the assignment at all. Ha-ha.*

Jett: *I "didn't" get it. I'm totally "not" thinking of a topic already. Ha-ha. You rock M!*

Melinda: *You rock J.*

Jett: *and our teachers rock. Smart kids represent! Ha-ha.*

Melinda: *Nerd flow.*

Jett: *Brain flow!*

Melinda: *#smartkidsrule!*

Jett: *#smartkidswillruletheworldoneday*

Jett: *Thanks for everything! Gotta go though. Gotta ride my bike to karate now.*

"Jett, do you mind if I drive you to karate today? It looks like rain. And can I please stay and watch? I've always wanted to see you do your karate. I'll keep a distance and stay quiet. I just want to sit with the moms and watch," Ashley asked, interrupting Jett's text conversation.

"I guess."

“Okay, good. And afterward, we’ll go out for dinner. Your dad is working tonight, and he didn’t want you staying home alone. You can hang out at my place after dinner until he is finished.”

“Okay, cool,” Jett said.

***

Ashley sat and watched Jett spar with Denise. Denise started with a few punches and kicks which Jett parried or moved away from. Her movements were fluid and efficient. She didn’t bounce around like a boxer but kept a firm stance and moved with Denise. They looked more like they were dancing than fighting. Jett was very patient and would wait for an opportunity to strike. At first, they fought in short bursts, but Denise gradually increased the number of strikes and combinations of strikes. Jett kept a cool head and continued to respond. Though she was sweating, Jett did not lose her wind and stayed very focused on her instructor. The volleys became more intense and Denise moved faster and worked to catch Jett off guard. While Jett hadn’t landed a strike, neither had Denise. At times Denise would stop and say something to her, to correct her technique. Ashley knew she could turn on the heat at any moment and overwhelm Jett, but she guided her through each round, escalating the intensity and speed and allowing Jett to adjust. Jett responded by moving and avoiding being kicked and struck. Finally, Jett saw her opportunity and threw a kick directly at her instructor. Her instructor blocked the kick, but Jett responded with two strikes with her fists and another kick, this time getting her leg almost as high as her head. Her instructor blocked the strikes, but Jett caught her by surprise with the kick.

"I like it when you are more aggressive. You can come at people fast, and that was a sophisticated combination. Just make sure you recover quickly because an experienced black belt will have several responses for that kick in tournament."

"Yes, ma'am." Jett looked at Ashley and waved, smiling. Ashley smiled and waved back, with a tear in her eye. Jett was growing up way too fast, she thought to herself. She looked like a confident young woman while sparring. Ashley was proud of the girl's skill but she was also sad; one day Jett will grow up, move away and she won't see her much anymore. She waved her hand in front of her eyes and told herself to stop being so damn emotional and just enjoy the moment.

Chapter Six: Diana Jones

Diana Jones was tall, blond, and beautiful. She was also bold and daring, but her best attribute was her intellect. Diana was brilliant. She went to all the best schools and universities and consistently graduated at the top of her class. She was also the lone heir to a huge family fortune. This gave her the freedom to take on the hard-luck cases most attorneys would ignore. She was an activist as much as she was an attorney.

Diana owned the swankiest law firm in Port City. Her firm had a contract with Markus Jackson. He provided investigative services for the people she represented in court. She also funded much of Jackson's work on missing person cases. Diana Jones was a private investigator before she was an attorney and investigating missing person cases related to human trafficking was her area of expertise. She uncovered a lot of corruption in her time as a private detective. As an attorney, she was relentless in her fight against corruption. She had the dirt on everyone, and she wasn't afraid to use it.

She discovered Markus Jackson in the clubs and bars of Port City and saw in him a person who was streetwise, analytical, and didn't much care if he rubbed people the wrong way when he was after something. He was rough around the edges, but she recognized his potential. She became his mentor and gave him cases to work through her law practice. Investigative Associates, the investigative agency now owned and operated by Markus Jackson and Ashley Garcia, belonged to Diana before she sold it to Markus Jackson.

When Diana met Ashley Garcia, she had come to Diana with a secret: she had a violent boyfriend and she was afraid to leave. She sent Ashley to Markus to rid her of the boyfriend; a service he often provided to people in dangerous situations. After working with Markus, Garcia took an interest in a career as a Private Investigator, so Diana suggested she work for Jackson as his assistant. Jackson needed someone to run the office and help with the books, and Garcia was organized and meticulous. He mentored her until she got her license as a Private Investigator. Jackson never liked having a boss and he never wanted to be anyone else's boss, so he offered Ashley Garcia the opportunity to be a partner in the business.

That was when Jett, Markus Jackson's ten-year-old daughter, arrived in Port City. Diana adored Jett, and they spent a lot of time together. While Ashley settled into the role of a surrogate stepmother, Diana became her cool aunt.

Diana and Ashley were at Joey's Italian Restaurant for Jett's birthday when Jett and her dad arrived. As they approached the table, Ashley rose first to hug Jett, followed by Diana.

"Well Chica, how did you like your surprise birthday gift, from your dad?" Ashley said.

"Ooh, what was it?" Diana asked.

"It's awesome. Dad set up a punching bag and a mat for me to practice my karate on. And he gave me my own customized gloves for competition. They're even my favorite colors: black and blue!"

"Like your opponents are gonna be when you fight in tournaments," Diana interjected.

“I’m gonna start working out every morning before school so I can get the extra work in. Now that I have a bag and gloves, I can work on my combinations. I want to be fast and strong.”

“Didn’t I tell you my kid would know how to throw a punch?” Markus was proud.

“Well, I’m happy for you Chica. You work so hard at your karate and I’m so proud of you.”

Joey Donelli, the owner of Joey’s Italian Restaurant, came to the table to tell Jett he prepared cannoli for her birthday. This was her favorite dessert and Joey made the best cannoli in town. Vinnie came to visit Jett and had a cup of coffee with her dad, as they discussed some business concerns.

Jett reflected on how things had changed since she was a lonely little girl, living with her mother, in Baltimore. They only had each other. Here in Port City, she had all these people looking out for her.

When she got home, she worked on another project. A secret project only she knew about. She took out her diary, where she recorded her data, and started a new entry. She placed the pen on her dresser; took several slow, deep breaths, and imagined the pen moving.

Chapter Seven: Fight Like A Girl

"You prepared for this?" Markus asked as they traveled to the tournament.

Jett was alert but tired, "I think so. I'm sleepy though. I could not sleep last night. I kept thinking about what I haven't done to get ready for this. It kept me up."

"Think about what you have done to prepare, kid. You've been working hard at it all year."

"I know. I kept watching videos of girls fighting in tournaments. Maybe figure out what to do. They weren't very good though. Most girls jump around during the match. I don't fight like that. It's like they're afraid to get hit."

"Shouldn't they be?"

"No. If you fight like you're afraid to get hit, you'll never be able to hit anyone back. Not while jumping around like it's boxing. It seems like it's better to be more confident and stand there and defend yourself and be in a position to hit back. I guess I'll find out today."

"You'll do fine. It's a learning experience."

"Yea, I want to do well."

Jett took a nap for the rest of the drive. Her dad woke her up and told her to get her things when they arrived. Jett got up, picked up her backpack, and followed him into the building. They found her teacher, Denise Williams, and checked in at registration. Her dad found a space in the bleachers.

Jett picked up a schedule for the preliminary matches. There were fifteen girls in Jett's division. It was the highest division in the tournament, including girls aged fifteen to seventeen with brown and black belts. Jett changed clothes and packed her regular clothes in her backpack and looked at her schedule. She would fight in four preliminary fights. She had to be in the top eight to make it to the finals.

Denise pulled her aside as they walked out of the locker room. "Your first fight is against the girl who won your division last time. She's very good. She also fights in the black belt division. She'll come at you fast, Jett. Be ready and focused. It will be a good test for you."

"Yes, ma'am," Jett was nervous. She was the lowest seed, so she had to fight the highest seed first.

"Relax Jett. You'll do well. Just breathe and keep your feet in the right place. Everything else will come together."

"Yes, ma'am."

Jett brought her backpack to her dad in the bleachers just as Ashley arrived.

Ashley hugged her and said, "How do you feel Chica?"

"Nervous. I fight last year's champion in the first round. Great."

"Just do your best and you'll be fine," Ashley said.

Jett spent a few minutes warming up. She did some of her moves, some kata, and stretched. Before she could finish her teacher gestured for her to come over.

"It's time Jett," she told her as she approached, "Just breathe and stay focused. Let her come to you and protect yourself. You'll score some points but be patient."

Jett walked to the mat and took her position. The referee checked the two girls in and they shook hands. "Good luck," the other girl said.

"You too," Jett replied, even though she knew luck was the last thing the other girl would need in this fight. The referee blew the whistle, and Jett Landry's karate career began.

Jett competed fiercely, but she lost her first match. She won each successive match and made it to the finals. Jett became confident and relaxed, and she was able to stay calm and focused. She kept finding ways to score points. She worked her way to the final match. She fought against the girl she fought in the first match.

Both girls elevated their performance and Jett made it to sudden death due to a tie at the end of three rounds. The final volley lasted an entire round with both girls fighting almost continuously, but Jett lost her focus for one moment and the other girl scored a point. Jett was disappointed, but Denise was very excited about her performance. Jett didn't realize it but she made quite an impression with the tournament officials and fans of the sport.

On the way home from the tournament, Jett fell asleep in the passenger seat of the car. As she drifted off, she promised herself she would never let her guard down again. She resolved to study every possible move and prepare a defense for it. She would visualize these moves and practice until they were instinct.

***

Jett's training escalated to a new level of intensity. She woke up early each morning and practiced techniques and combinations for at least an hour on the balcony of their flat. She moved an old stereo onto the balcony and hooked up her iPad, so she could play music while she trained. Her music was often relaxing. Jett's goal was to stay centered and focused while training; not to get fired up and aggressive. The music provided balance. She often did kata in a rhythm, so her movements would flow. Over time she would develop a routine: relaxing workouts, such as yoga and kata in the mornings, with more intense workouts in the evenings. As her technique improved, she began working on speed and intensity. The speed of the final rounds of the tournament surprised her, so she felt she needed to improve the speed of her karate, so she could keep up with the older girls. At five foot two Jett was small, but she was getting stronger and faster. She intended to be ready for anything.

***

Chapter Eight: A Shocking Turn of Events

Jett was at her locker putting her books away when she noticed a group of kids behind her. She turned around to see Mike and his friends staring her down. Angelique, his girlfriend, and two other girls stood off to the side of the boys. Angelique looked worried and annoyed. More kids started walking over, as they noticed something was about to happen.

"Ok. What's going on?" she asked the boys. She started to put her backpack on her left shoulder when one of the boys violently knocked it out of her hand.

"Are you seriously going to do this again?" Jett asked, annoyed.

"Go to hell, Jett," Mike said, glaring at the smaller girl.

"Damn," Jett said, sarcastic. "I thought we were going to make it the whole year."

"We're going to make the whole year," he said. "You're not. We're going to kick your ass this time."

"What did I do to you? We've hardly talked all year. Leave me alone."

"Nope. I still owe you for last summer and for the stupid story you wrote. I don't forget."

"You don't owe me nothing. I've got somewhere to be. Leave me alone." Jett tried to walk past the boys but one of the larger boys pushed her back against the locker. "Come on guys, let me by."

Jett again tried to walk away but another boy, standing to Mike's left, pushed Jett a few feet away until she was in a corner. The boys surrounded her and moved in close, staring at her menacingly. Jett felt crowded and trapped. She had no room to maneuver. It was strange; they said very little, just kept her in the corner, as if they were waiting for her to start the fight. Jett didn't take the bait. She held out hope she could talk her way out of this. All hope was gone in the next sixty seconds when Mike said some of the most hateful comments Jett had ever heard.

Melinda walked up in time to hear part of Mike's diatribe. She tried to interject, but she was shouted down by the other boys. She took out her phone and started to record, but another boy knocked it out of her hands. She scrambled to pick it up, but the boy kicked it down the hall. When she finally retrieved her phone, she was too shocked by the hatefulness of Mike's comments to think about recording. His words finally broke Jett down. Jett was sobbing and yelling as she spoke. She invited Mike to fight her instead of saying the hurtful things he was saying.

Mike stepped forward and started to hit Jett as another boy moved in from her right side. Jett moved away from Mike but was trapped in the corner as the other boy almost grabbed her arm. Jett swung hard at Mike, hitting him in the mouth. She stomped on the other boy's foot to back him up and followed with a kick to the stomach. The boy jumped back but took the kick. Wasting no time, Jett swung at the next boy coming towards her. Even though he was about to hit her, she hit him first, fast and hard, in the left cheek. He buckled at the punch and Jett saw blood drip onto his shirt. Without stopping, she hit Mike in the mouth again. His face was also bloodied from the punch as she busted his lip. Jett went on to hit the boy in front of her, who was trying to get a grip on her arm. Jett was still cornered, as the boys were not moving from their position, and Jett couldn't find a way to get around them. She felt vulnerable and scared as she couldn't use proper form when trapped and crowded. From the outside of the scrum, it looked to Angelique like there was nothing but a flurry of fists and feet, all coming from Jett and connecting with her boyfriend and his friends. When it was over, about thirty seconds later, all four boys were bloodied from strikes by Jett. None of the boys landed a punch. But they still had her cornered.

They stopped for a second, leading Jett to think they were giving up the fight. For just a moment, Jett let her guard down and started to say something to the boys. But one of the larger boys, a boy named Jeff, grabbed her throat, pinned her against the wall, and lifted her off the floor. Jett struggled for a moment and started getting dizzy. The boy seemed to get tired quickly and lowered her until her feet touched the floor, but he did not let go of her throat. The other boys cheered the boy on as he squeezed, not hard enough to keep her from breathing but hard enough to scare her into thinking he would.

Jett squatted down for a moment to get the boy to pull her back up. When he did, she jumped up, keeping her back to the wall for balance and, with both feet, kicked the boy hard in the ribcage. The boy let go of her throat and bent over in pain, gasping for air. Jett fell to the floor, but quickly jumped up and waited for the boys to make their next move.

"Okay. Plan T is in effect guys," Mike said to his friends, and, out loud, "Jett! Put the taser down. Come on, put it down before someone gets hurt."

"Taser? I don't have a taser. What are you talking about?"

"OK guys, on three, grab her and take the taser away. One, Two, Three!"

Three of the four boys moved towards Jett. Mike pulled a taser out of his pocket, activated it, and pressed it into Jett's arm. Jett grimaced in pain and dropped to the ground. Mike followed her to the ground, continuing to shock her as she went down. Once down, the boys crowded her and kicked at her. Jett felt disoriented and dizzy.

When the security officer arrived, Jett heard Mike say, "She had a freaking taser! She was going to shock somebody or something!"

Jett tried to respond, but the security officer pulled her to her feet.

"Stop resisting! Stop!" he yelled. His instructions became more confusing. "Stand up! Now, don't move. Put your arms behind your back. I said don't move. Now, put your arms behind you. Stop moving!"

The guard put the handcuffs on Jett's wrists, securing her arms behind her, and started dragging her away from the others.

"Assault, bringing a weapon to a school, fighting, resisting. You're going to Juvenile this time. I promise you," he yelled as the boys cheered.

Jett was still shaken up from being tased. “They started it, they had the taser, and they shocked me!”

“Shut up and stop resisting,” the security officer told her as he walked her down the hall.

“Call my dad!” Jett demanded through tears.

The officer put his left foot in front of Jett, took her by the shoulders, and shoved her so she would fall to the floor. He pulled her to her feet and started walking her to the office again. “Don’t resist!” he said. Jett froze; she was terrified at what the security officer may do next. “Walk!” the officer yelled. Melinda and some other kids tried to intercede, but the officer waved them off. “Say goodbye, you’re never seeing her again. She’s going to be locked up for a long time,” he said over his shoulder at the kids.

Angelique covertly put something in her purse and rejoined her friends. Some kids in the hallway were cheering for the security officer, while others were staring down the hall, scared, and unsure of what had just happened.

***

Ashley arrived at the hospital first. Markus had been in the field, north of the city, and was an hour away. He had received a call from the secretary who reported Jett was in a fight, had injured several kids, and brought a weapon to school. He called Ashley and asked her to check on Jett while he rushed back to town.

She rushed into the hospital room to find Jett handcuffed to the bed, with the security officer sitting in the chair across the room, watching her.

"Little Chica! Are you okay?" Ashley said when she saw the girl's condition. "What happened?"

"I'm okay, just sore. Those guys attacked me with a taser and lied and said I brought the taser. I tried to walk away but they wouldn't let me."

"Okay, we're going to figure it all out," Ashley said. Then she saw the handcuffs.

"What the hell is this?" she said, angry, to the school security officer.

"Handcuffs. So, she doesn't hurt anyone. She's done. Expelled for sure. Hopefully, she'll go to Juvenile Detention where she belongs."

"Take the handcuffs off *now*. I'm not asking."

"No, ma'am. She resisted detainment. They stay on."

"I'm sorry. Are you a law enforcement officer? Do you have a license? Do you have a warrant to detain this child? Do you even know what the law is regarding illegally restraining or detaining a child? What is your probable cause?"

"Are you her guardian?"

"No, I'm acting on his behalf until he gets here. And if he sees this, he won't ask. Take them off now."

"Fine. I'll remove them. You're responsible for her now. But the police are on the way. She's going to Juvenile Detention for this one. At the least, she'll be expelled."

"Just take the handcuffs off, asshole."

She looked warmly at Jett and touched her forehead. "They shouldn't mess with a momma bear, right, honey? You look like you got hurt this time. Are you sure you're ok?"

Jett looked up at her. "You should see the other guys."

Ashley smiled back worriedly. "That sounds like something your dad would say."

"About the other guys," the security officer said as he put his handcuffs away, "One has broken ribs, one is bleeding from all over his face and one is getting his stomach x-rayed as we speak."

"I got choked, shocked, and kicked repeatedly in the head and face and thrown to the ground," Jett said, angry. "And they started it. I tried to walk away. And they brought the taser."

"Shhh," Ashley said, "don't listen to him." To the security officer, she said, "Get out of this room and stay away from this child. If you say one more word to her, I will kick your ass myself. Do you understand me?"

He said nothing as he cut Ashley a dirty look and left the room. Ashley hugged the girl and took her hand in her own, as they waited for her dad to get there.

***

In the waiting room, Melinda paced, feeling anxious, and unsure of what to do. She found out they took Jett to the Emergency Room and she wanted to tell her parents, the police, someone, what happened. She saw the other kids there too, but they were brought to the back immediately.

Markus arrived forty minutes after getting the call. He walked up to the desk and asked for "Jett Landry" in a very worried voice.

Melinda ran up to him and said, "Excuse me, sir? I'm a friend of Jett and I saw the whole thing. Jett didn't bring the taser. She didn't, I swear."

He turned around and looked at her. She could see the worry in his eyes. He was wearing black slacks, a white dress shirt, and a matching jacket. His shirt was untucked, and he looked like he rushed over from another engagement. She noticed his blue eyes. They were the same as Jett's.

"I'm sorry sir," she said awkwardly, not knowing what else to say.

"What's your name, kid?"

"Melinda."

"Ok Melinda, I remember you from last time. Come on back with me and tell us what happened. And call your parents and let them know where you are." He rushed through the door, gesturing for Melinda to follow.

When they got to the room, he went to Jett and touched her forehead, brushing her thick black hair away from her face. "Hey kid, you ok?"

“I’m okay,” Jett said quietly.

“You don’t look so okay this time. Are you hurting?”

“You should see the other guys,” Jett said, smiling weakly.

“Your friend came to make sure everyone knows what happened.”

“Hi Jett,” Melinda said. “Are you ok?”

“I’ll be fine, thanks for coming.”

“Melinda,” Markus said, “Before anyone else says anything, can you tell us what happened?” He gestured at Ashley to record her statement.

“Yes, sir. It was terrible. I was walking to Jett’s locker, so we could go to the library. We go study and hang out on Tuesdays after school, and the same boys as always, had Jett cornered in the hallway. She tried to walk away but they wouldn’t let her. Mike said some horrible, horrible things to her. Even his girlfriend got upset by it. Jett said something back because she was upset by what he said, and they just attacked her. She fought them off, and they stopped for a second, and one boy got his hands on her neck and pinned her against the locker, choking her. Jett somehow managed to kick him in the ribs and he let go.”

“That must be the kid whose ribs she broke,” Ashley interjected.

“I hope the little asshole hurts. Every time he breathes, I hope it hurts,” Markus said. “I’m sorry, kid. Go on.”

“Yes, sir. I hope he hurts too. Anyway, that’s when Mike pulled out the taser and started yelling as if Jett had it. Really loud. They all jumped her again and this time he shocked her with the taser on her arm and she fell, and they kicked at her until security got there. Mike told security that Jett pulled a taser and he grabbed her around the neck and held onto her, yelling at her to keep still, and to put her arms behind her back, and telling her she was going to jail or something. When she asked him to call her dad, he threw her on the ground and picked her up again, telling her to stop resisting him.”

“And the guard handcuffed her to this bed when I got here, but I made him take them off,” Ashley said.

“Damn,” Markus said, “Is this your recollection, Jett?”

“Yes, they told me they were going to get me this time and when I tried to walk away, they pushed me into a corner. I tried to avoid the fight dad. I really did. Then he told me horrible things about you and my mom. I started crying and got upset. But I didn’t throw the first punch. I just told him off. I promise.”

“I understand. Melinda, we’ll need you to tell the police what you just told us. As far as this security guard, he and I are going to have words when this is over with.”

“Dad, don’t.”

“No, I will. I know his type. A grown man putting his hands on my daughter? No way.”

The police arrived shortly thereafter and were waiting to interview everyone. Jett and Melinda told their story, with her dad and Ashley present. Melinda’s parents showed up not long after. They were decent people, very concerned about Jett, and were glad their daughter had the courage to speak up. Melinda's mother told Ashley that her 'daughter' is welcome at their home any time the two girls want to get together.

After the police talked to the kids, they got the parents together by the nurse's station. Krayton was there. He glared at Markus Jackson as they huddled up in a corner to listen to the officer. There were two officers. An older officer and a younger officer. The older officer explained the situation:

"One of our detectives reviewed the tapes at the school and filed his report while we were talking to all the parties involved. Based on what we all found, we don't have enough evidence for probable cause for an arrest. There are conflicting reports regarding who brought the taser. The only non-involved witness claims the boys brought the taser and yelled that the girl had it. The boys said she had it, and she said they had it. When we reviewed the videos at the school, what we noticed was the boys provoked this conflict when they approached the girl at her locker. She tried to walk away, but they pushed her into a corner which, incidentally, isn't covered by video. This corroborates her account of who started the confrontation and conflicts the boys' account. It doesn't answer the question of who brought the taser. While the original complaint is against the girl, the situation is ambiguous enough that we could recommend the girl's family pursue an investigation as well. Our recommendation, though, is all of you talk to your kids about conflict resolution and fighting. Raise your kids yourself and don't involve the police department. It doesn't do anyone any good for kids to have a record this early in life. I personally don't want to put kids in jail over a fight at school."

Markus reached to shake the officer's hand and said, "Will do officer, we'll talk to our kid about getting along. Thank you, sir."

Krayton, however, wasn't satisfied. "I want an investigator looking into this, immediately. It's my right."

"Sir," the officer said, "I would be careful about this. Your son seems to have been the instigator in both the video and the witness accounts. Maybe you can talk to him about getting along with other kids in school."

"My son has broken ribs," one of the other parents, a mother with short, red hair, a sleeveless shirt, and jeans, said, "Do you think we can just talk to him about getting along when this animal is capable of this?"

Markus bristled at the 'animal' comment. He wanted to say something, but he suppressed the urge.

"Ma'am, the girl has contusions on her neck where your son was choking her. And three boys were fighting against one girl. She has the right to defend herself if attacked. The video clearly shows her attempting to walk away, and the boys shoved her into a corner instead. Are you sure you want to pursue this?"

The woman fell silent, as did Krayton and the other parents.

"If either of you wants to pursue this further, you're welcome to file a formal complaint at the station tomorrow. But as far as our report goes, we have three boys attacking a girl who defended herself and did a damn good job of it, and someone brings a taser, which was used on the girl, to immobilize her.

Sir," to Markus, "If anyone should pursue this further, I would encourage you to do so. As far as these boys, I think someone needs to teach them that men don't fight girls or women, ever. I think it would save them a lot of legal complications later in life."

As the police officers left, Krayton approached Markus. "This isn't over yet, Jackson. We meet with the principal tomorrow. I won't rest until your kid is out of our school."

"Drink plenty of coffee, you're gonna need it," he replied, as he turned to walk away.

When he returned to the room, a male nurse was in the room with Ashley and Jett.

"Well?" Ashley asked.

"No probable cause for anyone to be detained. Police even said the evidence supported the report that those assholes started this whole thing."

Jett smiled and relaxed. She was worried she would be taken to Juvenile Detention. Her nurse smiled back as he finished taking a blood sample. "Don't let those jerks push you around Jeticia Landry," he said, "keep on kicking butt."

Jett laughed and thanked the nurse, who had been kind to her. Her dad put his arm around her shoulders and said. "We still have to deal with the school tomorrow, kid."

"I know. And I still want to graduate first in my class. I'm serious about this, dad. Don't pull me out of school."

"Okay. Now, about the security guard."

Markus left the room and found the security officer in the lobby, getting ready to leave.

"Hey, you, a word?" he said to the guard.

"Yea," the officer said, "I only have a minute. I want to go home too."

"You're not worth much more time than that. You put your hands on my daughter today. You didn't listen to what she had to say, you put handcuffs on her, and you threw her on the ground. Is this true?"

"Well, she was-"

"It's a yes or no question. Is it true? Yes or no?"

"Yes. She was-"

"Ok. Never put your hands on my daughter again. Ever. Don't even talk to her. If you do, you deal with me. Got it?"

"Sir, I have a job to do and I'm going to-"

"Don't 'sir' me, asshole. Stay away from my daughter. That's it."

"Again, I'm responsible for..."

"You're responsible for staying away from my daughter. Got it?"

"I'm getting tired of you thinking you can tell me what to do. I work security, not you. You got it?"

Markus sighed as if he were exasperated, and looked the guard straight in the eyes, and said, "Here's what I got: you physically abused my daughter and illegally detained her using handcuffs after she had been injured by three knuckleheads with a taser. You didn't bother to find out what was going on before throwing her on the ground, while handcuffed. I deal with assholes like you all the time. See, I know your type. You were the cool guy in school. Not much different from these assholes that have been giving her a hard time. Truth is, you miss being the bully. It was the only time you ever thought you were worth a shit. When you graduated and got out in the real world, you realized no one gave a shit that you were first string whatthehellever you were first string at, and no one was intimidated by you anymore. You thought you'd be a cop. But they drummed your ass out of the Academy as soon as they realized you were another asshole wannabe tough guy. So, you became a security guard. At a school. Where you could go back to the last place anyone ever thought you were a badass. Now you're reliving all your high school memories about being one of the guys and picking on the smaller kids. Except you've messed with my daughter, which means you really messed up. I won't kick your ass right now, but I want to. Really bad. But one day I will see you somewhere, away from the school, away from all of this. And that day could be next week, or it could be ten years from now, but I'll run into you, and you'll be acting like an asshole. I will remember what you did to my daughter and I will mess you up like you've never known. So, don't mess with my daughter, and don't be an asshole. Because I will be watching. Got it, security guard?"

The security officer just turned and walked away, unsure of what to say. Ashley, who had walked up behind him, smiled and put her arms around his waist.

“Don’t mess with papa bear, right?” she said.

“Something like that.” He was still angry. “Thanks for handling this before I got here.”

“I love her as if she were my own child,” Ashley said impulsively, “they’re sending her home now.”

***

The next morning Jett, her dad, and Ashley arrived at school for the meeting. Mr. Preston’s secretary walked them to a conference room. As Markus and Ashley entered the room, she stopped Jett and touched her arm. “Are you okay Jett? I worried about you,” she said.

“I’m fine, thanks,” Jett said.

“Ok. I’m so sorry for what those boys did to you. I hope something good for you comes out of this.”

Jett thanked her and entered the room.

They walked into a room occupied by the parents of the boy who choked her, the mother of the other boy involved, and Mike’s parents. The security officer sat in the back of the room. Markus gave him a look, not threatening and not hostile, but somewhere in between, as they took their seats. Jett sat between her dad and Ashley.

Jett sported a black eye from a kick she took to the face. She was stiff as she walked into the room.

There was an intense hostility between the parents of the boys and Jett’s family. They were all quiet for a moment until the silence was broken by the mother of the boy who had tried to choke Jett.

"I hope you're happy. My son has broken ribs thanks to your child. Do you have any idea how much that hurts?" she said to Markus.

"Actually, I do. Tell him not to start a fight if he isn't willing to take a kick to the ribs. Maybe he'll learn something." Ashley touched Jett's arm as she glared at the woman.

Mike's mom retorted, "That's what you get. No responsibility. He just lets that ani... child run wild through this school. No discipline."

Ashley spoke up. "Were you going to say 'animal?' This young lady has more class than all of your little bastards."

"Ok," Markus recognized that this could escalate, "how about we wait for the principal?"

"No, she wants to talk about our boys," Mike's mother said, "fine. We'll talk about your child. She's finished at this school. She'll be lucky to avoid Juvenile Detention. I have friends on the school board, and they assure me this nightmare will be over soon."

"Your kids are going to have a hard time in the real world when they have real-world consequences," Ashley said. "Beating up a girl. Shocking her and kicking her when she's injured. Do you know what they do to guys who do this in prison? Ask them in ten years. They'll be able to describe it to you."

Mr. Preston walked in and looked at the people in the room. "I see you've started the conversation without me. Forgive my tardiness, but my secretary informed me that someone has sent her a video of what happened yesterday, and she is sending it to me. We can watch it once it downloads on my computer and maybe get a look at this incident."

"Who sent it?" Krayton asked. "Because I don't want some edited video making my boy look bad. We all know who the culprit is here. And I didn't give anyone permission to video my son."

"About that," Markus interjected, "I have a copy of the police report. As of this morning, I was encouraged to talk to a detective if I'm interested in filing assault charges on behalf of my daughter."

"That's another matter," Krayton said, "we're here to talk about what the school is going to do about this ongoing problem. We demand, and we've all discussed this at length, that you expell this girl from this school, effective immediately. You know the problems she's caused, Preston. You know this. You need to do the right thing right now. No need to wait for a video."

"I think we need to wait for the video," Ashley said, "and get the whole story. Why are you in such a rush?"

"Because this has gone on long enough. We want it solved today. Now. Everyone knows your child is the problem. This school didn't have problems before she came. Now, we keep having to come here and have this same meeting. Get rid of this child. Now."

"My boy was kicked in the stomach and punched in the face. Her boy was beaten in the face. And her son has broken ribs. Are you going to tell me this child isn't a menace to this school?"

Markus smirked to himself for a moment. He was proud of his girl for holding her own. "I'm sorry, is this funny to you?" Mike's mother said, "your child brought a taser to school."

"I did not!" Jett was angry. "They did. I've never used a taser in my whole life. I'm the one who was-"

"Shut your child up," one of the mothers snapped. "She shouldn't be talking to adults like that."

"No. She was there, and she can talk if she wants. Bring your kids here. Let them talk too. I'd love to talk to them."

"This is not productive at all. The video is almost ready. Let's just wait for it. In the meantime, I have requested the police report. And I understand that you," referring to Markus, "threatened my security staff last night at the hospital."

"I just told him what would happen if he pulled a stunt like that again with my daughter. It's not a threat. I stand behind every word I said." He looked over at the security officer. "Every single word."

The room was silent until Ashley spoke up. "We only want Jett to get fair treatment here. She is treated so unfairly. She makes straight A's. Her conduct is perfect in class. She is well mannered, and her teachers love her. The only time there is trouble is when these boys, who are known for bullying all the kids, are bullying her. She stands up for herself and you punish her for it. Something is going on with all of you. You won't discipline your kids for their behavior and you," pointing at the principal, "don't punish the kids who start these fights."

"I'm sorry," Laura Krayton, Mike's mother, said, "but you're obviously not this child's mother, she's a dead prostitute, so who are you?"

Markus flinched. Jett's face flushed, and her head went down. Ashley put her arm around the girl and said into her ear, "Don't listen to them, sweetie. They are terrible people who say terrible things." Jett started to cry anyway. Ashley pulled the girl close.

"Ashley Garcia and she can speak for Jett anytime she wants," he responded, "And don't talk about the kid's mother that way. You don't know anything about her."

"I'm sorry. Was her mother not a hooker, or a stripper? Isn't that how you met?"

Jett put her hands over her face and sobbed.

Mr. Preston let out a sigh. "I think we all need to just calm down a bit. None of this has been helpful in the least. Are you okay, Jett?"

"Yes sir. I'm okay. I don't want to watch the video though. May I please sit outside with your secretary while you all watch it? This is too hard."

"Yes, you may. I think the adults in this room have been very difficult."

"Thank you." Jett hugged Ashley and her dad on the way out. "Sorry dad, I just can't do this."

"Nothing to be sorry for, kid. We'll get this worked out."

Jett left the room and sat with the secretary in the lobby. The secretary, seeing the tears on the girl's face, hugged her before she sat down. "I'm sorry Jeticia. I know it's hard." Jett thanked her and sat down in a chair in the waiting area. She felt awkward not being in class during class time, but they may have already suspended her, or worse. The secretary tried to talk to her, but she had a hard time responding as she couldn't stop crying. So, she brought her some tissue and sat with her, not knowing what to say.

Back in the conference room, Mr. Preston had the video ready. He turned the computer to where everyone in the room could see it as it started playing. The video was from a cell phone and recorded from behind the boys. It started with Jett attempting to walk away and the larger boy pushing her into the corner while Mike started his diatribe:

'Nobody likes you, Jett. This school isn't for you. You're not wanted and you're not going to be tolerated anymore. Everybody hates you and it's never going to get better. We are never going to leave you alone. Our parents worked hard to create this school and your dad, who had nothing to do with it, just put you here. You don't deserve to be here; he doesn't deserve to have you here. You don't belong, and you never will.'

'Mike, just leave me alone.'

'Everybody hates you. You're in the way. We don't want you. You need to just drop out and go away.'

'Don't listen to him, Jett. We like you.'

'Shut up, bitch! The only reason they hang out with you because we're kicking your ass instead of theirs all the time. You're not one of us. My dad told me all about you and your family. Your dad is some asshole burnout alcoholic who gets off on screwing over wealthy people. And your mom? Your mom was a hooker, a whore. Apparently, she was sucking the wrong dick and your dad had to rush her out of town after getting off on her himself. I guess that's the only way she could pay him back. That's what you come from, A drunk and a whore. Maybe you should go back to your mom. Oh yeah, you can't go back to your mom because she's dead. She probably wanted to die to get away from you. Stupid bitch. You should join her. Just kill yourself, Jett. Do yourself, your family, and the world a favor and just get it over with.

'Oh look. She's crying. Like a girl. About time you act like one.'

Jett's trembling voice: *'Don't you ever talk about my mom. You don't know what it's like to lose a parent and then move across the country. It's hard. It's so hard I can't even explain it. It's just hard. It's always hard and it never stops. I'm already suffering enough, you entitled, privileged racist asshole. If you want to kick my ass, just do it. But stop talking about my mom!'*

The parents in the room saw the fight. They saw the larger kid pick Jett up by the neck and choke her. They saw Jett maneuver herself into a position to kick him in the ribs to get him to let go. They saw Mike holding the taser. They saw Jett get shocked and kicked while she was on the ground. They saw the security officer rush in and restrain Jett, giving her conflicting orders while handcuffing her.

Ashley cried while watching the video. Her dad was stoic, but his hand was shaking, exposing his departure from his usual cool demeanor. When the video was over, there was a tense, pregnant silence in the room, broken only by Ashley trying not to cry anymore.

Mr. Preston broke the silence by addressing his security officer. "You saw this child was shocked and kicked and you restrained her?"

"I thought she brought the taser sir," he said, "so I neutralized the threat."

"These are kids, not threats. This is not a war zone. I'll arrange a meeting with you and the security chief to review your conduct. Now leave my office, please." The officer got up and left the room without saying another word.

Ashley spoke up. "The things those boys said to her are horrid and disgusting. I'm in shock right now. This is so much worse than I thought. Ma'am," she addressed Mike's mother. "As a mother, can you imagine how it feels to hear someone say that to their child? Do you understand how awful this is?"

"They're kids. Kids get carried away," she responded but didn't seem convinced of it herself.

"I think you know how awful that is," Ashley said. "For someone to tell her such terrible, ugly things goes way beyond kids getting carried away. It's abusive. She said herself she would rather get beat up than hear all that. Jett has been through a lot.

None of this has been easy for her. She's very sensitive, especially when it comes to her mother. They were very close and when she died her life just changed overnight. And they planned to shock her and blame her for it. We all heard that, right? All three kids were in on this. Your son had the taser, and they all planned to make it look like she had it. Oh my god. I'm really upset right now. And to research Jett's mother's past to tell her those things. And you got it wrong. Her mother was a cocktail waitress, not a hooker or a stripper. Did you tell your son this?"

"I do my homework," Krayton said. "I didn't intend for Mike to tell Jett all this, though. But I like to know what I'm dealing with."

"What are you teaching your kids?" Markus said. "Dragging your adult issues into their lives? What's wrong with you, Krayton?"

"Don't tell me how to raise my son, Jackson," Krayton said. "I already raised a daughter. And she didn't just show up at ten years old from Baltimore. I was married to her mother when she was born. Some of us still have morals in this community."

"Morals?" Ashley said. "Are you joking?"

"No. I'm not joking. Sometimes we do what's best for the greater good, even if it doesn't always work out for everyone. I think you know what I mean, Ms. Garcia."

"You're gonna get yours one day, Krayton; but that's not what we're here for today," Markus said.

"We're getting off track," Preston started to say before Laura Krayton interrupted.

"I think you all are making too much out of this incident. They're just kids."

"Oh, come on, Laura," Jeff's mother said. "What if this girl would have tried to kill herself after that? It's going too far. There are limits."

"But she hurt our kids. Our sons. She's out of control. Can we still agree she should be expelled?"

"Or just allow her to home school as a compromise. We'll concede that. That's fair enough," Krayton said.

Markus held his rage at Krayton's proposal. In a firm voice, he said, "It's my daughter's goal to graduate from this school first in her class. She makes perfect grades in advanced classes; she deserves that chance. You're not going to take that away from her. Besides, you aren't in a position to offer a compromise. Your son planned and instigated this. He needs to be suspended or expelled. If he isn't, I may go to the police station today and talk about charges, now that we have evidence of what happened. Preston, what do you think?"

Mr. Preston looked at everyone in the room and, when no one said a word, he spoke up. "After watching the video, there is no way I can deny the boys instigated this. The girl tried to walk away and didn't want to fight. I cannot tolerate the emotional and physical abuse she endured. There is nothing to suggest she brought the taser, which is consistent with the police report. I have no choice but to hold the perpetrators of this incident, the three boys in question, responsible for what happened. They will each be suspended for one week. I know this will not affect their academics or their eligibility for sports, but district policy does not allow me to extend the suspension to the next school year. If I could, in this case, I would. I will instruct my staff to keep a more watchful eye on what goes on in the hallways. Are there questions?"

The room was silent until Krayton spoke up. "You're going to hear from the Superintendent. We're friends and we've talked about this at length. I want her out of this school. I will not accept any other outcome."

"Just stop, Krayton," Ashley said, tired of his relentless attacks on Jett.

"That's the outcome," Preston said. "Mr. Jackson, Jett can have an excused absence today, as she is probably very sore and tired from her ordeal. But she needs to be back tomorrow. We look forward to seeing her in class. We're finished here."

On the way out the door, Markus told his daughter what happened.

"We actually won a battle; how did that happen?" Jett was surprised.

"I don't think we won anything. We just had the evidence, and they didn't have any other option. I'm glad Preston finally saw the light. Get through next year and those guys graduate, and you don't have to deal with them anymore."

"This is going to be the best week ever. No one has to be anxious about going to school all week. By the way, do you really enjoy screwing over rich people?" Jett asked her dad as the three of them got in the car.

“No. I don’t enjoy screwing over anyone. But some wealthy people do tend to get themselves in trouble a lot.”

“Dad, what happened with mom? She wasn’t a prostitute, was she?”

Ashley looked at Jett from the passenger’s seat and said, “Your mother was a beautiful woman with a beautiful heart.”

Markus looked at her for a moment through the rear-view mirror and cleared his throat. “Your mom? She was not a prostitute. She was a waitress at one of those bars, that’s all. I was sitting in a bar getting drunk when your mom walked in, looking for me. She was beautiful. I just kind of fell in love with her. I tried to act cool, but she sat right next to me, in an empty bar, and asked me for a light for her cigarette. I lit her cigarette, and she just started talking and told me everything.

“She was terrified. She had just witnessed something illegal. She walked into the wrong room and heard the wrong conversation at her job. She had to leave town to avoid getting hurt. All she had was her tip money, so in a panic, she stole a couple of grand from the cash register and went to find me. I had a reputation for solving complicated problems and I had some connections that were useful.

“I didn’t want her money. I gave her the name to use for a motel to hide for a few days while I figured out how to sneak her out of town. She was in the bathroom when one of the Italian guys walked in, asking the bartender for her. I assumed there was a contract on her, so I punched him in the mouth while she snuck out the back door to go to the motel. Turns, out, he was there to help. He felt bad for her because she used to work for

Joey at the restaurant and he was fond of her. He got word of what happened, and he came to help her out, to help me get her out of town."

"So, you punched the wrong guy?" Jett asked, incredulous.

"Yea; I had it all wrong. To make things right with the bar she worked at, he replaced the money she stole and tried to work it out for her. He had already booked a room in one of the classier hotels. He figured they wouldn't bother looking at the nicer places. We also had to get her a new identity. She picked Elizabeth Landry. Landry is a common name. Easy to hide in plain sight with it."

"Landry's not my real name?"

"You were born a Landry, so yes, it is. It's what your mother named you."

"But what is mom's real name?"

"It's better we don't talk about that. Some things aren't safe to know."

Jett thought hard about this. She wanted to know if she had another family, but she remembered her mom telling her she didn't.

"Who was the Italian guy?" Jett asked.

"It was Vinnie, Jett. Joey's brother."

"Vinnie knew my mom? She worked at Joey's?"

"Yes. But don't ask them about her. They'll deny it."

"Do they know?"

"I'm sure they've figured it out. It's one reason they always look out for you. They liked your mom. Everyone did. She grew up here. She didn't have a family of her own, except a grandmother who took care of her; but she died when she was still a teenager. She was on her own after that. She was kind of a loner, but the Donelli's always looked out for her. The same way they look out for you. Working at the restaurant is like being family to them. The restaurant, the neighborhood means a lot. They wanted to protect your mom. But those secrets saved her life, and it's better not to talk about them."

"When, uh... did, how did I come about if you sent mom to Baltimore?"

"We waited about a week to let things settle down. They had people everywhere looking for your mom. We stayed in a nice hotel. I stayed with her, so I could protect her. I had a bad feeling I was going to get killed for helping her, but I didn't care about the risk. We spent all our time together in that room. We knew we could never see or talk to each other again. And those guys never give up. We chose Baltimore because it's not the city people usually go to. New York, Los Angeles, Chicago, those are the obvious choices. She would go to Baltimore, start over, and make a new life for herself. She was going to go to college. Something she always wanted to do. She was very intelligent. Loved to read. She wanted to be a therapist or social worker. She had dreams. Once things settled down, I drove her to an airport six hours away, in disguise as a college student, and got her on a non-stop flight to Baltimore. We said goodbye, and she got on the plane and left. I went on with life."

“I always thought it was just a fling,” Jett said.

“Well, it would have been much more if it weren’t for some really unfortunate circumstances.”

“Little Chica, I remember when I met your mom. I could see in her eyes how much she loved you. She was a very warm and loving woman. A woman can tell these things.”

“I loved her too. I miss her so much,” Jett said. “I feel so guilty for not being there when she died. I should have been with her. I wish I could have seen her one more time, just to say goodbye.”

“Things happen for a reason, Chica. Your mother was very sick, but she held on as long as it took to know you would be with family. She didn’t want you to be alone like she was. She said it over and over to us. I’m sure she died in peace, knowing you were here.”

“Her parents died when they were very young. She was only seventeen when her grandmother died, and she had been on her own since. She was smart, figured out how to survive.”

“I can’t stop being mad at myself for not being there. She died alone. Without me.”

“You got to stop beating yourself up for that, kid. She ain’t mad at you for it. She never was. You were exactly where she wanted you to be.”

“That’s what she hung on for, Chica. Now you’re making her so proud. A mother always sacrifices for her child. Sometimes she gives up everything, without giving it a second thought. It's what makes parenthood a beautiful thing," Ashley added.

The rest of the ride continued in contemplative silence. Jett didn't feel any better. She still felt like she let her mother down.

Chapter Nine: The Sisters

Later in the afternoon, Jett, her dad, and Ashley were at the office when Angelique and her sister walked through the door. Her sister was about ten years older. She had straight brown hair, freckles and wore a yellow dress with sandals and a denim jacket. Angelique wore jeans, a black tee-shirt, and a sweater.

"What?" Jett asked Angelique, frustrated.

"It's okay Jett, I'm not here to start shit with you. This is my sister, Annette. She made me come here to talk."

"Shut up and be polite," Annette said to Angelique. "Are you Jett? It's good to meet you."

"Nice to meet you too," Jett said as they shook hands.

Ashley, along with Markus, walked into the lobby. "Can we help you?" Ashley said.

"Yes. I'm Angelique's older sister, Annette. Angelique goes to school with your daughter. I brought my sister here to talk to you guys about what happened and to apologize to your daughter for her role in all the abuse that's been going on. My little sister is Michael's girlfriend, and she has been passively complicit in the bullying."

"Do your parents know you're here?" Markus asked.

"Nope. My parents don't care for me anymore. To them, I'm the lost soul of the family. The wayward hippie daughter who rejected all their country club, elitist bullshit. I brought my sister here because someone needs to teach her how to take responsibility for herself. I will not let her go down the same rabbit hole of craziness they subscribe to. She has something important to tell you, Jett, and she's afraid to say it. I'm here to make sure she gets over it and does the right thing. Angelique?" Annette gave her sister a stern look.

"Okay, I appreciate you bringing your sister here, but Jett's been through enough today. It's been a long day. Could we..."

"I understand that sir, but I'm not sure we'll get this opportunity again. I really want her to make this right."

"Okay, fair enough. Okay with you Jett?"

"Uh, sure dad, that's fine." Jett was too curious to know what was happening to wait another day to find out.

Angelique was uncomfortable. She looked up at her sister, who nodded back and turned to Jett. She stood in front of the girl and said, "Jett, I'm really sorry that Mike and his friends are so mean to you and I don't do anything about it. I really did try to talk to him when we were alone to get him to stop, but he doesn't listen. I'm so sorry for how they are so mean to you. I'm sorry." Angelique started crying and wiped her eyes. "You don't deserve it and it really bothers me."

Jett didn't know what to say, so she just stood there.

"And," Annette said, "the rest. She deserves to know."

"I'm the one who recorded the whole thing and sent it to Mr. Preston's secretary. I just don't want anyone to know because if it got back to my parents I would be in huge trouble."

“I wanted her to tell you this, so she could feel vulnerable for once,” Annette said. “Now she has to trust you not to say anything. I assume you won’t, but if you do, it’s okay. It’s up to you.”

“Please don’t tell anyone Jett,” Angelique said.

“Thanks for apologizing. I won’t tell anyone. You were nice to me last summer.”

Annette continued, “Most parents would be glad their kid did something like record the fight and send it to the principal to keep the wrong kid from getting in trouble, but ours aren’t like that. They would lose their shit if they found out. She’d probably have to stay with me, which honestly wouldn’t be bad for her. They worship status, and to them, that asshole Mike’s family represents the status they want. This relationship has been orchestrated since those two were little kids. All those kids in that crowd are brainwashed to believe they are special, and the rules don’t apply to them. It’s like they are raising a generation of dictators. They have all kinds of crazy ideas that kind of affect your daughter.”

“Don’t get started on that. Please?” Angelique said.

Markus spoke up. “Jett, why don’t you and your friend sit in my office while we talk. I’d like to hear this, but I don’t want to make the girl uncomfortable.”

“Angelique, do you want to go upstairs to our apartment on the balcony where I practice my karate? It’s cool. Can we dad?”

“That sounds kind of cool, actually,” Angelique said.

"Okay, you two go ahead. Bring your phone so I can call you when we're finished here," Markus instructed.

Jett and Angelique went to the stairs to go up to the apartment. "My dad rents the office and the apartment from the woman who used to run her detective agency here. He worked for her before she finished law school and became an attorney. Now she pays him to investigate stuff on her legal cases and all. It's a cool place to live. My dad lets me use the balcony for my punching bag and mat."

Jett let herself and Angelique into the apartment and turned on the lights as they walked through the living area towards the balcony. "That's my room there. I do my homework, reading, research, and stuff in there. Here's the balcony." Jett opened the door to the covered balcony. They walked past the table and chairs and approached the workout area in the corner.

"This is where you learn to kick ass? It seems like a small space."

"I train at Downtown Karate and I also run on the track and lift weights at the recreation center. I use this for my morning workouts and to get some reps in after karate class. I compete in karate tournaments."

"So, you do this to win tournaments? Cool. I didn't know that."

"It's a fun sport, but I can handle myself if I need to. I just don't like to fight. I hate fighting for real. I like tournaments because it's a sport. No one is trying to hurt each other. But real-life fighting, I hate it."

“How does it work? What do you learn?”

“Well, first you learn to breathe and get your feet right, then the individual moves. When you master using some of the moves, you learn to put them together, kind of like a dance. I practice those with music. It helps me get fluid.”

“Did you take dance?”

“No, never did. I was never really interested in stuff like that until karate.”

“Show me what it looks like.”

“Okay, let me take my shoes off first.” Jett slipped her shoes off. She took her stance, took a few slow, deep breaths, and started working through her kata, moving around the floor as Angelique watched.

“Usually I do it to relaxing music, like jazz or Spanish music or something.”

“It’s beautiful,” Angelique said. “It’s like a dance, with purpose.”

“Thanks.” Jett smiled. “It’s not hard. I can show you what I just did. Watch.”

Jett demonstrated each step, including breathing and footwork. Angelique got up, stood beside her, and copied her movements. Within a few minutes, both girls were doing the movements together, like a dance routine. Jett said, “Next I learned to do this kata in coordination with another person, like a choreographed fight. Then they taught me to make the same movements but react to my teacher. Soon we were reacting to each other, like a real fight, but in slow motion. Now we spar all the time, sometimes up to tournament speed. That's how I learn."

"So cool. What about the bag? Show me what you do with the bag."

"Okay, but it's much less interesting, it's just hitting and kicking. Karate is more about the movement than it is about hitting and kicking."

"I wanna see though."

"Okay, watch." Jett took her stance in front of the bag and, after a few warm-up strikes, she began hitting and kicking the bag with controlled ferocity. Angelique's eyes got big as she watched the girl work the bag.

When Jett stopped, Angelique said, "You were not hitting or kicking that hard in the fight yesterday. Not even close. If you had, it wouldn't have lasted more than a few seconds. What gives?"

"If I fight like that, I'll hurt someone. So, I control myself. I have to be responsible for how I use my skills. I don't want to fight, and I don't want to hurt anyone."

"When you kicked Jeff in the ribs with both feet while he was choking you, I got to admit, that was some badass Jackie Chan stuff there. How did you practice that?"

Jett looked down at the ground and looked up again. She was not proud of herself for injuring the boy, but she had to do something, he was choking her. "I kind of made it up on the spot using some of the principles they teach us in karate. I didn't intend to hurt him though. I feel bad about it."

"He's an asshole, so you shouldn't. He deserved it." Angelique said, and with a more personal tone, "Jett, I wish we could be friends, I really do. You're so much better than us. If I broke up with Mike and we became friends, I would ruin my family life. My parents, they don't understand any of this. They just want me to marry Mike after graduation and then stay home and have his babies while he becomes his dad. I hate it. I hate school and I can't wait for it to be over, so I can just do what I want. I'm secretly glad you're kicking their asses. Ever since last summer when you stood up for me when you had no reason to, I've been thinking a lot about what's right and wrong. But if I don't keep up the act, my life is ruined, and I don't know how to deal with it. So, I'm sorry that I'm such a bitch. I'll try really hard from now on to keep them away from you, but I can't change much until I graduate. Maybe, just maybe, after I graduate, we can hang out and be friends, if you're still around and you want to. You're so much more real than the barbies I hang out with."

"It's okay, Angelique," Jett said, "I understand. I've never had much of a social life, but I get that sometimes you just get stuck somewhere and can't get out. I may be better off being more of a loner because of it. You should move in with your sister. She seems really cool."

"My mom would kill both of us if I did. Literally. She wants to be a part of Mike's family so bad; I probably shouldn't disappoint her until I can afford to buy my own food."

Angelique approached Jett and hugged her. "I am so sorry for how we treat you, how we've been all these years. I really am. I hope you can forgive me."

"I understand," Jett said, pulling away from the hug after a few seconds. While she appreciated Angelique's honesty, the whole conversation made her uncomfortable. She was not accustomed to having friends.

Angelique looked at Jett. "And next time Mike messes with you, please; please kick him in the balls like you kicked that bag. So, I can get a break from him trying to get me to have sex with him. Just let loose." Both girls laughed as Jett put her shoes on, so they could go back downstairs.

"So, what are they talking about downstairs?" Jett asked as they walked down the stairwell.

"They are talking about my parents' crazy ideas regarding white nationalism and Texas leaving America or something like that. It's nuts. They think Texas and a bunch of other states are going to leave America soon and become the Confederate states again and bring back their old ways. They are all into that bullshit. They believe there's some secret plan for people like them to make a shit ton of money off of something like that. It's why my sister left home; she couldn't deal with it anymore. I just smile and nod and try to ignore them when they talk about it now."

Downstairs, Annette continued talking about her parents' ideas. "They truly believe this stuff. They think they're the elite and it's their right to rule over everyone else, especially people of color, gay people, poor people, etc. And they think this secessionist movement will bring it about."

"Unfortunately, more people think this way than you may realize. It concerns me how their kids treat Jett since she's black," Ashley said. "Since they've been conditioned to feel justified in their racism, they may not have the normal restraint most people have."

"This is why I wanted to talk to you. Just so you'd be aware of what's driving all this. That kid, Mike, his dad is all up into this stuff. He's kind of the leader and his goal is to be mayor one day. Mike Jr. is brainwashed to believe that what he is doing is righteous and good. They created that school to segregate their kids. Some parents bought into it, others just took advantage of the opportunity to be in a better school than they were before. It's their own taxpayer-funded private school. Your daughter, being biracial, messed up their carefully planned status quo. I think it's awesome that she's there and showing em all up, but I worry about how they react. She would have no trouble in any other school, but that school was created for white kids only and they are super pissed about her being there, and they're pissed she makes good grades. She contradicts their white supremacy thing."

"Jett is testing their system. She challenged their belief in their own superiority. Now, they have to figure out if they are willing to act on those beliefs," Ashley replied.

"My parents are, and Mike's parents are too. Some other parents, well, they are followers. Pathetic sheep blindly following the herd. They don't think for themselves. Mike Krayton exploits this to his benefit. I don't know that they believe this stuff as much as they just go along with it to fit in. Most of the parents are ambivalent at best."

"Well, I appreciate you looking out for your sister and trying to keep her from falling into this trap. She's lucky to have you," Ashley said.

"Well, my little sister isn't the smartest person, but she isn't stupid either. Our parents haven't forbidden her from seeing me yet and I care too much about her to let her go like this. She came to me last summer with this story of the 'brown girl' who stood up for her when Mike threatened to hit her. It made a difference with her. I don't think she ever saw someone who could just do the right thing, even for the wrong people. The cognitive dissonance challenged the worldview our parents instilled in her, and she came to me to talk about it instead of them. She was taught that 'those people' are inherently bad and need to be 'controlled.' She now questions this. She seems to have put your daughter on a pedestal because she is the only kid that can stand up to Mike, who, I'm sure, is just as much a bully with her as he is with everyone else."

Jett and Angelique walked into the lobby, sat down on the couch, and listened to the adults talk.

"It's okay," Angelique said. "I already told Jett about mom and dad's insane beliefs. It's no secret."

"Hey kid," Markus said. "I don't want you to talk to anyone about this. If this gets around school and someone hears you talking about it, everything will get worse, for both you and your friend, okay?"

"Okay, dad. I get it."

Angelique and her sister, Annette, said their goodbyes and left the office, leaving Jett, her dad, and Ashley sitting in silence for a moment.

"Okay," Jett's dad said, "let's go get some food. You need to explain to me how you came up with the double kick to the ribs thing to get out of being choked. It sounds like something out of one of those martial arts movies on Saturday mornings. We should go out for ribs to celebrate."

Jett rolled her eyes at her dad and walked out ahead. Her dad turned off the lights and locked the door behind them. Dad's got jokes now, she thought to herself, as the elevator doors closed.

Chapter Ten: The Fierce Warrior

Markus Jackson woke to the smell of the coffee Jett made before she started her karate workout. He poured some of the coffee into a mug and went out on the balcony to read the paper. He noticed Ashley's car on the curb, so he sent her a text asking if she was at work. She texted back that she had fell asleep working the night before, so she slept on the couch in the office. He invited her up to the apartment for coffee and she accepted.

It was summer, after Jett's sophomore year.

When Ashley arrived, she came to the balcony with a cup of coffee. She sat down and sipped her coffee as she watched Jett work through her karate moves.

"She's so graceful. She's not a little girl anymore," she said.

"You keep saying that, but I want her to hold off on growing up a bit. There is still so much I need to teach her."

"You're such a good dad." Ashley smiled at him.

"This summer, she needs to learn to drive, change a tire, jumpstart a car. And I want to take her to the shooting range and teach her how to shoot a gun."

"Why?"

"Because one day she will be old enough to choose for herself. If she chooses to own a gun, I want to be sure I teach her how to use one. I don't trust anyone else with this."

"That makes sense. Why can't you let her go to a driving school to learn to drive?"

"I want to teach her to drive. I also want her to learn to drive a standard. It's important."

"She'll enjoy that."

"I need her to learn these things the right way."

"Aww, you're so sweet. You're a good papa."

"I'm just trying to do this right. Tonight, I'm taking her to an art opening. Want to join us?"

"An art opening? Sure. What brought that on?"

"I think it will be good for her. I saw a write up about it in the paper."

"Thanks for the invite. What time?"

"Seven."

"I'm on a case in the late afternoon, but I'll meet you two there as soon as I'm finished."

He nodded and took a sip of his coffee while he watched his daughter work out. Now she was working on the punching bag.

"Look at the intensity. She's working the shit out of that bag, and she isn't going all out, just including the bag in her exercises," he said.

"She's a strong, determined girl. She's getting ready for tournaments with the black belts?"

"Yea, later this summer."

Ashley sipped her coffee and watched the girl. “I’m so proud of her. She’s growing into an amazing young woman. She was just a shy little girl a few years ago.”

“She’s still a shy little girl, but she kicks ass too.”

Ashley laughed. “She’s not a little girl anymore. She’s growing into a young woman.”

“I can hear you talking about me over there,” Jett said. “I’m right here.”

“We’re just saying how proud we are of you, Little Chica. You make our hearts full.”

Jett smiled and went back to her exercises.

***

Later that evening, Jett and her dad were driving to the art gallery.

“So, why are we going to an art opening?” Jett asked.

“Because we need some culture in our lives. I used to do this kind of stuff all the time when I was young. I think you’ll enjoy it.”

“Ok. I guess.”

“Ashley will meet us there and afterward we’re going to Joey’s for dinner.”

“What was your dad like? Was he like you?” Jett asked, out of the blue.

“My dad,” he said after a pause, “did two things: work and drink. Every day he would come home from work and sit and watch television and get drunk. My mother always tried to fix everything, because my dad had a bad temper. We were told not to provoke him, and we got punished if we did anything to set him off. I had a bad habit of being an asshole, which didn’t help. My older sister just spent her time alone in her room, drawing and working on things. She’d try to protect me, but I wouldn’t listen. You remind me of her.”

“I have an aunt? Why haven’t I met her?”

“Because she lives in Chicago and we don’t talk much. She’s still angry at me for what happened after our parents died. But I email her about you, pictures and all. I think she should know she has a niece. But we don’t talk about anything else.”

“What does she do for work?”

“She’s an artist and an art teacher. A very good one. I often google her and look at her work. She’s quite successful.”

“I want to meet her. She sounds cool. Oh, and she probably has an Instagram. You should follow her there.”

“An Instawhat?” Jett sighed at her dad’s old-fashioned outlook on the world.

Markus pulled into the parking lot and found a parking space. Before they got out, he looked at Jett. “We’re going to see a lot of people who will remember me from the old days when I was a stupid kid. If you hear someone say: ‘Remember that time we…’ I want you to walk away, ok?”

Jett laughed. “I can’t wait to hear those stories.”

The gallery was crowded. Most people were milling around, drinking wine and visiting instead of looking at the artwork, but others were admiring the pieces on the wall. Jett straightened out her white blouse as they walked into the building. She wasn't used to dressing up and felt awkward in heels. At least her slacks were comfortable. Her dad was wearing a pair of black slacks too, with a blue shirt and a matching black blazer.

It didn't take long for Ashley to find them. She arrived before they did. She wore a black skirt, a white blouse, and a black jacket. Jett and Ashley matched.

"Hey Little Chica." She hugged Jett. "I got finished early and came straight out."

The three of them walked around the gallery and looked at the paintings. Jett was quiet as she perused the artwork. Soon she saw a painting of a young mother, with a young girl, on a busy sidewalk.

"This one reminds me of Mom, back in Baltimore." She teared up as she spoke. Ashley put her arm around her and gave her a quick squeeze.

Ashley took her hand. "Do you want something to drink? A soda or something? Or a snack? I'm about to get a glass of wine. Would you join me?"

"Okay," Jett said and went with Ashley to get refreshments. Her dad, meanwhile, went looking for a very specific painting. He hoped he wasn't too late. By the time he found it, he also ran into an old artist friend, who turned out to be the current director of the gallery.

“Whoa! Who is this guy?” his friend said, excited. “It’s been years, brother. Where’ve you been?”

“Hey! Good to see you. I’ve been running the business, working late nights; and raising a kid.”

“You have a kid? No way! Didn’t see that coming.”

“She’s over there.”

“With the attractive Latina woman?”

“Yea. The kid is my daughter.”

“She’s your daughter? You did good.”

“I got lucky to have a good kid. She’s better than we were ... Speaking of, I need to talk to you about this painting. Can we speak in private?”

They went into his office and shut the door. The artist soon joined them. While they were talking, a volunteer placed a red sticker under the painting.

He was back on the gallery floor when Ashley and Jett returned with refreshments. Jett handed her dad a cup of coffee and they resumed looking at the paintings. His friend approached and introduced himself.

“I hear you’re the daughter of this crazy guy here. It’s nice to meet you. And you too, Ms. Garcia.”

Jett and Ashley shook hands with the gray-haired, jovial man. “You know my dad?” Jett asked.

“Oh, yea. We go way back. We used to run in the same crowd when we were young. Your dad was quite the guitar player, you know. He used to sit right back there in the corner with his guitar, his amp, and his gadgets and play beautiful guitar pieces during exhibits like this one. He was the man."

Jett's eyes lit up, surprised at this little piece of her dad's history. There was so much about his past he never talked about. But a painting caught her eye, and she walked across the room, to the far wall, to look at it. It was the same painting her dad was looking for earlier.

"What do you think of this painting Jett?" her dad asked when he caught up with her. Jett just stared at it. In the painting, a young African American girl, about Jett's age, was holding a book in her hand. There were books strewn around about, some open, some closed. The girl was looking to the upper left corner of the painting as if she were daydreaming. In the corner was an African American woman dressed as a warrior. The warrior looked confident and strong, and she stared with intensity and purpose at the horizon.

"It's awesome. I want to be her so bad." Jett said, dreamily.

Her dad's friend, the director, touched his arm and said, "I'll be right back," and smiled as he walked off.

There was a note below the painting with the title, 'The Fierce Warrior,' written on it. Ashley put her arm around Jett's shoulders and leaned her head against hers as they both looked at the painting. "She's you, Jett."

"More like you. You're a fierce warrior," Jett said.

"I wish Little, Chica. But thank you."

"She reminds me of you, kid," her dad said.

"Not quite. I'm just a girl."

The gallery director returned and said, "Hey, I found the artist and she would like to meet Jett."

"Go ahead, we'll catch up with you in a minute," her dad replied.

"That was so sweet. You're such a good father," Ashley said as Jett walked off with the gallery director.

"Nah. I'm sure all dads do stuff like this for their kids."

"If they did, we wouldn't be in the business we're in, you know?"

Jett walked across the floor to an attractive woman in her late twenties wearing a burgundy dress with black heels. She was a petite woman, not much taller than Jett, with dark skin and dark eyes. She wore her long hair in braids that framed her face. She smiled when she saw Jett. She had a magnetic smile, drawing Jett in with her warmth and beauty.

"Kilanna, this is Jett Landry, daughter of an old friend of mine. She's really enjoying your work, so I thought she would like to meet you."

Kilanna gave Jett a huge smile and extended her hand. "It's very nice to meet you, Jett. How old are you?"

"Nice to meet you," Jett said. "I'm fifteen years old. I turn sixteen in the fall."

"You look like you've been crying. Are you okay?"

Jett wiped her eyes. "Yes. I was looking at one of your pictures, the Warrior one, and my dad was telling me how I'm like the girl in the picture who is going to grow up to be a Fierce Warrior. It made me cry."

Kilanna looked at her. "Is this a good thing?"

"Yes. I'm just too sensitive all the time. It made me feel good because I said I want to be the warrior in the picture."

"It makes me feel good that my painting moved you and your dad. Can I give you a hug?"

Jett turned to the side and allowed Kilanna to give her a side hug. "You're talking about the painting, 'The Fierce Warrior?'" Kilanna asked.

"Yes. I love it."

"Oh, me too. This piece means a lot to me. Tell me about yourself, Jett. Why do you want to be the Fierce Warrior?"

"I don't know. It's been hard. My mom died when I was ten and I moved to Texas to live with my dad, who I hadn't met before. My mom didn't tell him about me until she was sick. I go to this school with all white kids, almost all of them are nice, but there are about five or six boys who bully me all the time. For years, because I'm biracial, and they aren't used to that there." Jett was eager to tell her story to Kilanna so, in a rush of emotion, she told her everything. Kilanna took her hand and looked her in the eyes as she listened to her talk about the bullying, and her anxiety, and her karate, and how she is becoming more confident, but the anxiety and the sadness never go away. Jett kept talking, telling her about how she insisted on staying in her school, so she can graduate first in her class to prove they can't stop her no matter what. When she finished Kilanna looked at her and said, "Jett, you ARE the Fierce Warrior. Don't ever lose that spirit you have. You have a fire in you that few people will ever experience. I am so glad I met you. You are going to be a superhero or something one day."

Jett smiled and put her head down. "Thanks, but I'm just a girl."

"Don't ever underestimate what 'just a girl' can do. Women have changed the world. You can do amazing things if you believe in yourself."

"It looks like someone bought this piece as soon as the exhibit opened tonight. It's a popular piece," the director said.

"Yes, the gentleman over there, in the black suit, with the pretty woman," Kilanna said.

"That's my dad!!!" Jett exclaimed. "He bought it???"

Jett, in a rush of emotion, started crying again. Kilanna took her hand and said, "Let's go talk to your dad." The two of them walked across the gallery floor. Jett ran up to her dad and hugged him, crying again. "Why are you crying, kid?"

"You bought the painting I love so much."

"I did, it resembles you too much not to buy it."

***

After they left the gallery, Jett and her dad drove to Joey's Italian Restaurant. Ashley arrived first and was sitting in the lobby. There was a younger couple, a man and a woman, sitting to her left. Jett sat next to Ashley and her dad sat next to her.

Joey's décor was relaxed and inviting. Behind the cash register were pictures of the casts from various Italian American television shows and movies, such as The Godfather and The Sopranos. The lighting was low for ambiance. Traditional Italian music played in the background. The smell of marinara, garlic, and fresh-baked bread wafted from the dining room into the lobby, enticing people as they waited for a table.

Jett's excitement was almost crushed when she saw who walked into the lobby and checked in at the front desk. It was Mike and his parents, along with an older couple. Mike glared at Jett as he walked to the lobby with his mother. Jett looked back and looked down, not wanting to engage Mike. Mike smirked, taking this as a victory. Mike's mom looked over and saw Jett, her dad, and Ashley and shook her head.

Krayton and the other couple walked in and took their seats, sitting next to Mike's mom. This put the wife of their friend sitting next to Ashley. Markus put his arm around Jett as he watched them sit down. Jett smiled and looked at Ashley, who smiled back at Jett. Ashley was showing grace under pressure, something she often told Jett she needed to master.

Mike's mom leaned into his dad's ear and whispered, loud enough for Jett and her family to hear, "I didn't realize they allowed people to bring their pets here for dinner."

Mike laughed out loud and stifled it. Krayton was confused. "The city ordinance allows for therapy animals if they're certified."

“No, silly, look.” She gestured at Jett.

“We can hear you,” Ashley said out loud.

“Hear what?”

“Your comment about allowing pets in here.”

“You’re mistaken,” she said back. “I wouldn’t say such a thing.”

“You heard no such thing,” Krayton said, “and you’re interrupting our private conversation.”

“About my daughter. We’re interrupting your private conversation where your wife insulted my daughter,” Markus said. He looked to the other couple sitting in the lobby. “Did you guys hear her too?”

The younger couple looked at each other and the woman said, “Uh, yea. We heard it too. That lady there looked right at the pretty girl sitting here and made a comment about them allowing pets. It was petty, racist, and disgusting.”

“He’s running for mayor,” he said to the couple. “I’m sure he would love your support.” Ashley, Jett, and the couple laughed when he said this. “I mean if you’re into his kind of thing.”

“Not hardly.” the woman said. “Thanks for the heads up.”

He looked back at Krayton and gave him a sarcastic thumbs-up gesture. He noticed the younger Mike shifting his glare from him to Jett.

“Watch how you look at my daughter, boy,” he scolded. “I’d warn you not to mess with a man’s daughter.”

Mike shifted his glare back to Jett’s dad. “I’m not scared of you,” he said without taking his eyes off him.

“Wouldn’t matter either way,” he said, looking back at Mike.

“Mike, stop it,” his mother admonished him. “You know how these people are.”

“These people?” Ashley responded. “Well, either way, you’re not going to ruin our night. I hope you have a wonderful dinner with your family and friends. And I hope you enjoy whatever it is you are going to do after dinner.”

The couple sitting off to the side giggled as they read something dirty into Ashley’s statement. “Couple swap,” she heard the woman say to the man, and they both started laughing.

“I can’t un-see that mental image now, thanks,” the man said and they continued giggling. The hostess then called their name, and they got up to leave.

“Have a nice dinner!” Ashley said as they left.

Krayton leaned into the other man and pointed at Jett’s family. “They are the people I was telling you about.”

The other man looked over at them as if surprised and said, “How did this happen?”

Markus spoke up. “We live in the same school zone. And that boy over there has been bullying my girl for five years, but now she has his number and they don't like it. She stopped putting up with his constant abuse, but somehow it's her fault."

"You, sir, do not live in our area. I would know if you did," the man said.

"We live downtown."

Krayton smiled with his best 'checkmate,' look and said, "Meet the superintendent of the school district, and a very good friend of mine."

"I know who you are," Markus said. "And we're the ones who screwed up your re-segregation plan. What does 'how did this happen' mean?"

"I'm not following you, sir," the Superintendent replied.

"You seem surprised that my daughter would be zoned for your school. Why are you surprised?"

"I'm not going to answer your question, sir. I don't like the implications."

"You don't have to. It's a rhetorical question. We all know the answer. But rest assured, she represents herself and your school very well. Makes perfect grades, works hard. All honor classes. You're lucky to have her in your school, and I'm sure you're very proud of her academic accomplishments. Maybe you can look into the bullying and do something about it. It's not just her, but she does get the bulk of it. I'm sure you can figure out why."

The hostess called out "Garcia, table for three!" Markus continued staring at the Superintendent for a few more seconds, waiting for a response.

"That's our table," Ashley said, standing up. "Come on, let's go get some of that bread. I'm starving."

Markus stood up, straightened his jacket, and said, "Nice to meet you, sir. Enjoy your dinner," and walked off behind Ashley and Jett.

***

Chapter Eleven: Melinda Brown

Melinda's mom contacted Ashley and invited Jett over for pizza and movies. It was the weekend before her first black belt karate tournament and Jett was glad for something to do to get her mind off her anxiety. As always, Ashley volunteered to drive.

All the houses in Melinda's neighborhood were new and beautiful, and the yards were perfect. Jett studied the houses, as they drove through the neighborhoods where most of the kids in her school lived.

"Have fun Little Chica," Ashley said as she pulled into the driveway.

"Why am I nervous to do normal stuff that kids do?"

"You're just used to being in your comfort zone. It's time to stretch your boundaries so you can grow. Now go and have fun!"

Melinda opened the door as Jett walked up the drive. Jett was nervous, and she didn't feel like she had any idea how to act in another kid's home.

"Hey, Jett!" Melinda said. "OMG! You've gotten taller." Melinda gave Jett an unexpected hug. Jett hugged back. "And you're solid! You've been getting crazy strong, haven't you?"

"Hey Melinda," Jett said. "I've been training hard all summer. Big tournament next weekend."

Melinda had already ordered a pizza, and it was sitting on the kitchen table with two plates. Melinda's mother came out of a room adjacent to the kitchen. She looked to be in her early forties, wearing jeans and a short-sleeved black shirt. She was taller than Melinda, with straight sandy brown hair pulled up in a ponytail and a light complexion, with a few wrinkles around her mouth and eyes. She had a wide mouth with very white teeth. Jett felt comfortable with Melinda's mom. She looked at Jett and smiled, a very warm smile, as she extended her hand for a handshake. "Hello Jett! It's so good to see you."

Jett extended her hand to shake. "It's good to see you too, ma'am." Jett felt like she didn't belong there, with these nice people, intruding on their family life.

Melinda's mom looked at both girls. "Well, you have the pizza. There are drinks in the fridge, so help yourselves. You can hang out in the den after you eat." She looked at Melinda. "We'll stay out of your way, so you can just do your thing, ok honey?"

Jett stood there, feeling awkward, as Melinda gestured for her to sit down at the table. Melinda's mom pulled up a barstool and looked at Jett for a moment. She could sense Jett's discomfort. Her maternal instinct activated, and she felt like it was a good time to make the girl feel at ease.

"Jett, honey," she said, doing her best to convey a warm sentiment. "I know you've had a hard time with some of the other kids in school, but when you're here with us, you're family. We are so glad to get to meet you and spend time with you, and we're glad you and Melinda are friends. She speaks so highly of you, about how you always look out for the other kids and all, and how intelligent you are. We appreciate you."

Jett, embarrassed by the compliment, blushed a little and put her head down. "Thank you."

"And if there is something you ever need to talk about and you don't know who you can talk to, don't be shy to come to me, ok? It takes a village, you know?"

"Yes ma'am; thank you." Jett wasn't sure how else to respond. Melinda took her plate and put a slice of pizza on it. Jett was too shy to even get a slice of pizza.

"What do you want to drink Jett? We have cokes, iced tea, bottled water?" Melinda asked as she went to the refrigerator.

"Bottled water please," Jett said, "I'm staying off soda and caffeine while I'm in training, which is pretty much all the time."

"What are you training for, Jett?" Melinda's mom asked.

"I'm competing in a karate tournament next weekend. My first with the black belts. All the other girls will be older and probably better than me. And stronger too."

"How exciting. Black belt already? You must have started really young."

"She just started a year ago," Melinda said. "She's just really good at it."

Jett blushed again and put her head down. Melinda's mom saw how Jett was reacting to compliments. She smiled at the shy, insecure girl.

"You're good at it, huh? I think that's awesome. I bet your parents are very proud."

"It's just my dad and me," Jett said. "And Ashley. She's not my mom, but she's kind of like my mom. My mom died when I was ten. That's why I came here."

"Oh. I'm so sorry Jett. Where were you before you were here?"

"Baltimore. Where my mom and I lived. When she was dying, she called my dad and told him about me. He and Ashley, she's his business partner, came to Baltimore to meet me. Then I came here for a visit later in the summer and that was when my mom died. I've been here since." Jett wondered if she was telling too much family business, but part of her was dying to tell her story to someone who would understand, and Melinda's mom seemed to be the person who wanted to listen.

"What an amazing story Jett. I'm so sorry about your mom though. Your dad must really love you to just want to raise you after not knowing about you all that time. Is Ashley still in your life?"

"She brought me here tonight and is gonna pick me up later. We do lots of things together. She even taught me to speak Spanish. She's part Cuban and part black like me."

"Are you part Cuban too?"

"Oh no ma'am, my dad is white, and my mom is black. But I didn't know my dad was white until right before I met him. So, I didn't know I was biracial. I always thought I was black. My dad told me if that's how I see myself, that's who I am."

Melinda's mom nodded her head and smiled again. "And now you're a karate champion too. And you're also a beautiful and intelligent young lady. I bet your mom is up there somewhere, watching over you, and is very proud of you."

Jett looked down again and blushed, this time she shed a tear as Melinda's mom mentioned her mother.

"Oh my God Jett, I'm so sorry," she said and rushed over to hug the girl. Melinda buried her face in her hands and shook her head. Melinda's dad walked into the room and heard her mom apologize. Her dad was a middle-aged man, tall, thin with thinning hair and glasses. He was still wearing slacks and a dress shirt from his job as an engineer, but his shirt was untucked, and he was shuffling around in his socks. He had a confused look on his face.

"What's going on?" he asked.

"Mom made my friend cry," Melinda said.

"It's okay," Jett said, "I cry a lot. Teenage girl hormones. That's what Ashley tells my dad all the time."

"I'm sorry, honey," Melinda's mom said, "Sometimes I get all sappy and turn everything into a Hallmark moment or something."

"Hey!!" Melinda's dad said as he realized who Jett was, "you're the kid who beats up all the bullies at school. Good job! Where did you learn to fight like that?"

"Dad!" Melinda said, mortified now. "We covered this already. Jett has a black belt in karate. I'm so sorry for my parents, Jett."

"No, it's ok. I like them. They're very nice."

"I'm sorry you had to fight those boys, Jett. I hate that they target you," Melinda's mom said.

“It’s scary. I hate fighting other people. Tournaments are fun because it’s a sport, we don’t try to hurt each other, just score points. Everyone is really nice. Fighting in the real world is different and scary and I don’t like it.”

“But you’re plenty good at it,” Melinda’s dad said.

“Dad!” Melinda yelled. “Y'all are embarrassing me!”

“Ok,” Melinda’s mom said, “I’m sorry, Mel. Let’s let the girls eat in peace. Come on, honey. I’m sure there is something with a ball being thrown around on TV for you to yell about. Let’s go. It was so nice to meet you, Jett.”

“Nice to meet you too, ma’am.”

When they left, Melinda said, “I am so sorry about my parents. They are freaking crazy. My mom, ugh, prying into your personal life.”

Jett sat there a minute and didn’t say anything, took a bite of her pizza, and said, “It’s okay. She seems sweet. It’s no big deal.”

“Is your family like this too?”

Jett thought for a second. “Not really. It’s just my dad and me at home, even though Ashley is around a lot. It’s always quiet. My dad is serious a lot. But he’s cool. I like hanging out with my dad and Ashley. It’s different than most families, I think. I stay in my room and read, study, work on stuff a lot.”

“Your dad is a private eye?”

"Yea. I work in his office during the day. Answering the phones and doing some of the paperwork. He pays me for it, so I have some money to spend on stuff."

"I remember when I saw him at the hospital. He reminded me of one of those private eyes from those old movies. Really cool. And kind of hot if you don't mind me saying so."

Jett almost choked on her pizza, laughing. When she caught her breath, she was still laughing. "My dad? Hot? Wow! As far as the film noir thing; I think he used to be like that, and he's street savvy and knows how everything works. I think he's mellowed out since then. But to see him handle people, he's really cool. Like, cool as ice. Last summer Mike's dad and a few of the dads came to the office to threaten him about the fight we all got into when I was riding my bike from karate. They thought they were going to get the best of my dad. But they walked out of his office angry and defeated. It was awesome."

"Wow! Your dad *is* cool."

"Usually, but he can be weird like most dads. But he has lots of cool stories of cases he's worked on over the years. He's dealt with a lot of gangsters and such. Now, he and Ashley do a lot of work on missing person cases."

"Wow. Your dad is hot and cool."

Jett started laughing again and couldn't stop giggling at her friend thinking her dad was hot. "I wish Ashley thought of him like that. I have this secret fear that my dad will meet someone else, fall in love, and that person would want to do what Ashley does with me. The thought of it scares the crap out of me. I love Ashley. She's so cool."

“What’s she like?” Melinda asked as they put their plates away and started walking towards the den.

“She’s kind of like a mom. She’s cool, like my dad, and tough, but graceful too. But she’s also really emotional. She was so angry about what happened at school that day you came to the hospital. She was madder than I was.”

“You weren’t scared when you got in that fight?”

“I was, but once I got focused, it was almost automatic. I kind of go into a zone.”

They were sitting on the couch now with the television on in the background, but they were too busy talking to watch.

“What do your parents do for a living?” Jett asked.

“My dad is a chemical engineer for a huge consulting company, and my mom is a CPA and works for an accounting firm. Not nearly as exciting as your parents, but they make lots of money.”

“That’s cool though. They get to use math and science all the time. That’s geek cool. I love that.”

“It’s okay. They don’t have any cool stories to tell about it though. And I PROMISE you my dad has never dealt with a gangster before.”

“Yea, but your dad is hot,” Jett said, laughing. Melinda started laughing too. Jett was getting comfortable and having fun.

“Excuse me?” they both heard Melinda’s mother in the background, talking on the phone. “She is my guest, a friend of my child's. I can have ANYONE I want in MY home. I don't care what you say or think."

"What's that?" Jett was alarmed.

"I bet it's Mike's mom. His parents act like they run this entire subdivision. It's like a Homeowners' Association from hell. They are just like Mike and his friends. They bully everyone and tell everyone what they can and can't do all the time. My mom will tell her off any minute, listen."

"What kind of element? She's a child. No, ma'am. You will NOT talk about a child like that to me. <long pause> No, there is nothing in the contract that governs who I can have as a guest. <long pause> Now you listen here: I paid for my property like everyone else. You don't tell me what I can do on my property or in my home."

"She's winding up for the big tell off. Wait for it..." Melinda said.

"and another thing. You have a lot of nerve to talk about a child like that. She's a very polite, intelligent child. Your son would do good to be more like her."

"Here it comes... get ready," Melinda said, giggling. Jett was nervous because she knew they were talking about her.

"Your son is an asshole and a bully. Maybe you need to clean up your own mess before you bitch at everyone else. <long pause> yea, I said it. He's an asshole. I'll say it again, listen up: YOUR SON IS AN ASSHOLE. Like your husband. And like you. <long pause> I don't care what you think. She's a sweet girl and they are having fun. What? You don't like it. Let's all guess why.

It's because you're a <long pause> Dangerous? Not hardly. The only dangerous thing here is your toxic attitude towards everything. You know what."

"Here it comes in 3 2 1"

"You can just go to hell and leave us alone!"

"Told ya. My mom has some fire in her."

"I feel bad because they were talking about me."

"Don't. If it's not that, it would be something else. Their family, and their little circle of friends, are literally Nazis."

"They're that bad?"

"Literally Nazis. Like they have all kinds of bizarre beliefs. I only know because they've been here at parties and I've overheard them talking. My mom and dad hate them. But they try to be social because they run the HOA and they don't want to get fined."

"What beliefs?"

"Oh, well, they are into this whole 'the south will rise again' thing for one. They also believe that Texas should be its own country instead of being part of the USA. And I'm sure you've figured out; they are racist as all get out. They don't even try to hide it. And Mike's dad has the freaking nerve to think he could be mayor one day. And he's such a bullshitter I'm afraid he may pull it off. They're loaded with family money and property. That's why this neighborhood is here. They just bought up tons of property, tore everything down, zoned it as residential, created a huge, gated community, and created an oppressive HOA just so they could control who could buy in. They just wanted white people, so they could create their own personal school zone for privileged white kids. A lot of people, like my parents, just liked the houses and the new school so they bought in before they realized what they were getting themselves into."

"Mike's mom has called me an 'animal' and a 'pet' before. I can't stand her. She's gross."

"Wow. Who the hell does she think she is, anyway?"

"Why doesn't Preston do anything about Mike?"

"Oh, yea. Preston. He's sold his soul for his job and is owned by them. They run the school board and are friends with his boss. He's kind of forced to do what they want all the time. Does it make you feel uncomfortable to talk about all this racism stuff?"

"Nah. It's good to talk about it. It's hard to be the only brown kid at school. I feel like Franklin on Peanuts." Jett laughed at herself. "Like, I'm just there so they can say they're not racist. I'm glad you're my friend. I felt so alone for so long at school. It's so much better now."

"You're really cool Jett. And you're a rock star with the karate and all. How did you end up in our school, anyway?"

Jett laughed at being called a rock star. "Oh. It's kind of cool. My dad said that when they zoned the school district, to keep some neighborhoods out, they had to claim other parts of town, so they would have the same amount of territory. So, they claimed downtown, where NOBODY lives. It's just a bunch of buildings and businesses. But my dad rents a flat on the top floor of the building his office is in and lives there, so he could be close to work. Because we live downtown, we live in your school zone. So, I have to go to school there, or a private school or home school. My dad and Mike's family had a 'talk' about this when my dad told Mike's dad and the Superintendent that we messed up his 're-segregation' plan."

"Your dad is SOOO cool. That's awesome. Can I ask a personal question?"

"Sure."

"Is it hard to live with people of a different, uh, ethnicity than you?"

"It was weird at first. I didn't even know my dad was white until my mom told me right before I met him. So, I didn't see myself as biracial, but as a black girl. Except for the blue eyes and bright skin. I never knew how to explain that. Anyway, it was but it wasn't because Ashley has always been there. So, I had a woman around as well as a person of color. My dad didn't know what to do at first either, so he just gave me enough space and time to figure it out. He always wanted to talk and do stuff together though, like go to the coffee shop or out to eat and stuff. As I got to know him, I started realizing that we're a lot alike. I'm kind of weird myself. I never really fit in with other kids, black or white. My dad said that my mom is a survivor, always has been, and she handed that down to me. I guess, but my mom never gave up. She was strong and smart. My dad said I get my brains from her. I'm like my dad too, though. He keeps to himself, only has a few friends, but knows a lot of people, and is content to do his own thing instead of doing what everyone else is doing. So, we have that in common. Ashley has always been the one to make me do things and get out more. And we have a friend, Diana, who is an attorney, who spends time with me too. Sometimes I get to hang out or work in her office or stay with her when dad and Ashley go out of town. I just kind of gradually got used to stuff. This is my first time to hang out at someone else's house. I'm sorry, I'm just rambling now." Jett again felt relieved to just talk about these things with someone besides her family. She could probably go on forever.

"Don't apologize Jett. That's really neat. Your life is kind of an adventure. My life is boring compared to yours. Just like everyone else on this street. Same stuff. It is really cool to hang out with you."

"Thanks, it's cool to hang out with you too."

Melinda's mom entered the den with a sad look on her face. "Jett, honey, I'm sure you heard that conversation on the phone a few minutes ago. I'm sorry it happened. Just so you know, you are always welcome here and I think that crazy woman is, well, crazy. Or crazy mean. But don't let it make you feel uncomfortable or unwelcome. We do what we want here. And we enjoy having you here. Ok?"

"Thank you," Jett said, "I don't want to cause any trouble though."

"Nonsense," she said, smiling. "We'd rather you than them. You're a sweet girl. Those people are terrible. Anyway, I just wanted you to know that."

Jett and Melinda talked for another hour before Ashley arrived. Jett heard the doorbell and Ashley's voice. She made small talk with Melinda's mother as Jett came out from the den to hear Melinda's mom say, "She's such a sweet girl. We enjoyed having her. They've been in the den just talking up a storm the way teenage girls do, this whole time."

"We like her too," she heard Ashley say, "Hey Jett, sorry I'm late. You ready?"

"Yes. Thanks for having me! I'll text you later."

"Later Rock Star!" Melinda said.

When they got back in the car Ashley asked, "So, how did it go, Little Chica?"

"Her mom was very nice. Like, sweet. We had fun. Talked about a lot of stuff. I just didn't know how to act for a while. I'm so awkward."

"You'll get better at it. It's good that you spent some time with someone your age, even though I think your dad missed you. I stayed with him and we had coffee and played cards. But he kept checking the time."

Jett smiled and looked out the window. "It was fun. Maybe Melinda can come to our place sometime? It would be different. She thinks Dad is hot. How funny is that?"

"It's funny, but your father is a very attractive man. He's always had a quiet, strong intensity about him and he's very reliable. You can always count on him to do what's right, even though he'll never make a big deal out of it. It's a very admirable quality these days. And he loves his daughter very much. He's a good father, and women like that."

"So, do you think Dad is hot?"

"Ok. No more of this line of questioning. You suckered me in on that one. We'll have to get you to interview people on cases since you're so smart."

Jett laughed at Ashley's response; Ashley laughed with her. They were quiet for a moment, until Jett said, in a quiet, nervous voice, "I just think we'd make an awesome family," blushing after she said it.

"Little Chica, we are an awesome family. Just not a traditional one. We are different. But I hope you know that we will always be family. I love you with all of my heart. Forever, no matter what. You'll never be rid of me, ok?"

"Thanks, Ashley. I love you too. And I'd never want to be rid of you. You're the best," Jett whispered.

"Thank you, Jett. Thank you," Ashley whispered and smiled in the dark, as they pulled into the parking lot.

Chapter Twelve: The Karate Kid

From the *Port City Times*:

Local Student Wins Regional Karate Championship

Houston, Texas

Port City, Texas, competitor Jett Landry won her first karate tournament Saturday. Seeded an underdog, Landry fought with skill, precision, and speed to outmaneuver her opponents and win five consecutive matches to qualify for the final match against a seasoned opponent in the 15 to 17-year-old black belt division. Katie Bracket, last year's champion and number one seed, turns eighteen in one month after this tournament and lost her final match, in dramatic form, to Port City's Landry. After two sudden death rounds with no points scored, Landry won the championship match by maneuvering her opponent off the mat to score the game-winning point. "She kind of came out of nowhere and no one knew how good this competitor was," Roderick Sumarro, League President, said of Landry. "She's got a future in this sport if she keeps this up. I look forward to seeing her in Port City." Landry said she is doing the best she can and will work on getting better. Her next tournament will be the District Tournament, two weeks from today, at home in Port City. If Jett wins, she will qualify for the league's State Championship Tournament in Austin, Texas. Her Karate Instructor is Denise Williams at Downtown Karate.

Melinda and her mother surprised Jett by showing up to watch her compete. Diana also texted Markus during the prelims and asked how the tournament was going. When he told her Jett needed one more win to qualify for the final rounds, she drove to Houston as fast as she could to see the last two bouts.

On the way home, Jett fell asleep in the backseat. Her dad woke her up and, after a shower and change of clothes, they all went to Joey's Italian Restaurant. Joey congratulated her and recognized her accomplishment publicly, which drew a round of applause and cheers. In the evening, she went to sleep exhausted and happy, on the couch, under a blanket, with Ashley, watching a movie while her dad fell asleep on the recliner.

Chapter Thirteen: Enter the Jett

Jett, her dad, and Ashley arrived at the Port City Events Center for the District Tournament. Being the only local competitor was a thrill, but in a community that was obsessed with high school football, basketball, and baseball, other youth sports were under-represented, which only made her feel special about her success. As she warmed up for her first match, she noticed a few of her friends were there to support her: Melinda and her mom, Greg, and two other kids she knew from school. She smiled and waved. Melinda pointed over her left shoulder. In the bleachers, towards the top, sat Mr. Preston and two of her teachers. Shocked, she smiled even bigger and waved. Diana showed up right before her first match and blew her a kiss from her seat, one row below and in front of her dad. Ashley, as usual, was nervous for Jett. Jett waved and reported to the competition area. She stepped onto the mat to face her opponent. The referee blew the whistle, and the fighting began.

Jett Landry Advances to State Karate Tournament

Port City, Texas

Jett Landry, the local 'Karate Kid,' wins her second consecutive tournament and advances to the Summer League Karate State Championship Tournament in Austin, Texas. Set for August 21, Landry will compete against girls from all over Texas for the State Championship title in the Girls' 15-17 Black Belt Division. Landry went undefeated in the preliminary bouts and fought her way to the final match, where she overwhelmed her opponent with superior speed, accuracy, and skill. "The state championship will be very competitive. She will be the youngest person in her division, so this will be a wonderful learning experience for her. It will be quite a challenge," Denise Williams, Jett's coach at 'Downtown Karate' said about her star pupil. "I'm just going to work hard and do the best I can in Austin," Landry said. "And I'm excited about the challenge."

Chapter Fourteen: Gracias Mi Madre

"If I thought that I wouldn't have let you drive. You did fine. Don't second guess yourself," Markus said as they arrived home. Jett spent the afternoon learning how to drive her dad's truck. Her dad insisted Jett learn how to drive a stick shift. She may be in a position where she needs to drive a standard one day, he told her. He already taught Jett to drive on the sedan he used for work. The truck was his second vehicle. He bought it when Jett first arrived from Baltimore, and they used it for running errands around town. It was a dark blue Toyota Tacoma with dark-tinted windows and black trim. He insisted she will get her driver's license when she turns sixteen, so she can learn how to be independent.

"Thanks, dad. Ooh look, Ashley's here!" Jett said as they pulled into the parking lot.

"Yea. She's at the apartment helping me with something."

As they entered the apartment Jett saw the painting her dad bought at the art opening, hanging on the wall, behind the couch in their den. Ashley had just finished hanging the picture.

Jett's jaw dropped when she saw it. "You like where it's at, Little Chica?"

"Yes! It's even cooler hanging on our wall."

"Just in time for state. You're our Fierce Warrior."

"Thanks, I'm just a girl though."

"You also have a note from the artist." Ashley unfolded the note, written in cursive on personalized stationery, and handed it to Jett.

"Dear Jett, I so enjoyed meeting you at my opening and I am in love with the fact that you shared your story with me. When I read about your accomplishments in the news, I immediately thought again about this painting and what it means to me and what it means to you, and what it means to your dad. Like your dad, I believe this picture is YOU. You are the little girl who becomes the Fierce Warrior. You have the spark in you and you inspire hope in others, whether it's your dad, or me, or your friends in school. In whatever you do in life, always keep the spark alive. Protect it, nurture it, and fire it up when you need it. I will always be here for you too, so stay in touch. Love, Kilanna."

He put his arm around her shoulder. "I'm glad you like it. It goes along with what I was saying about having confidence. Everyone that knows you has faith in you, kid."

Jett put her head down and cried a little. She looked up and smiled at her dad and hugged him.

"Thanks, Dad, thanks, Ashley."

"Just don't ever stop being mi chica."

"No, nunca detendra'. Te quiero."

"Yo tambie'n te quiero," Ashley said back.

"Whoa, you two have your own language now?"

Jett smiled. "I took Spanish in middle school. Ashley and I have practiced ever since."

***

They arrived at the hotel Friday afternoon, the day before the tournament. After checking in, they went to their rooms to unpack. Ashley changed clothes but Jett wore her jeans and a Guns and Roses hoodie. Ashley and Jett went back downstairs to sign in for the tournament. There were gift shops with overpriced items, chic' coffee shops, elegant restaurants, and a jazz bar on the first floor. Nothing in the hotel caught her interest until she saw the vendor setting up outside of the conference area, where the tournament would take place.

Jett and Ashley went to the tournament area while Diana and Markus made their way down to meet them for dinner. Once Jett registered and received her tournament schedule, she went to see the vendor across the hall from registration.

The vendor was selling traditional African goods. He was a middle-aged African American man; friendly and polite, he greeted Jett and Ashley with a smile and welcomed them to browse and ask questions. Jett's eyes widened as she took in all the trinkets, jewelry, and artwork laid out on the two tables he occupied. Ashley excused herself to go to the restroom while Jett looked over the products.

"Do you know what part of Africa your people are from?" the vendor asked.

"No, my mom never talked to me about that. She was too worried about the present to think about the past. That's what she always said."

“I understand. Life can be very hard. What about your father?”

“He’s my father,” Jett pointed at her dad, who was walking down the hall with Diana. They stopped to investigate a shop near the conference area.

“Yes. Is this your mother?” he gestured to where Ashley had been standing.

“Well, my mom died when I was ten and I came here to live with my dad, and Ashley is kind of like my mom now. I mean, that’s how I think of her. But my mom was my... my mom. It’s complicated.” Jett often felt guilty thinking of Ashley as a mother figure. She feared it was hurtful to the memory of her mother.

She recognized the compassion in the vendor’s eyes as he looked at her. He broke eye contact after a second and said, “do you see anything here you like?”

“I like the bracelets and necklaces. They look like nature or organic or something.”

“They are traditional, handmade in Ghana. Each with their own meaning.”

Jett picked up a bracelet. “This one just calls to me. What does it mean?”

“This is part of a set of bracelets worn by warriors. There are three of them, each with a separate meaning. Warriors in an ancient tribe who once occupied Ghana wore these, when going into battle, to remind them of their code. This one means to fight with courage. This one means to fight with honor, and this one means to live with compassion. Why do they speak to you?"

"I'm fighting in the karate tournament tomorrow. Maybe that's why. And the necklace? What does it mean?"

"It means God is with you and you are with God, even when you don't think about God, or even forget about God. It means God is always with you."

"Ok. I want to buy the bracelets if I have enough money. How much?"

"Five dollars each, ten dollars for the whole set."

"I have ten dollars. I can buy the set."

"Good. And I'll give you the necklace, because you need to be reminded that God is with you, always. Your mother, who is in heaven, watches over you, loves you very deeply, is very proud of you, and she prays for you. She prays for God to be with you, no matter what. And she is very happy that you have a mother here on earth who loves you as deeply as she does. So, be joyous and fight in your tournament with," as he handed her each bracelet, "Courage, honor, and compassion."

"Thank you, sir." Jett was confused and she tried to hide her emotions. She cried as soon as she turned away from the man.

Ashley was returning and saw her face as she turned around. "What's wrong, Chica?"

"Nothing, I'm just happy and sad. Thought of my mom just now."

"Your mom is watching over you and she is so proud of you. I can feel this. With every cell in my body, I can feel this and know it to be true. She'll never leave you. And neither will I. No matter what. So be happy. Because you have her and me."

Jett took Ashley's hand, and they walked down the corridor together, returning to her dad and Diana.

"What did you buy from the vendor?" Ashley asked.

"Three bracelets and a necklace. Well, he gave me a necklace. I bought the bracelets for ten dollars. The bracelets are for warriors and they are for courage, honor, and compassion. The necklace he gave me is a symbol. It means God is with me." Jett pulled the necklace out from under her hoodie as she showed her the three bracelets she wore on her wrist.

***

The next day Jett felt confident and ready. She talked with Denise about strategy. She fielded texts from her friends wishing her luck, and multiple texts from Melinda. Her favorite was a message telling her that she will kick so much ass that ass will hide from her in the parking lot to avoid getting kicked. Jett loved Melinda's sense of humor.

Many of her fellow students, teachers, Mr. Preston's secretary, and Mr. Preston himself posted encouraging messages on the school's official Facebook page. Melinda said that her mom would be in touch with Ashley for updates throughout the tournament. Taking this in, Jett reflected on all the support she was getting from her family, friends, and school. Despite her efforts to isolate herself, she had people who cared about her now.

Before her first match, she approached her dad, Ashley, and Diana. Ashley looked nervous while her dad tried to project calm. Diana gave her a 'go for it, girlfriend' with a hug and a big smile. Jett felt an intense feeling of urgency. She was tired of waiting and ready to compete.

She took off her bracelets and put them in her backpack. She took off her necklace, that reminded her of her mom, and handed it to Ashley. "This is very important to me, it's why I thought of my mom yesterday. I want you to hold on to it for me while I fight because I thought a lot about what you said yesterday. Okay?"

Ashley carefully took the necklace and gave Jett a tight, warm hug. "I will. I am so proud of you Little Chica. I love you so much and I know what you mean."

Jett whispered the words, "Gracias Mi Madre" into Ashley's ear, pulled away, and ran to the mat for her first match. A tear ran down Ashley's cheek as she watched the girl run.

After a brief talk with Denise, Jett stepped onto the mat and faced off against her opponent. Jett looked the girl straight in the eye, bowed, took a few deep breaths, and cleared her mind. The referee blew the whistle, and the tournament was underway.

Breaking Sports News: Local 'Karate Kid' wins State Karate Championship

Austin, Texas

In a stunning display of grit, courage, and determination, local karate champion Jett Landry won the SKA State Karate

Championship in Austin, Texas. "Jett just took it to another level tonight. I've never seen her fight with such skill and poise before, against girls who are much older and more experienced than her. She took everything they threw at her, stayed calm and focused, and returned it in greater measure," her coach, Denise Williams, said. Landry was ranked at the bottom of a field packed with established talent. Landry worked her way through the prelims and qualified for the finals, only losing one match out of four. In the quarterfinals, she faced off against last year's SKA state champion, Rhonda Gibson. After losing the first point of the match Landry scored five points in a row and dominated her opponent. The semifinals were challenging but Landry persevered and won. The championship match went to Sudden Death overtime, but Landry managed, after 2 minutes of continuous exchange, to score a point with a well-placed kick to the abdomen of her opponent, earning her the first State Championship for Downtown Karate. At fifteen years old, she is the youngest athlete to win the SKA State Karate Championship. School starts next week, and one kid will have the coolest story about what she did this summer.

Chapter Fifteen: Throw Justin in the Pool

Jett got her books from her locker and started down the hall. It was the first day of school and she was getting a lot of high fives and fist bumps from the kids for her state karate championship. She was taller than last year, almost five feet, four inches tall. While she was still lean, she was strong. With her strength, she was developing confidence.

When she got to her first class her teacher handed her a pass. "Hey, Jett! Welcome back! Mr. Preston has summoned you to his office."

Jett's heart sank. "Already? I haven't even sat down yet. What did I do?"

"Don't worry about it. I'm sure it's okay."

Jett walked into the office and saw Mike and two of his friends, Jeff and Nathan, sitting across from Mr. Preston's desk. Jett knew Jeff, but Nathan was new to her. She knew of him, had seen him around, but never met him. Mike looked like he had gained even more muscle mass over the summer and was wearing jeans and a tight-fitting white tee shirt that showed off his biceps when he bent his arms. To Jett, all three boys looked like they spent the summer taking steroids and lifting weights. Jett felt tiny.

Angelique was there too, but she looked different. Her hair was straight, and she wasn't wearing makeup. Angelique had freckles. She wore jeans and a light sweater over a tee shirt. Jett noticed Angelique didn't seem comfortable with the boys.

Mr. Preston, from behind his desk, gestured at the empty chair next to Angelique. "Ms. Landry, take a seat please." Jett sat down and waited for him to begin.

"I want to talk to you about the year each of you needs to have. I hope each of you has matured enough to put your differences aside and to try to get along with each other.

"Michael, Jeffrey, Nathan. This is your senior year. I hope you would want this year to represent the adults you would like to be when you graduate. I would ask you all to be leaders and to be positive role models for the younger boys who look up to you.

"Jett, congratulations on winning a very competitive state tournament in karate. Gentlemen, I had the pleasure of watching Ms. Landry compete, and I think our athletes can learn a thing or two about competition, character, and determination from Jett's performance."

Jett smiled at his compliment and murmured, "Thanks, Mr. Preston."

Angelique put her fist out for a fist bump. "Congrats." Jett looked at her and returned the gesture.

"Ms. Angelique. I'm not sure where you stand at this point. I am a bit confused."

Angelique perked up. "Jett, I broke up with Mike this summer. For good. I am so over his bullying and racism and misogyny. I'd rather be your friend than his girlfriend."

"God, I'm gonna vomit," Mike said. "Don't encourage it. It'll start thinking it's someone. And the karate stuff. Big deal. It's not like football."

Before Mr. Preston could respond, Jeff looked at Mike and said, "Man, why you gotta be such a jerk? We haven't won a game in two years and she wins state. At least she's doing something." Jeff looked at Jett. "Congratulations Jett. It's cool that you won state."

"Thank you!" Jett was surprised.

"Thank you, Jeff. Michael, Nathan?" Mr. Preston said.

Nathan looked at Mike to see his response. Mike looked perturbed. His arms were folded, and he was sitting back in his chair, staring at Mr. Preston. Finally, he looked at Jett and said, "Okay, fine. I won't be a jerk to you this year if you stay out of my way and mind your own business. But if you step out of line, I'll put you down. Karate, no karate, don't test me with that crap. I've worked out a lot this summer and I'm ripped. Karate doesn't do any good against strength and size. There's nothing you can do if I decide to take you out. But don't worry. I won't. I'll leave you alone. Just mind your business and stay out of my way and I'll stay out of yours."

Nathan smiled and nodded menacingly at Jett. Then he looked at Mr. Preston and said, "Me too."

"Fine with me, Mr. Preston. I'll stay out of their way to avoid trouble."

Mr. Preston looked at Mike, then Jett, and said, "Thank you, Jett. As for you Mike, I will not tolerate bullying this year. Last year was disturbing in the least. This year I will have zero-tolerance. Do you understand me?"

"Whatever, sure," Mike said. "In November my dad is going to be mayor. And he's friends with your boss, the superintendent. He has dinner at our house a lot. Just saying."

"Say what you want Michael, but I expect responsible behavior this year and I will not tolerate the bullying and violence we endured the last few years. I have had enough. Now, go back to class."

Jett stood up, trying to comprehend what happened. It was like she rounded a corner and walked into an alternative universe where Mr. Preston was taking her side and admonishing Mike. She wasn't the bad kid anymore. She wanted to high five Mr. Preston. Instead, she said, "Thank you sir" and left the room to return to class.

Two weeks later, Jett was having lunch in the cafeteria with Melinda and a few other kids. Jett dipped a carrot stick in yogurt when she dropped some yogurt onto her black tee shirt. As she was wiping it up, Nathan walked over to their table with an angry look on his face.

"All you dumbasses, sitting at a table together. One day there will be a time when no one gives a shit about any of you. Hope you're ready."

Jett looked up and said, "No one gives a shit about us now, so it'll be a smooth adjustment." She went back to wiping the yogurt off her shirt. The other kids laughed nervously.

"You got a problem half-breed?"

"Yes. I spilled some yogurt on my shirt, and I think it's gonna stain. I was trying to clean it off, and I missed most of what you said. I love this shirt. I hope it doesn't stain. You were saying?"

"Unlike those other assholes, I'm not scared of you."

"Ok," Jett took another bite of her sandwich.

"I can beat your ass, easy. No girl can kick my ass."

"Cool."

"Are you some kind of smart-ass?"

"I don't care about anything you're saying. I'm worried about this shirt. So, you're not scared of girls, cool. One day no one is going to give a shit about us. Got it."

The other kids were now chuckling, but still nervous.

"What are you looking at, homo?" Nathan said to another kid, a boy named Justin, sitting at the table.

"Uh, you. You're talking. It's normal and considered polite to look at someone when they're talking. You knew that, right?"

Nathan turned and walked towards the boy and leaned over and got in his face, trembling with anger.

"Give me a reason. Just give me a reason." Justin turned red and started shaking.

"Hey, we're trying to have lunch. There's no need for that," Jett said.

"Screw you and your lunch, mongrel."

"Screw me and my lunch? Now you're going too far. I like this lunch," Jett said. "And just to clarify, now I'm being a smart-ass."

Melinda spoke up. "Nathan wants to have sex with Jett's lunch. How weird is that?"

The boy who drew Nathan's ire, Justin, said, "And Jett too."

"No, I think he meant it figuratively, not literally. I doubt he really wants to have sex with a sandwich, fruit, vegetables, and yogurt. Maybe my yogurt." Jett held out the yogurt. "Nathan, if you want to have sex with the yogurt, I'm finished with it. You can have the rest if you want."

Nathan stared at all the kids, angry but confused. He didn't know how to respond. They were all trying not to laugh now. "I don't want to screw your yogurt, half-breed bitch. And I don't want to screw your genocidal ass. I just want you to go away. That's all. Stay out of my way and there won't be trouble."

It was quiet for a moment, and Jett looked up at Nathan. "Ok. Sounds good. I mean, you came to our table so..."

Nathan stormed off without saying another word.

"Lunch-perv," Greg, who was also at the table, said.

"He went straight to anal," Justin said, and the kids started laughing.

"You offered to let him screw your yogurt," Melinda said, giggling. "That was epic."

"I think he actually thought about it," Jett said. "Gross."

"What's the deal with the genocide comment?" Justin asked.

"Who knows? They just say stupid stuff. Mike has said twice that he will 'own me' one day," Jett said. "Now Nathan is talking about some time in the future when we won't matter anymore. They say stupid, creepy stuff."

"They're delusional. No telling," Melinda said.

"They like to drop stuff like that into conversation when they're mad at me. Like they are going to get even with me someday," Jett said.

"Weirdos. Anyway, it's time for class," Melinda said.

"And my shirt. I love this shirt." Jett cringed at the yogurt stain.

"Let's stop in the bathroom and put some cold water on it. That may help," Melinda said as they walked down the hall with their group.

Two weeks later Jett got a text from Melinda after their last class of the day.

Melinda: *Jett! Urgent. Mike, Nathan, and Jeff just grabbed Justin and are dragging him to the pool. On my way there to help him out.*

Jett: *Melinda, be careful. I'm on my way too.*

When Melinda arrived, the boys held Justin by the arms and were dragging him towards the water.

"I knew it. You're gay. All it took was a few messages, and it all comes out," Mike yelled.

"Come on! I didn't know it was you."

"Secret's out now. Everyone's gonna know. And your parents are gonna find out too."

"Leave me alone. I wasn't bothering you."

"Your existence bothers me. You're not wanted here. We don't need gays at this school. Trying to force your lifestyle down everyone's throat."

"Force my lifestyle? I kept it a secret."

"You were all ready to meet someone after school. That don't sound like no secret to me."

Nathan joined the conversation. "Enough talking. Let's throw him in the pool."

"I can't swim! Seriously, guys, I could drown and die! Don't!"

"What do we care?" Nathan said. "You're gay."

Melinda arrived and took off her shoes, saying, "It's okay Justin, I can swim. I'll get you out."

"I don't want to go in. Please just leave me alone."

"No, you're going in the pool. And you, don't let her jump in."

Suddenly the door swung open, and the room went dark; someone turned off the lights. The room was eerily quiet for a moment. The door slammed shut again. The three guys let go of Justin and looked around the dark room. Melinda used the moment to grab Justin and pull him away from the pool.

The lights came back on and Jett was in the room. "Leave him alone, Mike." Jett's voice was stern.

"Shit," Mike said, "Why can't you just mind your own damn business. You were gonna stay out of my way this year."

"Leave him alone, Mike."

Mike circled Jett until he was between her and the door. Jett turned to keep Mike in her sight while also keeping track of the others.

"Come on, Mike. Let's throw the ni-" Nathan started to say before Jett cut him off.

"Don't say that word. If that word comes out of your mouth, I'm putting my fist in it. And you can't stop me. Ask Mike how it feels."

Mike pleaded with Jett. "This is none of your business, Jett. Just leave it alone. It's between us and Justin. We're just goofing off."

"I don't want anything to do with you guys," Justin said.

Jeff tried to explain. "Jett, Justin is gay. We looked it up on a gay dating app, put up a fake profile, pretended to be someone in the school, and Justin showed up to meet us. He was willing to meet another gay at this school. That's just wrong."

Jett looked at Jeff for a long moment and said, "I thought better of you, Jeff."

Jeff looked down. "You can't help what you are, and I understand that. But, being a homosexual, that's different. He can help it. Or at least keep it to himself."

Jett sighed at Jeff's ignorance. He didn't even know how many bigoted things he had just said.

"Who cares," Nathan said, angry. "Let's beat the shit out of them both. She started it. She didn't need to butt into our business."

"Business? That's business? Just walk away, guys. I don't want to do this," Jett said.

"Let us throw him in the pool. Your friend can get him out and we all walk away," Mike said. Nathan laughed.

"I want to beat the shit out of Jett, though," Nathan said.

"That's just the steroids talking, Nathan. You should get some help." Jett shook her head.

"See. She's practically asking for it."

"Walk away guys. That's it. No one is getting thrown in the pool. No one. And no talking about Justin. What he does is none of your business."

"I've had enough of her shit," Nathan said and made a move to punch Jett. Jett turned and kicked him hard in the mouth before he could get close enough to punch her. His lip burst and blood ran down his chin to his shirt. He stood there, stunned, for just a second, and he started to throw another punch. Jett kicked him again, this time in the chest. Nathan stopped. Jett turned to face Jeff as he was the next closest person to her.

Jeff put his hands up. "I don't want to fight. I don't want to fight."

"Good," Jett said. "Neither do I."

Mike reached for a metal rod he saw lying on the floor. When Jett turned to him, he flung it in her direction, but Jett reflexively flicked her wrist and the rod veered slightly off course.

"What the...?" Nathan said.

"Back off Nathan," Jett said, anxious now, keeping Mike in her peripheral vision, "you too Mike. Just back off, both of you."

Both boys backed off, stunned by what they saw with the metal rod.

Mike stared at Jett for a moment and said, "I know. That was crazy."

"Anyway, we're done. Leave Justin alone. Justin, Melinda, let's get out of here."

Jett, Melinda, and Justin made their way to the door and down the hall. Justin was shaking and started crying in the hallway. When they got to the front door, school security and Mr. Preston were waiting.

"What just happened? Why is Justin crying?" Mr. Preston said.

"Mike and Nathan just tried to throw Justin in the pool, and he can't swim. We just went to help him," Melinda said.

After separating all the kids and placing each group under supervision, Mr. Preston interviewed each student to find out what happened. In the meantime, Ashley arrived to bring Jett home, but a teacher told her Jett was in the office. Krayton had already shown up to speak for his son.

"You did the right thing. Hopefully, they'll understand this time. And that poor boy. Everyone is going to know about him now, before he is ready. That poor boy. This will be hard in this school," Ashley said after she joined Jett and Melinda in the office.

"I guess they've done sexism and racism, now they've moved on to homophobia," Melinda said, "Why are they so hateful?"

"I don't know. I wish I did," Ashley said.

Mr. Preston brought the parents and kids into the conference room and explained what he found out about the incident. "I have talked to each of these kids about this incident and I've put together what seems to be the truth of the matter. Now, these two boys," gesturing at Mike and Nathan, "had two different versions of what happened and, amazingly enough, the only thing they seemed to have in common is that they both agree they are innocent of any wrongdoing. I talked to the two young ladies and the other boy and their stories are the same. Now, this brings me to the last person I interviewed. Jeff had the integrity to tell me the truth. They were bullying this young man and were going to throw him in the pool knowing he can't swim.

Three of them, picking on one boy. This young lady," pointing at Melinda, "showed up to help him get out of the water and Jett showed up to confront the bullies, so they wouldn't hurt this young man or her friend."

The room was quiet for a moment. Mike and Nathan glared at Jeff. He looked back and shrugged. "I told the truth."

"Mr. Preston," Krayton said, in a grim voice. "Surely we can agree that the same problems with this child are occurring again. When are we going to address the core problem?"

Ashley started to speak up, but Mr. Preston spoke first. "No sir, we don't agree. We've had a bullying problem in this school for about three years now. Bullying always seems to start elsewhere. In this incident, the 'problem child' you refer to wasn't part of the incident at first. But your son was. We have a unique opportunity to address the problem head-on. Surely you agree we should do this. I will impose some tough love today. Your son, and sir, your son," pointing at Nathan's dad, "are suspended for two weeks. During those two weeks, they will NOT be eligible for any school activities. That includes football practice and games. Maybe they will learn to treat these other kids with respect. As far as Jeff, because he spoke up and told the truth, I will ask two things of him: to apologize to the young man for his part in the incident and to serve one week of on-campus detention, and he will also be ineligible for football as long as he is in detention."

Jeff sighed and looked at Jett. Jett gestured with her head at Justin. Jeff looked at Justin, stood up, and walked over to him. Justin looked up. "I'm sorry I took part in trying to throw you in the pool. It was wrong." Jeff put out his hand and Justin shook it.

Mike and his dad looked like they were going to burst. "You mean to tell me you're taking this boy's word over my boy's word?"

Mr. Preston looked at Mike's dad and didn't say a word. Krayton continued. "You know, I will be mayor soon. I have a lot of support on the board and I'm good friends with the superintendent. I hope you're planning on retiring soon, Preston."

"Oh, I just may be retiring soon. I'm not interested in your political ambitions. I'm responsible for the physical and psychological safety of the students in this school. Today, your son and his friends started an altercation. Today, they will learn the consequences of their behavior.

"I am also aware, Jett, even though you did not state this, Michael threw a metal rod at you and missed. This was confirmed by two other witnesses. Because Mike is eighteen years old, your guardian can opt to pursue assault charges. You have a right to know of this, according to school policy; policy approved and signed by our superintendent."

"Thank you," Jett said.

Jett's heart went out to Justin. His dad wanted to know why those boys targeted him, so Justin said he would only tell him with Mr. Preston present.

"Melinda, your mother asked me to give you a ride home since I'm already here. Is this okay?"

"Yes, ma'am. Thanks."

Ashley walked between the two girls and put her arms around both of their shoulders. "I'm so proud of you two. Standing up to the bullies and protecting your friend. That took a lot of courage. You're superheroes."

***

"I'm gonna need cash, man. That's the only way this is gonna work," the grimy, sweaty man sitting across from Markus Jackson said.

Jackson regarded him a moment. "You realize they kidnapped this girl, right? Give me the info first and then we'll work out the details."

"I wanna do the right thing like the next guy, but I want that reward in cash. I can't go to no bank to pick it up. This is confidential, right?"

"Of course. My only concern is finding the girl. I'm not interested in whatever else you got going on around here." He was meeting with this man, who wouldn't disclose his name, in the back room of a diner on the edge of the woods, about fifteen minutes north of Port City. The man was homeless, living in a camp in the forest, and contacted Investigative Associates from one of the last remaining payphones in Texas. His informant was in his early thirties, balding, and thin. He wore torn-up jeans, worn-out work boots, and a white tee shirt.

The man leaned in and whispered, "I have warrants. I need to stay away from cameras. Burglary, no big deal, but I don't feel like going to jail. So, I want the reward in cash.

Otherwise, I'm not sayin' nothin. I'm not gonna risk getting myself killed without some kind of cash reward attached to it. Besides, it's not just the girl you're looking for that's the thing here. It's other girls too. The same situation."

"I'll talk to our attorney and see if we can swing it. Regarding the warrants, would you accept legal representation as part of the deal? Maybe we can help clear your name."

"Man, I don't trust no damn attorneys. I'm fine. I have a place to sleep, I can move around without being seen. I can get by with enough stuff to sell off for food and weed. Your ass is gonna have me on probation wearing a damn ankle bracelet with the cops watching every damn thing I do. Plus, I won't be able to smoke weed or drink booze, and they'll make me get a damn job. No way. Just give me the cash and I'll tell you what I know."

"If you're able to move around without being seen," Jackson said, "why do you have to hide and spy on these guys?"

"I don't have to hide as much as you think. Nobody gives a shit about what some paranoid, drunk homeless guy thinks, sees, or talks about. I can do what I want out here. I'm not the only one either. It's a great place to hide from warrants, if you know what I mean. Hell, the cops in Port City know it, but as long as no one is complaining about us, they leave us be. The only reason I'm here, besides the cash, is because I don't wanna see no one get hurt. I can't imagine what they're doing to those girls. We got a deal or what?"

"Okay, we got a deal. I'll get you cash, on one condition though. It doesn't stop here. I'll give you some of the cash right now as a down payment, you tell me what you know. Then, if you agree to continue collecting information for us, we'll keep paying you for it. How does that sound?"

"It sounds like a job."

"Consider yourself an independent contractor."

He was prepared for this; Diana provided him with an additional two hundred dollars in cash. He pulled the envelope out of his blazer pocket and set it in front of the man.

"Now, what've you got?"

The man leaned in and started talking about what he described as a safe house for human traffickers, corrupt politicians, out of state militia types, and a motorcycle gang of violent neo-Nazis.

Chapter Sixteen: The Long Night

"Remember, if a boy tries to touch you, you have my permission to punch him in the mouth," Markus said. "Or if he looks at you, or if he thinks about looking at you," he added gruffly.

Jett rolled her eyes. "Okay, Dad."

It was Homecoming night. Jett and her friends were going to the dance. It was Jett's first high school dance. She didn't know how to dress. She wore black slacks, matching heels, and a dark blue blouse. Her dad was happy she chose something modest, but he kept it to himself. He didn't trust any of those boys.

"Here are some rules, kid: don't let a guy bring you a drink. Get your own drinks. Don't let your drinks out of your sight. DO NOT let a guy talk you into drinking alcohol. They act all nice and talk you into drinking just a little bit of alcohol. Then they slip something into your drink. Don't go outside with a boy, not even for a few minutes. Use the buddy system, stay with your friends, and look out for each other. You and Melinda be buddies and do not let each other out of your sight. And remember the most important rule: EVERY GUY IS YOUR ENEMY AND IS NOT TO BE TRUSTED. Got it?"

Jett sighed. "Got it. First off, I'm not interested in meeting a boy. Second, what kind of drinks do you think we'll be having? It's a high school dance, not a bar. I wouldn't go outside with a boy. And I'll be looking out for all my friends. Especially this one kid, who is gay. He is bringing along another friend, who is also gay. I'm not sure if they are dating or not. Between having the only black kid, the geeks, and the only two gay kids, we're going to be a target-rich environment for bullies."

"Just leave if they give you trouble. Don't make a stand. If it's that bad your friends can hang out here. I'll stay out of the way, as long as you all don't act like a bunch of jerks."

"Aww, dad. A party?"

"Maybe not a party but hanging out is okay. Your friends are good kids, so I don't mind. If it were me and my friends, when we were in high school, there is no way they'd get invited here to hang out. We'd of trashed the place. We were a bunch of stoners and drunks."

"I'm sure you weren't that bad."

"Little Chica," Ashley said.

"Yes, Mi Madre?" Jett responded.

"Quieres probar un maquillaje?"

"No es posible!" Jett said emphatically.

"Solo para resaltar tu belleza natural?"

"I don't like stuff on my face," Jett said.

"What are you two talking about?" her dad asked, alarmed.

"Makeup dad. She asked me if I wanted to wear makeup."

"You two have your own language. Great," he said with a small chuckle.

“Us ladies have to help each other out with the girl stuff. Right Little Chica?”

“Los hombres no entienden de todos modos, derecho, Mi Madre?”

“Si’ little Chica,” Ashley said, smiling at Markus.

“I need to go now. I’m supposed to pick Melinda up in a few minutes.”

“Ok. You promise, to follow my rules at the dance?”

“Yes, Dad.”

“And you promise, no alcohol or drugs?”

“Yes, Dad.”

“Okay, because it’s your first time to go out on your own, I’m worried. So, do you promise to be safe and responsible in your truck? No showing off, or being reckless, or speeding or doing anything stupid?”

“Do you know me?”

Her dad had surprised her by giving her his truck, as a birthday gift, on her sixteenth birthday. He had planned to do this when he first bought the truck, thus the reason he insisted she learned to drive a stick shift last summer.

Ashley had a concerned look on her face. “If anything happens, you can call, we’ll be there in no time.”

“Yes, I know. I’ll be fine.”

Ashley put her arms around Jett and hugged her. Her dad gave her a wary look and patted her on the back. “Have fun kid, but not too much fun, got it?”

“Y'all are too much. It’s just a dance.” Jett grabbed her keys and went out the door.

“It’s so exciting to see her do things with her friends. I was afraid this would never happen,” Ashley said.

“I don’t know,” her dad said. “I hate being worried all the time. It sucks.”

***

Jett and Melinda arrived at seven in the evening. Melinda wore jeans, black heels, and a red blouse. She wore a black blazer over the blouse. She looked like she was dressed for work on casual Friday.

When they walked into the gym, they found the rest of their friends occupying an area near the restrooms. Justin approached the girls, introduced his friend, pulled Melinda aside, and told her he felt stressed out. He pointed at the dance floor and she saw why. It was Mike, Nathan, their girlfriends, and several other big guys with their girlfriends.

“Oh. It’s the sad little wolf pack and their alpha,” Melinda said.

“If he thinks we’re together, he’s going to start something,” Justin said, with urgency.

“You’re together? That’s awesome!” Melinda said.

“It’s awesome until we get the shit beat out of us.”

"Okay, just relax and try to have a good time. Don't be obvious about being together. If anything goes down, we'll leave and go somewhere else. Okay?"

"Ok. I'll try. But be ready to leave."

Justin's friend was Michael. Greg rode with the two boys to the dance. There were two more girls in the group. A tall, awkward, blond girl with braces, named Marsha, and Lara, a red-haired girl with freckles, who was pretty and had a nice smile. After they high fived and fist-bumped each other, they stood there awkwardly, looking at the dance floor. Greg left to get something to drink from the drink table. Jett went with him and they picked up sodas for all the kids in their group.

After a few minutes of awkwardness, the kids started doing what they usually do in social situations: isolate themselves and make snarky comments about the popular kids.

"Hey Jett," Melinda said, "remember when Nathan wanted to have sex with your lunch earlier this year?"

"He talked about it. I offered him the yogurt."

"Oh yeah," Justin said, "And he totally went anal."

"He looks like the type to do that," Justin's friend, Michael said.

"What do y'all think? Nathan: closet or no?" Melinda said.

"Closet," each of the kids rattled off, laughing.

Jett snorted when she laughed and said, "This is like a new game, 'Closet or no?'"

“The funny thing,” Greg said, “is that they dance like they think they’re cool or something. I mean, we know we’re not cool and we can’t dance without looking stupid. But they dance like they think they can dance. It’s like watching someone who sucks at singing go off at karaoke. You feel bad for them, but you just want them to stop.”

“Look at Mike,” Melinda said, “his face. It’s like he’s doing this funky overbite thing when he dances.”

“That’s his ‘O’ face during sex, you know,” Marsha said.

“Ew,” Lara said, “I feel sorry for whoever has to see that.”

“Oh, it’s okay,” Greg said. “Nathan has his back to him and is all bent over so he never sees it.”

Now the kids were laughing so hard they couldn’t control themselves. Jett had to sit down because her stomach hurt from giggling. None of them noticed Mike’s date was walking towards them and overheard their conversation on her way to the restroom.

She listened for a moment and started laughing too.

“What so funny?” Mike asked as he joined his date.

The group got quiet. “Shit,” Jett said out loud. “We drew his fire.”

Mike’s date was still laughing and said, “It’s nothing babe. They were just cracking jokes when I walked up, and they were cracking me up. They’re hilarious.”

Nathan, who followed Mike, puffed out his chest. He was wearing slacks, a white dress shirt, and a tie, but he loosened his tie and approached Justin.

"Why don't you tell us your jokes then?"

Justin got nervous and didn't say anything.

"You're crashing our buzz guys," Jett said.

Mike glared at Jett. "You're at a dance? You got balls half-breed. I'll give you that."

"Ovaries actually, but thanks," Jett said. Greg chuckled.

"About the half-breed thing," Michael said to Mike but was cut off by Nathan.

"What about it, dick rider?" Nathan said.

"Ok. That's bad too. My name is Michael."

"Your name is 'Homo.' I guess you're with this dick enthusiast here?"

Jett inserted herself between the guys. She pulled off her heels when Nathan was in Michael's face, just in case. "Come on, guys. It's a dance. Why don't you do your thing and leave us to do ours? We didn't come here to see you guys."

Mike looked at Jett. "Why don't you shut up and mind your own business, half-breed?"

"Don't escalate this, Mike. I don't want to fight."

"Then leave," Mike said.

"Babe," Mike's date said, "Come on. They aren't doing anything to you. Leave them alone. Let's dance."

Nathan looked at Justin. "I still want to hear your jokes."

"The mood is gone now," Justin said.

"Come on, let's dance. Nathan, you too. You have a date, you should spend time with her," Mike's date said. She looked at Melinda and mouthed "I'm sorry" as she walked Mike away from the group. Mike's date seemed nice, Jett thought. She wondered how she ended up with Mike.

There was a long silence until Justin said, "Damn."

Jett put her heels back on while Greg said, "We should have challenged them to a dance-off or something. Winner gets to stay. I mean, look at 'em. It's a dead heat."

The kids started laughing again, but this time with less enthusiasm. It was an anxious laugh.

"I got an idea." Melinda took charge of the group. "Let's dance. As a big group. Not as couples. Just all of us together."

"I don't know," Jett said nervously. "I don't dance. I don't know how and I'm going to feel self-conscious."

Melinda took her hand and pulled her towards the floor. "Come on Rock Star. We're going to have fun and we're not going to worry about what other people think. If you're not a good dancer, then dance bad on purpose. Be silly."

The group nervously followed Melinda to the dance floor and started moving around. Melinda took Jett's hands and tried to loosen her up as she moved around awkwardly. Greg, always the comedian, took Lara and Marsha's hands and said, "Ladies, the king of boogie has arrived."

"King of boogie? More like the king of boogers!" Lara said. They were relaxing and starting to have fun again when Mike and about six of his friends approached them on the dance floor, surrounded them, and started herding them off the floor by pushing them to the edge.

"What the hell?" Greg said, but one of Mike's larger friends had him by the arm and kept moving him backward. They were a moving wall, and the kids couldn't stand their ground. They were helplessly and continuously being shoved to the edge. None of the chaperones at the dance seemed to notice. They weren't paying attention to what the kids were doing on the dance floor. Jett had noticed earlier that many of them were the mothers of the kids who were pushing them.

"No. No. No. No," Mike was saying as they moved them off the floor. "The floor is for the cool kids with dates, not a bunch of stupid assholes who can't dance." He looked at Justin and Michael and said, "Opposite gender dates. Not gays. The dance floor isn't for gays." He looked at Jett and Melinda. "It's not for lesbians. No lesbians on the dance floor. That's the rules."

Jett felt angry and embarrassed. "There's plenty of room for everyone Mike. You can't just kick people off the floor."

"We just did. And no, there isn't plenty of room for everyone. Some people try to force their way into everyone else's space. Not tonight, bitch. This is our space. Go find your own."

Nathan stepped in front of Mike. "Hey, I think I figured out what jokes they were telling. Y'all ready. Here goes: Three gays and four ugly ass bitches get kicked off a dance floor for being ugly. And, here's the punchline. One of the ugly ass bitches is the only black kid at the dance and she's the worst dancer in the room. It's the one thing her kind is good at but, because she got some white genes in her, she didn't get the black people can dance gene. How hilarious is that? That's what you were laughing at, right?"

Marsha put her head down and started crying. Greg put his arm around her, and she leaned against him. Jett stepped in front of Nathan and looked him right in the eyes. Her heels were lying on the floor beside her again.

"Screw you, Nathan. Screw you and screw all your friends. We didn't approach you or say anything to you. You approached us and started shit. You pushed us off the dance floor. At what point do you think we push back?"

Nathan stared at Jett. "I don't care. I hope I find that point, so I have a reason to beat the shit out of all your friends."

"I already beat the shit out of all of you. I've been doing it since the ninth grade. If you try to hurt my friends, I'll do it again. It's up to you."

"You? Only with that cheap shot that you threw at the pool. Give me a reason to go off on you again. You're not shit. You're just a worthless, stupid, trashy, ghetto nig-"

"Don't say that word, Nathan. If that word comes out of your mouth, I'm putting my foot in it."

Nathan and Jett stared each other down for almost five seconds. It was Greg who broke the tension, by saying: "Actually, you got the joke wrong. We were joking about how you and Mike are probably gay, and you take it up the ass."

Nathan stared at Jett with a searing, hateful intensity. Jett didn't blink. She wasn't backing down to Nathan this time. Nathan looked at Mike, who shrugged, turned around and they all walked away, without saying a word.

After they walked away Jett exhaled in relief.

"What just happened?" Melinda felt confused.

"I have no idea," Jett said, "But you guys totally threw them off. I was sure Nathan was gonna get punched in the mouth."

Melinda put her arm around Jett. "You're a brave girl. I wish I had your courage."

"It's there. We all had it just now. But let's go. These guys won't let it go. It'll fester and then someone will stir it up again."

"You're right," Greg said. "Let's go to the coffee shop."

"Melinda and I will ride together and meet you guys there. I can fit two more if anyone needs a ride," Jett said as they walked outside. She didn't notice a guy standing near the door waving at Mike and Nathan as they exited the building.

"We're good. We came in two cars," Greg said, then to Marsha and Lara, "Ladies, can I ride with you?" Greg was getting brave.

They were halfway through the parking lot when Nathan ran up to Greg and shoved him in the back, hard. Greg fell to the concrete. When he started to get up Nathan started to swing at him. Jett, who was still carrying her heels, dropped them in time to kick Nathan in the chest before he could hit Greg. The air went out of his lungs as he took the kick. One of the other guys tried to get to Jett, but she turned and punched him in the chest too. Mike stayed out of the way, wary.

Nathan recovered from the kick and approached Greg again. "I'm going to beat his ass for what he said. Stay out of my way."

Jett stepped between them and said, "I could kick your ass for what you said to me. But we chose to leave instead. But I told you what happens if you try to hurt one of my friends."

"Get out of my way, bitch. I'm kicking his ass."

"Not today, bitch." Jett was angry and determined.

Nathan started swinging at Jett. Jett gave ground to Nathan's wild punches until he was off balance. Jett sidestepped Nathan and pushed him in the back, causing him to lose his balance and stumble to the ground. When Nathan tried to get up, Jett kicked him in the face. When he tried to get up a second time, Jett kicked him in the mouth. Nathan tried to get up again, and Jett kicked him again. Jett waited for him to try it a fourth time, but Nathan stayed on the ground this time. None of his friends were helping him. He looked up at Jett, angry, and said nothing.

"Go ahead. Keep trying to get up. I got plenty of these for you, asshole. Try it again."

Nathan didn't move. The ferocity of Jett's aggression stunned him.

"Good. Stay on the ground. We're leaving. If you follow us and try something, you're going to get a lot more than that. You do not understand how much I'm holding back. You're lucky I took my heels off."

Nathan still said nothing.

"We were leaving," Jett said, angry. "You could have let this go. We said shitty things, you said shitty things, we were even. But because you're stupid and can't let things go, you literally got your ass kicked. I didn't want to do it, but I told you what I would do if you tried to hurt my friends. Now you know."

Jett gestured for the other kids to leave while she and Melinda waited for them to drive away. When her friends left, they got in her truck and drove out of the parking lot.

***

Greg started applauding when Jett and Melinda entered the coffee shop. Other young patrons in the coffee shop joined in just for fun.

"Ladies and gentlemen, our own Superhero, fighting the forces of evil," Greg announced. Jett cringed and plopped down in a chair.

"That was crazy," Lara said. "What the hell happened?"

"Oh, I don't know. That was messed up," Jett said. "I'm just glad we're cool here."

"Did they follow you?" Greg asked.

"No. We doubled back twice to make sure they didn't follow us," Jett said.

"Seriously?" Greg said.

"My dad's a private eye. He worries about stuff most people don't think about. That makes me a little warped."

The kids ordered coffee and continued their lively conversation. Jett noticed a room in the coffee shop populated by a group of adult men and women, with a glass door separating them from everyone else. On their PowerPoint projected on the wall was a Confederate Flag and a map of the city. Jett got the other kids' attention and said, "What's going on over there?"

"Some kind of meeting? The Klan?" Greg said.

"I'm curious too," Melinda said. "What are they talking about?"

"It makes me kinda nervous," Jett said. "I don't know how to take that."

"My brother told me about this guy who comes to history classes and talks about the 'truth behind the Civil War,'" Justin said.

"It's bullshit. They always try to make it look like slavery was okay or something," Greg said.

"OMG. My parents went to some kind of thing where they started talking about the Civil War, and slavery, and segregation, like it was a good thing. My parents left, came home, and freaked out about it. They said it was creepy," Marsha said.

Melinda tugged at Jett's arm. "I'm gonna go listen. Wait here."

“Oh, me too,” Lara said. “We’ll take turns, come back and compare notes.”

One at a time, the kids took turns walking by the room, stopping to check their phones, and going to the restroom. They’d return and share what they overheard. The people in the room were quiet when Jett attempted to listen. She waited a little longer to check her phone, but they seemed to be waiting on her.

When she returned from the restroom, all the people in the room were watching her. Now she felt anxious. Melinda noticed and approached Jett as one of the people in the group opened the glass door and got their attention.

“Can we help you kids? You seem to be eavesdropping on us,” an older, graying man said. The man looked like he could be anyone’s grandfather, Jett thought. He had gray hair and a kind smile. He was short, maybe five foot four, thin, but with a protruding stomach under his white dress shirt. He wore gray slacks with suspenders and black dress shoes. He looked normal, and this bothered Jett even more.

“We’re curious what you’re talking about in there,” Melinda blurted out.

“Just ask. Don’t need to sneak around. Come on in,” he said. “We’re just people talking about ideas. What're your names?”

“I’m Melinda, and this is my best friend, Jett,” Melinda said.

"Well, I'm Frank and I lead this group. There's Burt, Jason, Paul, Loren, Mark, and a few others who aren't important." They all laughed and greeted the girls.

"Now," he continued, "we're talking about some of the ideals of the post-Civil War period. Where we succeeded, but more importantly, where we failed, and how we can do better."

"Like abolishing racism?" Melinda said. Jett nudged Melinda.

"Actually, yes. That's our goal. But we have some different ideas on how it should be done. Are you girls familiar with Louis Farrakhan?"

"He's the leader of the Nation of Islam group in America. That's all I know," Jett responded.

"Did you know he advocates that the races be kept separate from each other? A black man advocated for this."

"Segregation? That wasn't right," Melinda said.

"Minister Farrakhan, who is black, thinks it's a great idea. A lot of other black folks think that too. And a lot of white folks agree with them."

"None of those black folks are here," Jett said. "But it didn't work. Segregation was just a way to oppress people and take away their rights and opportunities."

"Well, that's how it failed. We did it wrong. We used it to exploit our advantage. But in and of itself, it wasn't a bad idea. It was the execution that didn't work."

Jett looked disgusted. “Are you saying there should be segregation again?”

“Why not? If we do it fairly, it should work out best for everyone. You’d have your community, we’d have ours, and we’d all have the same opportunities. It’s scientifically proven that people prefer to be with their own kind. That’s just nature. We fight our nature way too much.”

“If ‘WE’ do it fairly, meaning you. I think I found the problem with your idea. It’s still something YOU would do to everyone else. And I’m not so sure that anything you just said is scientifically accurate,” Jett said.

Frank laughed and looked at his companions. “These young ladies don’t understand. They’re too young and naïve to know how the world works. Girls, what would be different about your lives if you only lived among your kind? You go to school with your kind; you socialize and go to church with your kind; you marry your kind. We can still work together, but we go home to be with our own people. What would change about your lives if the government persuaded people to do that?”

Melinda put her arm around Jett’s shoulders and Jett put hers around Melinda’s waist. “First off, Jett’s my best friend. We wouldn’t get to meet if we didn’t go to school together. See that boy over there? Another boy was going to beat him up at a dance, a bully, but Jett made him stop because she’s a badass. If it weren’t for Jett, I wouldn’t have a best friend and he would have been beaten up tonight.”

Jett looked at Melinda, smiled. “If everyone only married or dated or had kids with their own kind, I wouldn’t exist. My dad is white, and my mom is black. She died when I was ten and my new mom is part Hispanic and part black. She's Afro-Cuban. My existence depends on it."

Frank narrowed his eyes as he looked at Jett. "My sincere condolences about your mother, but it's unfortunate that your dad and her got together. It's not fair to the black or white races to mess around and violate the racial purity of either one. It's never fair to the children. Nobody accepts them."

"Jett's my best friend. Those are OUR friends. My family loves Jett. We're gonna be roommates in college so we can keep hanging out together."

"And you, young lady, need to understand that even if you didn't have your best friend here, you'd have another, and she'd look like you. You'd be just as happy about her as you are about this one here."

"I like diversity," Melinda said. "I like being around different kinds of people."

"Diversity doesn't work. It just causes discord and people to feel like things are being forced down their throats. You'll understand that one day. And you," to Jett, "probably won't, because you're confused. Not your fault though. Your father should have known better."

"My dad said that who you are is more important than who people say you are. He also said stereotypes and discrimination are for weak-minded, stupid people. And he said that the government should mind its own damn business. So, it shouldn't be telling people where to live. No offense, but I'm going to listen to my dad instead of you. And my dad and my mom were in love, so of course I was born. That's how it's supposed to work."

Melinda abruptly said, "We better go. Bye," and waved as they left the room and returned to their table.

When they got back and sat down, Melinda said, "Whoa, that was so weird."

The girls told their friends about Frank and his ideals. After a twenty-minute discussion of what they observed, the kids realized they were hungry and decided to go to a late-night diner.

***

"This diner is a little sketchy," Lara said. The kids were sitting in the back, huddled around the table, and whispering. There was a group of guys from a biker gang across the dining room. One guy had a swastika tattoo and a few of the others had 'SS' tattooed on their arms. They were large, weathered, and scarred. They watched the group of kids as if they thought they were up to something.

"My dad said that some of the gangs engage in human trafficking," Jett whispered. "He showed me some of the tattoos and patches to avoid and, well, those guys have those tattoos and patches. He says they are hardcore racists too. He helps the police bust those guys and finds people who are lost."

"Jett's dad is hot," Melinda said. The other two girls laughed.

"Do you think they want to do anything to us?" Lara asked.

“I don’t know,” Jett said. “I can call my dad.”

“Call him,” Melinda said, smiling.

“We can all go hang out at my house tonight. You want to go?”

“Yes!” Melinda said.

“Your dad is cool?” Michael said, gesturing at Justin.

“Yea,” Jett said. “I’ll text him and tell him we’re coming.”

Jett texted her dad:

Jett: *We’re at that diner on 10th street. Can we hang out at home?*

Dad: *What the hell are you doing at a diner? I thought you were going to a dance? Bring your friends over.*

Jett: *Long story. I’ll explain later.*

Jett surveyed the crowd. Two more guys showed up and joined the bikers sitting across the dining room. One of them side-eyed her as he walked in. Outside, two more bikers sat on their bikes and talked with each other.

“Okay,” she mumbled, “here’s the situation. We have several of the racist biker guys in here, and two more outside. We can play it cool and just walk on out, no big deal. Or we can wait them out. Any ideas?”

Greg lit up and said, “We can summon demons that will drag them to hell in exchange for a sacrifice. We’ll need one of us who is a virgin to step up, which means we all qualify so we can draw straws or something.”

Jett replied, “Ok. We have the sacrificing a virgin to summon a demon idea. Any serious ideas?”

Greg spoke up again. “What about aliens? This is gonna sound crazy, but I swear me and Tommy Dugas did it last year to get out of a jam and it worked. We can get aliens to abduct them. They can get anal probes and be in experiments and stuff.”

“Tommy Dugas was born stoned, Greg. Chances are you were smoking something laced with something else,” Melinda said. The other kids giggled.

“Shit,” he said, “they’re looking at us. Do they hear us?”

“Calm down, we don’t do any good if we don’t stay calm, ok?”

“Sure, Jett. You probably don’t wanna do your karate thing again tonight.”

“If that happens here, my dad will never let me leave the house again.”

“We should just call your dad. He’ll know what to do,” Melinda said.

“He would, but I’m afraid I’d never get to go out again if he found out about this,” Jett replied.

“Well, I’m pretty sure our social lives would suck if we get abducted and sold off as sex slaves. Make your choice,” Marsha said.

“Ok. I’ll text my dad if it makes you feel better.”

Jett group texted her dad and Ashley to explain the situation and got an immediate response.

Dad: *I'll call the police to send someone out there to check the place out. Don't move until they get there. Everyone stays at the table and no one goes outside or even to the bathroom. Of all the diners in town, why that one?*

Jett: *I didn't think it mattered.*

Dad: *It matters. We need to have a talk about this town, kid.*

Ashley: *Don't move Chica. I'm on my way. I'm already out getting snacks for your party. I'll come by.*

Dad: *I'm heading out too. Don't leave your table until we get there.*

Jett: *Ok.*

"Ok. Ashley and my dad are on the way and my dad called the police to send someone by to check things out."

Ashley arrived first. She walked in wearing a blue blazer over a black tee-shirt and a pair of jeans. She saw the kids and smiled. Jett waved back, relieved. The bikers stared her down, so she casually adjusted her blazer, so they could see the pistol on her hip. She looked back at the men for a moment before she approached the counter to pay the bill for the kids.

One of the bikers approached Ashley at the counter and said, "What kind of heat you packing?"

"The kind I need to do my job," Ashley responded while signing the receipt.

"You a cop?" he asked.

"Are you?" she replied.

"Ashley is a badass," Jett whispered to her friends.

A police officer pulled into the parking lot and got out of her car, eyeing the men on the bikes as she entered the diner.

"Hello Ms. Garcia," she said as she recognized Ashley.

"Hey Mary, how are you tonight?"

The kids all sighed in relief as they got up to leave.

***

Back at Jett's house, the kids rode up the elevator, acting goofy and giggling. Snacks and sodas were sitting out. This was Jett's first time to have friends over.

"Make yourselves at home. I got some records if you want some music and grab some food and sodas if you want." Her dad said.

"Chica, could you tell me what happened at the dance? And after?"

"Yea, I want to know too. Am I getting a call from the principal Monday?" Markus asked.

"Seriously, I don't know Dad. But the usual suspects started messing with us, so we decided to leave and go to the coffee shop instead. But one of the guys tried to jump Greg in the parking lot. So, I stepped in and we had a very short confrontation, and he gave up."

"Ok. Greg, why did the other kid want to fight you?" he asked.

"Uh, I may have made some jokes about him or something. But not to his face. Well, not at first, but eventually, I did, because he was about to start a fight with J so I distracted him by... uh... insulting him and his friends. It's kind of my super-power."

"Insulting people is your super-power?"

"Yes, sir?" Greg replied.

"You may need to be a little more careful about how you use your super-power from now on."

"I'm sorry. I crack jokes when I'm nervous, or scared; or excited; or bored; or... whenever," Greg said.

"Relax kid, I'm just trying to figure out what happened."

"Sir," Melinda said, "Jett didn't start a fight, and she tried everything to avoid it and she didn't escalate it. That's why we left."

"And you went to the coffee shop? Which one?"

"The one off the Interstate. A lot of kids go there at night," Melinda said. "Usually geeky kids like us. That's where we ran into the creepy segregationist guy."

"Creepy whom?" Markus was concerned.

"Uh, creepy segregationists. They were a bunch of old people having a meeting about segregation," Melinda said.

“So, you left the creepy segregationists, you went to the diner and ran into the Nazi Bikers?”

“Uh, yes sir?” Jett said.

“This would make a great movie,” he quipped.

“You’re not going to let me go out again, are you?” Jett asked.

“You need to have a better idea of where you should and shouldn’t go. I’m glad you called when you recognized the danger.”

‘Cool, because we actually had fun. We had a lot of fun together.”

“Aww. I’m glad Chica, but next time more fun, less adventure, si’?”

“Si’, Mi Madre.”

“Ok kids. You need some music. What do you guys listen to? I got tons of records here, and I mean vinyl, the real thing,” Markus said.

“What you got?” Greg asked.

“I have everything. You name it.”

“Can I see your record collection?” Greg asked.

“Sure thing,” he replied and showed him the closet where he stored his records.

“Whoa, y’all check this out. I don’t even know where to start.”

“You kids are subversive; rap-metal protest music is your genre,” he said. “Ever heard of Rage Against the Machine?”

“Dude, I’ve got to check out this Rage Against the Machine That sounds badass,” Greg said.

He pulled out an album and handed it to Greg. “Put it on. Start at the first song.”

Jett never listened to Rage Against the Machine before. She was thrilled to listen to it with her friends.

Justin looked at the top of the closet and saw a board game. “Risk?” he said.

“Yea, you play?” Markus asked.

“Hell yeah. I used to play with my dad’s friends and sometimes we get together for a Risk night.”

“I haven’t played in years, but I was in a band when I was young, and we used to get together on off nights, sometimes while on the road with lots of time to kill and play Risk. Y’all want to play?”

“Yes, Sir!” Justin said. “Come on, Michael, Greg. Let’s get a game going.”

Greg looked from the guys to Marsha and Lara.

“Oh... Greg is lovesick for Marsha. I knew it. Dude. Jett, you wanna play?” Justin said.

“Dude!!!” Greg said. “But you guys go ahead.”

“I’ll play,” Ashley said, “I’ve played before, with some guys when I was in college.”

Jett, Melinda, Lara, Marsha, and Greg stayed in the living room, with Jett and Lara on the floor and Melinda and Marsha on the couch. Greg sat awkwardly next to Marsha, who didn't seem to mind.

"This is the coolest night. We survived the bullies, the creepy segregation guys, and the Nazi bikers, all in one night. Now we're hanging out in a loft downtown listening to your dad's protest music," Melinda said.

"It's been fun. Kind of like a movie," Lara said.

At midnight, after hanging out and having fun at Jett's place, her dad walked the other kids to the parking lot to make sure they got to their cars safe. Jett wanted Melinda to stay the night, and her mother said it was okay, so they sat on the living room floor, listening to records until they both fell asleep. Ashley walked into the living room a few hours later and saw the two girls asleep on the floor. She covered them with a blanket, turned out the lights, and went back to the bedroom.

Chapter Seventeen: Good Cop, Bad Cop

Melinda was waiting in the driveway when Jett pulled up in her truck. Melinda climbed in and Jett backed onto the road and headed towards the party. Jett had a Rage Against the Machine CD in the CD player. She pressed play and the music was blasting through her speakers and the girls were getting pumped. It had been about a month since their first dance and all the adventure that ensued. Since then Melinda and Jett, and often the rest of their friends, went out on weekends regularly. Sometimes they went to the coffee shop, sometimes to the movies, sometimes they went to one of their houses and played games. Tonight, they were going to Greg's house for a party. His parents were out of town and he was taking advantage of his temporary freedom.

Jett turned the radio down. "This song is about propaganda and war, Melinda; do you know that? And power. War and power."

"People with power fight wars. To get more power."

"Or to keep others from having power. Or freedom. But why?"

"Because if they can get more wealth or power, they are going to get it. Look what's happening in Europe."

"What's happening in Europe?" Jett asked.

"Russia. They moved into Eastern Europe, stirred up civil wars just so they could back the side they can control, and now they control most of Eastern Europe. They are now sending troops to the borders of western European countries. If there is a war, because of NATO, we have to fight with Europe. China is threatening our allies in the Pacific and Asia. We have allies there we have to defend. And Iran is threatening our allies in the Middle East. We have to help them too. How messed up is that? It's like they all want World War III."

"It's pretty messed up. I hate the whole idea of war. It's stupid. Why can't people just get along with each other?"

"Because they don't want to, Jett. They just don't."

"It's scary. Like what's going on here, with all the racism, and hate getting worse. People just go off on people. Human trafficking is getting worse. No one seems to care. My dad investigates those cases. He says it's terrible what people do to each other these days. I don't know where we're gonna stand, what we're gonna do when we grow up."

"We'll look out for each other, that's what we'll do."

Jett pulled into Greg's driveway and parked the truck. The girls got out and went to the door. Greg opened the door and welcomed them to the party.

"Ladies! We have food all over the place, just get what you want. We have sodas, beer, and other stuff too. I know you don't drink and all, but we have stuff if you want it."

Greg introduced two older guys as his cousins. They looked to be about eighteen to twenty years old.

Jett and Melinda sat on the couch feeling awkward while more kids showed up. The music got louder, the kids got louder, and they felt more uncomfortable.

"Greg," Melinda yelled, "Are Marsha and Lara coming?"

"What?" Greg said, scrunching his face up.

"I said, Are Marsha and Lara coming?"

"Are marshmallows coming? How would I know?" Greg yelled, confused, but not passing up an opportunity to make a joke.

"Are Marsha and Lara coming tonight?"

"I don't know if they're coming. They're not here," he said, laughing.

"Ew, Greg!" Both Melinda and Jett said.

"They're not coming to the party. Apparently, they have something else to do."

They didn't know a lot of the kids at the party and most of them were boys who seemed a little older. Melinda gestured at the back door. "Let's go outside, get some air."

Jett nodded, and they went out the back door. They walked through a patio where Greg's cousins and a few other people were sitting outside in lawn chairs, talking to each other.

"Hey, girls, What's up?" Greg's cousin said, in a mellow voice. Jett smelled smoke.

"Hey, bye," Melinda said as they walked past them and went to the yard.

"Whoa, come hang out with us," Greg's cousin said.

Jett and Melinda felt awkward and uncomfortable as the guy approached them.

"Hey, look," he said in a serious, mature voice. "I don't mean to come across as some kind of stupid-ass stoner douche bag. I'm Gary. What're your names?"

"I'm Melinda, and this is Jett."

"Hi, Melinda and Jett. You two seem kind of shy. Which is totally cool. I mean, that just means you're careful who you associate with. But it's cool to have fun too. Why don't you join us?"

"We're kind of taking a break. It's crowded. Not our thing," Melinda said.

"Cool. I get it. You're into the low-intensity thing. You know what helps that?"

"Leaving?" Melinda said.

"Nah. Take a hit. Here, I'll help." Gary blew smoke in Jett's face right as she was inhaling. Gary laughed. "You may as well take a hit now; you're getting a contact high anyway. Here." he held the joint in front of her.

Jett looked at the joint. She always wondered what this was about. Her dad smoked when he was young, and he's okay. Before she could talk herself out of it, she put it in her mouth.

"There you go. Take a deep breath. Breathe it in and hold it."

Jett sucked the smoke into her lungs and held her breath. After a few seconds, the sensation hit her. She felt relaxed. Calm. At peace.

"Right on babe. How does it feel?"

"Weird," she said.

"You want some," Gary said to Melinda.

"No thanks. I had marijuana for lunch. It's a family thing."

"Here, have some more, Jett. Where you from?"

"Baltimore. But I've been, like, here since I was ten. My mom died, and I came to live with my dad. Never met him until then. He's white. It's cool."

"Sucks about your mom. My parents don't talk to me."

"That sucks too. My parents talk to me all the time."

"Parents? I thought your mom died. She still talks to you?"

"My earth mom," Jett was feeling stoned. "I have an earth mom. She treats me like a daughter."

"Stepmother? Your dad's girlfriend?"

"She's his business partner. But get this, I was buying this necklace in Austin, and this guy told me, like he knew, that my mom still watches over me in heaven and she's happy I have a mom on earth who loves me too. So, she's like my earth mom. It's like he just freaking knew."

"Dude. That's cosmic of epic proportions. Or epic of cosmic proportions. I'm too stoned to know which. Cool though. You got two moms."

"And a dad."

"So, are your parents hippies or something?"

Jett burst out laughing, stopped, thought for a second, and started laughing again. "They're private investigators."

"Private investigators? Like in the movies?"

"Yea. My dad is all like 'it was a hot night in south Texas as I sat in some dive in the south side of town, waiting for a call that wasn't going to come. That's when she walked in.'" Jett laughed hard at this. "That's my dad."

Melinda took Jett's arm and pulled her away. "You okay, girlfriend?"

"Yea. I'm fine." Jett hugged Melinda. She was either stoned or she thought she was stoned.

Gary's friend joined their group. "Hey Gary, what the hell, man? You joining us? You're hoggin' the joint. Who is this piece of black ass? She's hot."

"I'm not a piece of black ass. I'm the entire, biracial Jett."

"Bitch's stoned. She's smokin' my shit, Gary?"

"Gary offered it to her," Melinda said.

"I don't give a shit. Shit ain't free. You got money, bitch?"

"I'm not a bitch," Jett said, "and I don't have any money on me."

"My shit ain't free. What you gonna do to pay for the weed you smoked?"

"Be cool. I gave it to her," Gary said.

"Okay, fuck my friend, that'll pay for the weed."

"No," Jett said.

"Stop it, man, I'm not like that," Gary said.

"Fuck you. I am like that. Bitch, give me a blow job. For the weed."

"Fuck you," Jett said.

"You can do that too, but I'll settle for a blow job. Come on, let's go."

He reached for Jett's wrist and started pulling. Melinda grabbed Jett's other hand and held on.

"Get your hands off of me," Jett said, suddenly more coherent.

"You smoke my weed and don't pay for it. Now you tell me what to do? Do you know who I am?" he asked.

"Don't piss him off, Jett," Gary said.

"Do you know who I am?" Jett said.

Greg came running over, scared.

"Bitch, you're gonna get knocked out. Give me a blowjob for the weed. Let's go."

He grabbed her wrist again and started pulling. Greg jumped in between them and said, "Dude! Stop. She's a friend of mine from school. She's just a kid."

"Well, little Greg. She's in some grown-up shit now."

"It's not like I asked you for the weed. I'm not doing anything for you. And you better keep your hands off me."

"What are you going to do about it?"

"You don't want to know the answer to that question." Jett looked to her right just as something hit the privacy fence surrounding the yard. Small rocks and tree limbs were continuously falling on the fence. The guys stood there for a moment, confused, before going to investigate.

While they were distracted, Jett took Melinda's hand. The two girls went back inside, through the house, and straight to the truck.

When they got inside the truck, Jett banged on the steering wheel and yelled, "Damn it!! Can I just go somewhere, relax, have fun, and not have a conflict with someone? Am I that horrible a person?"

"Jett. Stop! It's not your fault. Those guys were douche bags."

"I'm sorry. It's just so hard. I don't want to get in fights, but it seems like some people just want to push. I hate myself sometimes."

"It's okay Jett. It's okay. It's not your fault some people, a lot of people, are dicks. That guy was a dick. I'm sure the other guy was too. They were playing good cop bad cop. They were going to convince you to do something with that Gary asshole to keep the other guy from losing it. It's a scam."

"You think? That's terrible."

"Seems like it. Assholes. And you're not a horrible person. You're the best. And I know you better than anyone. I'm the expert on you; I'm a Jettspert."

"You're right. Screw those assholes. I should go back in and tell them."

"NO! Let's go. Let's go to the coffee shop for a little while. And we'll ignore any creepy segregation guys who may be there. Or argue with them. Whichever seems more fun."

Jett started the truck and headed towards the coffee shop, with tears in her eyes.

***

When they got to the coffee shop Melinda stared at Jett while she parked the truck.

"What?" Jett cut off the engine and putting the stick in neutral.

"Girl, I need to ask you something."

"What?"

"How did you do that?"

"Do what?"

"When you distracted those guys, so we could leave."

"What about it?" Jett said.

"I knew it! You did it. Just like the metal rod by the pool earlier this year. I knew it!"

"No. No." Jett was upset again.

"Girl, it's okay. I know. Ever since those chairs hit Mike and the other kid in the ninth grade. I knew it. You can make things move with your brain."

"That's crazy, Melinda."

"It's crazy true. How do you do it?"

"Do what?"

"Telekinesis. Moving stuff with your brain! Come on Jett. I know you can do it."

"No..." Jett said, panicked.

"Jett, it's okay. It's me. I won't tell anyone. I promise. I've known this since the pool. Remember it with the chairs."

"I didn't try to move the chairs. Just when I'm upset or scared. I can't just do it."

"I won't tell anyone."

"Please, not even my dad or Ashley knows. Okay?"

"Okay," Melinda said, "It's our secret."

Jett felt terrified. Another person knew her secret. She didn't want to talk about it. She didn't want to believe it. She wasn't even sure if it was true, or if she reads too much into coincidences that work out in her favor.

"Let's just... Let's just never talk about it, okay?" Jett said to Melinda as they walked towards the door. "I don't even know if it's real or not. It's just too freaky."

"I'll never bring it up again." Melinda opened the door to the coffee shop.

***

When Jett got home, she let herself into the flat and went straight for her room. She was still anxious about someone knowing her secret. Her dad was in the living room waiting up for her.

"Hey kid, how was the party?"

"Fine. I'm going to bed."

Jett walked right by her dad and kept walking as he tried to get her attention.

"Whoa, stop. Come here first."

Jett ignored her dad and kept walking towards her room.

"Hey! Stop and come here."

"I'm going to bed! Okay?" she yelled, without looking back.

"Get your ass over here, now!"

Jett stopped in her tracks, turned around, and looked at her dad. "Seriously?"

"Get over here right now and tell me why I smell marijuana on your clothes!"

"Dad, you've never raised your voice at me before. It's weird."

"I know. It is weird. But do it."

"Okay, fine." Jett walked to the table and plopped down in a chair.

"Did you smoke weed?"

"Yes, I did. Can I go to bed now?"

"No. What all happened?"

Jett was ashamed to tell her dad about smoking marijuana, but she told him some of what happened. How she did it out of curiosity, how there were older guys there who brought it. She explained how one of the guys became belligerent because she didn't have money. She left out the part where the older guy tried to coerce her into doing a sex act on him. Her dad sat and listened.

When she finished talking, he put his hand on her hand, ran his other hand through his hair, looked into her eyes, and said, "I am so glad you didn't get hurt by those guys."

Jett looked back at him and said, "Me too," in a small voice.

"But there is a bigger problem here. And there will be consequences."

Jett put her head down for a second, frustrated, and then looked at her dad again. "You're going to punish me?"

"I'm going to ground you for a week. No truck. I'll take you to school, Ashley will pick you up. For one week. Then you can have your truck back."

"Dad! I thought you're glad I'm safe."

"I am. And for the next week, I'm going to make sure you stay that way. Do you understand what all happened, and what all could have happened tonight?"

"Sorta."

"Let's start with the guys. Some guys use drugs to control women. Tonight, you saw a little bit of that. They use drugs or alcohol to lower your inhibitions and try to pressure you into doing things. Some guys take it further. You have no idea what you and Melinda could have gotten yourselves into.

"You also drove under the influence of a drug. If you get pulled over, you're not going to get a fair shake. People are going to treat you different. It sucks, but that's how it is. They put your mug shot on social media, people make ugly, racist comments. Your friends see it. Remember this kid, the higher you rise in life, the harder you fall.

"If you ever give in and smoke again, or drink alcohol, I want you to let me know. If you're at a safe place, ask if you can spend the night. If not, I'll come get you. You won't be in as much trouble if you just call me or Ashley for a ride. Okay?"

"Okay, Dad. I'm sorry. I'll try to do better."

“No one bats a thousand in this league, kid; and you’re doing a lot better than I was at your age. But I expect better out of you because you’re better than me. Now, move on to bed. And your keys. I keep them for the next week.”

Jett reluctantly handed her keys to her dad. “I’m sorry kid. But I got to do my job as your dad.”

Markus Jackson sat at the kitchen table with his head in his hands for a long time after Jett went to bed. He didn’t sleep.

***

“So, we have this homeless guy, lives in a camp in the woods, and all he wants is money to buy food and weed. He gets around by navigating the old train tracks. Says people forgot about ‘em a long time ago and he gets to most places by staying on those tracks, out in the woods. He’s got warrants for burglary, and I don’t think he’s retired, but he’s willing to work with us. I also contacted the head of a bike gang who rivals these Nazi biker guys. He’s willing to work with us. He says he can’t abide the human trafficking and these guys are riding all over their territory, starting trouble for his guys, trying to run them off. So, he’s in,” Markus Jackson said. He was meeting with Ashley, Diana, and another man who was taking part over speakerphone. Jett assumed he was their client. She was working in the office when the meeting started. Jett wasn’t invited to the meeting, but she made it a point to bring everyone coffee so she could eavesdrop.

“Thanks, Chica,” Ashley said as Jett set her mug down in front of her.

“Yea, thanks kid,” her dad said.

“You’re so sweet,” Diana said, “do you mind if I ask you to do something else for us?”

“I’m sorry. It was just late so I... I just figured you’d like some coffee,” Jett stammered, embarrassed because they figured out her ploy to eavesdrop.

“It’s okay Jett.” Diana smiled. “I want to ask you to research something for us online. Could you look up...”

“Wait,” the man on the phone said. “Is there someone else in the room? This is confidential.”

“It’s okay Doug. It’s my daughter, Jett. She just brought us coffee. She’s a thoughtful kid. A curious kid, too.” He chuckled at Jett’s anxiety over causing a disruption.

“That’s fine. But let’s get her out of the room,” the man, Doug, said. “She doesn’t need to hear this. Or talk about it at school or with her friends or anything. You know the drill.”

“I’m giving her a job to do,” Diana said. “Jett, research the old train lines in the country-side north of here. Apparently, there is a network of abandoned train lines the homeless people use to stay out of sight while moving around. That could be very useful in this case. You can make a report later.”

Jett went to Ashley’s office and researched the train lines, land titles, and geography of the counties north of Port City. It was amazing. She compiled her report in one hour and texted Diana, telling her she was finished. Diana texted her back to return to the meeting.

“Okay, I made a presentation,” Jett said when she walked into the Conference Room. She put together a PowerPoint for everyone in the room. Her dad was impressed as Ashley prepared to email the PowerPoint to the man on the phone so he could see it too.

"Wait," Diana said as Jett turned to leave the room. "Aren't you going to give us a verbal report of your findings?"

"I… Guess?" Jett looked at her dad.

"Doug, my daughter just typed up this report, in less than an hour. We're going to have her walk us through it if it's okay."

"That's fine," Doug said irritably. "Let family hour begin. But, Jett, right? You don't talk about this outside this room. It's a national security issue. It would be treason to spread this info around."

Diana shook her head. "Doug's just being dramatic. He works for the government. But he's right. Don't talk about it to anyone."

"Okay," Jett said. "First off, there is a massive network of trails left behind by train tracks from various lines that were discontinued at different times throughout the history of this area. They would discontinue one line, start another, and discontinue that one, and so on. This went on until trucking became the preferred mode of delivery for industrial products. The land the trains ran on is owned, to this day, by a private railroad line, but they don't utilize the property. It's probably just a tax write off or something. The trails the tracks were on are sustained by the various gravel and rocks they used to stabilize the ground for the tracks. Judging by this map, it would be easy to get lost on these lines, but they intersect with state highways and roads at various places. They also intersect with farms and ranches in the area. Most of this land around these lines are part of a state forest, but it's not developed for hunting leases or walking trails. It's very isolated. Some property near the trails, however, is owned by various companies. I couldn't find much information about these companies. They are in the middle of these small communities, farms, and other businesses that support the ranches and farms. These communities are very isolated. There is a local sheriff, a county judge, and not much else in terms of local government that I could find. No one knows much of what goes on there.

"When looking at the maps, I found some cool stuff. I love maps. There is an old road that runs from the very edge of downtown, by the river on the north of downtown, it goes along the riverbank and runs into the country. You could literally drive into the woods, near these trails, without having to go through any other cities along the way. It takes longer, but no one uses this road much anymore. It's called the 'Old Port City Road.' Back in the day, it was a trail people used to drive into town to trade goods by the port.

The room was quiet after Jett finished. Doug spoke up over the speakerphone, "How old are you, Jett?"

"Sixteen, sir."

"Hey Jackson, your sixteen-year-old daughter just provided more useful information in one hour than you guys have been able to get me in the last several months. We now know why they use this area and how they get in and out of town without anyone noticing. All this time we've been staking out the wrong areas trying to get an idea of how they move. We need to work on tracing those shell companies and individuals who own the land back to the actual owners. Good job, Jett. You should work for the CIA or something when you finish college. You'd be one hell of an analyst."

"Thanks!" Jett said. "The CIA, dad?"

"You'd be a good lawyer too, kid. Like Diana. You'd make more money with that brain of yours."

"You would be a fantastic attorney!" Diana said, smiling.

"Jett is a brilliant young lady and we're very proud of her. She's also a state champion karate competitor," Ashley said, beaming.

"Okay you guys," Jett said, embarrassed, "Anything else you need me to look up?"

"Thanks, kid, go upstairs and relax a little. I'll be up soon, and we'll all go get some dinner together."

"Give the kid a raise, Jackson. She's earned it," Doug said, as Jett left the room.

Chapter Eighteen: Mall of Fears

Jett and Melinda talked about school while Jett drove them to the mall. Both girls were hungry, so they went to the food court first. After eating tacos, they hit the stores. Jett wanted to buy sunglasses. She tried on several that Melinda picked out for her. The girls took selfies, giggled, and goofed off, annoying the older people shopping around them. Jett picked out her sunglasses and Melinda talked her into trying on hats. She tried several hats, but she didn't like anything over her hair, so she picked out a new scarf for her hair instead. Jett often used scarves to hold her hair back, especially while working out. Melinda pointed out how the scarf and sunglasses looked cool together.

Melinda wanted to look at tops. They went to a boutique in the mall known for reasonably priced clothes for teenagers and young adults. An employee approached them as soon as they entered the store.

"Hi! My name is Angelique. Can I help you? Hey!"

"You work here?" Jett asked.

"Yes. I have to work now that my parents hate me. No allowance."

"Wow. No wonder we haven't seen you around much," Melinda said.

"Yep. Not every day, it's only part-time, but it's the only way I can afford to do anything."

"Why do your parents hate you?" Melinda asked.

"I broke up with Mike. Ruined their lives. And they found out that my sister took me to see Jett to apologize. That was the final straw for them. As soon as I graduate, I have to leave. I'm going to move in with my sister."

"I'm sorry, Angelique," Jett said.

"I'm not doing my part to keep our family relevant. Whatever that means. I was supposed to graduate, marry Mike, have his gross little demon babies, and join the Country Club. But I don't want it. I'd rather jump off a bridge than marry him. My parents would probably opt for the bridge, even give me a ride and a push at this point."

"Oh Angelique, I'm so sorry," Jett said again, distressed at the girl's plight.

"Oh, don't be. It's not as bad as you think. My parents are crazy. Racist, conspiracy-theory crazy. I don't have to pretend to believe what they believe anymore. I do my thing, they do theirs. I work as much as I can. Once I move out, just like my sister, I'm not ever going back."

"That sucks!" Melinda said.

"You've changed," Jett said, "a lot."

"I'm woke, Jett. Seriously. There are people in this town who are crazy. We'll have to get together sometime, and I'll tell you more about it. Seriously, crazy with crazy ideas and crazy talk. Just, crazy."

"Yea, we need to talk about it sometime." Jett wasn't sure if she wanted to talk more about this, though.

"Oh yeah and let me tell you something else that is really ridiculous," Angelique moved closer to Jett and lowered her voice. "I'm supposed to follow you around and keep an eye on you, according to my manager."

"What?" Jett exclaimed. "I'm not a thief!"

"I told her that. But she told me I need to be *realistic* about people and not assume I know so much," Angelique used her fingers as quotes for the word 'realistic.'

"She's profiling black people?" Melinda was shocked.

"Yea. She says it's 'corporate policy,' but they don't write it down anywhere. It's something she said the regional managers tell them when they visit."

"It's time to go," Jett was frustrated. "Sorry, Angelique. I can't shop here. I hope it doesn't affect your job."

"Jett, I understand. I would quit, but I need this job. I don't have anything else going for me right now. Jobs are hard to find."

"I get it," Jett said, "but I can't shop here if they make you profile people."

"Ok. But I want to hang out with you guys sometimes. So much I want to talk about. I'll message you."

"Ok, bye, Angelique. We'll get together soon," Melinda said as they walked back into the mall.

Melinda and Jett left Angelique's store and took a break to get coffee at a coffee shop near the food court. When they arrived, there were two women in their mid to late twenties, with dark hair and light brown complexion, in line, with a middle-aged woman with a pale complexion behind them. The middle-aged woman was in her early forties, with her blond hair pulled into a ponytail. Jett and Melinda got in line and talked about Angelique and the incident at her store, oblivious to what was going on around them.

The two women were carrying on a conversation in Spanish as they waited for their orders. The older woman ordered as her husband arrived. He wore cargo shorts, high-top sneakers, and a tee-shirt. The man was taller than his wife and about the same age. He looked as if he worked out but also had a large belly.

Jett and Melinda ordered their coffee and stood with the others to wait for their order. As the two women continued their conversation, the older woman sighed in exasperation. Her husband nodded but said nothing. Finally, she said, "I don't understand why they come to this country and refuse to learn the language," to her husband.

"I know," he said, looking stern, "probably illegals too."

Jett and Melinda overheard their conversation and fell silent. The woman looked at Melinda. "You know what I mean, right?"

Melinda just stood there, not sure what to say. The woman looked past Melinda, saw Jett, and said, "What? What are you staring at?"

Jett was speechless too. She didn't know how to react, so she stood there, saying nothing.

“Listen to me, young lady, don’t come in here with that attitude; looking at me like that.”

“Mm, okay,” was all Jett could manage, followed by a confused, “yes ma’am.”

The woman looked at Melinda, looked at Jett, and made a gesture to indicate she was annoyed.

“She’s with me, ma’am. We’re friends.”

The man looked at Melinda and shook his head.

“At least they’re legal and they know the language,” the woman said.

“Still,” the man said, “people ought to associate with their own kind. None of my business though.”

“I would agree with that,” Melinda said.

“Really? About associating with your own kind?” the woman asked.

“No, ma’am. That it’s none of your business.”

Jett snorted and stifled her laughter.

“You have no respect, young lady. That’s what happens when you- oh, never mind,” the woman said.

“We weren’t minding in the first place. You started this,” Melinda replied.

The woman looked flustered. At about this time the coffee started coming out. The two women got their coffee first, then the couple got their coffee. Jett and Melinda got their coffee last.

As all six people collected their coffee and started looking for tables, the older woman turned red at hearing more of the conversation of the other two women.

"God Damnit! Could you please speak English? It's the language here. This is not Mexico. Learn the language if you're going to leech off of us, okay?"

"Are you okay?" one of the women said, confused, to the angry woman.

"I'm perfect. I see you speak English. Great. Why don't you use it here? You're supposed to speak English."

Jett found herself interjecting. "Ma'am, they're having a private conversation. They can speak anyway they want."

The woman slowly turned to Jett and said, while clenching her teeth, "And WE'RE having a private conversation too, honey, so butt out."

The man stepped between Jett and his wife. "Why don't you take your coffee and leave. And take your little friend with you."

"Get the manager, honey. I'm feeling very threatened right now. These people are being belligerent. We just came for coffee, not to be attacked."

Jett looked at the two women and said, "Lamento que te traten así. ¿Te gustaría unirte a mi amiga y a mí a tomar un café?"

"You speak Spanish?" one of the women said, smiling.

“Mi madre es afrocubana. Me enseñó a hablar español,” Jett responded.

“You’re freaking awesome!” Melinda said to Jett.

“How sweet!” one of the women said, “We’d love to join you girls for coffee. There’s a table for four across the room.”

The four of them left the couple while the other woman said, “Just get the manager, get the manager, get the freaking manager. They’re mocking me. Of all the disrespectful things those stupid kids could do.”

Jett, Melinda, and the women were sitting at the table introducing themselves. They all had a good laugh at what just happened.

“It happens more these days,” one of the women said. “People are just so put off by anything different. It’s like they want us to just be white. No offense honey, but it’s not happening. I am a Latina.”

“I understand,” Melinda said, “they got an attitude with me because I’m here with Jett.”

“And I’m half white and they hate me the most. I should get a half-off discount on racism,” Jett said. The other ladies laughed.

The manager approached their table and looked down at the four ladies. He was a serious-looking man, with a protruding stomach, male pattern baldness, and a graying goatee. He had the look of a man who wasn’t particularly pleased with his current vocation.

“Excuse me, but there’s been a complaint about you all from the couple over there.”

They looked at him, waiting for him to continue. After an awkward pause, Melinda asked, “What was the complaint? They were harassing us and these ladies here.”

“Well, they feel you were all being very threatening to them and it’s making them uncomfortable?”

What?” one of the Hispanic ladies said, “They were harassing us.”

“Then why didn’t you report it?” the manager challenged them rudely.

“Because we just walked away. We didn’t want trouble,” Jett said.

“Well, I think you didn’t report it because you started it,” the manager said as if he were annoyed.

“Seriously?” Jett said, “I think you’re siding with the two racist people over there because you don’t have the guts to stand up to them. It’s easier to pick on us, isn’t it?”

“Look, I don’t know what happened, but I think it would be best if you all just leave. I won’t have to call mall security.”

“Do they have to leave too?” Jett asked, pointing at the couple who were casually sipping their beverages as if nothing happened.

“Maybe we should go,” Melinda said.

Jett was angry and defiant. “No. We don’t leave. We didn’t do anything. We tried to ignore them. But they kept on being jerks.”

Melinda stood up with the two Hispanic ladies. “Jett, let’s just go. If they don’t want us here, we leave. We go where we’re wanted. Leave your coffee. We’ll buy more somewhere else.”

Jett stood up, glaring at the manager and the couple.

She walked out with the group. The shop was quiet, and everyone was staring. Her face was hot, and she was angry and humiliated.

The four kept walking until they were back in the mall, with their bags in hand.

***

Jett spent the night at Melinda’s house, talking about school, playing on social media with their other friends, and having fun. But she couldn’t shake the gloomy feeling from the mall. Later in the evening, she woke Melinda while they were lying in sleeping bags on the floor of Melinda’s room.

“Why were those people so hateful? It’s not like Mexican people, or biracial people, are new. We’ve been around forever. What’s happening?” Jett asked, worried.

“I don’t know Jett. People are just angrier. They’re just looking for a reason to go off.”

“Why racism though? I thought things were getting better.”

“I don’t know. With all the Nazi bikers and creepy segregationist guys, Mike and his family, Angelique’s family, Angelique’s boss, the racist coffee shop couple... Something’s going on.”

“I just want it to go away. It scares me. I’m afraid it will keep getting worse.”

“We’ll stick together, Jett. You and me. We’ll look out for each other. Help each other. It’s scary, but hey, we’re the Renegades of Funk!”

“What?” Jett said, laughing.

“Renegades of Funk. Rage Against the Machine. Everyday people, like you and me, change the course of history with new philosophies.”

“We need some new philosophies.”

“We’re going to make the world a better place, Jett. Racism is gonna hate us when we’re finished.”

“That’s silly,” Jett said, giggling. “But I hope so. Somehow. The world can get better. It only seems to get worse all the time.”

The girls kept talking until they dozed off and went to sleep.

***

“All you’re supposed to do on these cases is find the missing person and inform law enforcement. We get the warrant, and we pick up the person. Let me repeat, all you’re supposed to do is tell us where she is,” the tired, frustrated detective on the night desk explained. Ashley had arrived earlier with the missing woman and Markus Jackson showed up after he made sure Ashley and the victim made a clean escape.

"Okay. I found her. She's right over there. Over there, sitting at the desk drinking a cup of coffee, next to Garcia. I am now informing you that I found her," he quipped while pointing through the window at the woman they had rescued from a trafficking operation earlier in the evening.

"Shit. I like you, Jackson. You get things done. I appreciate that. But you cause us a lot of headaches. How many laws did you break to make this happen? I got the sheriff yelling at me through dispatch and he's on his way here. I had to drag my boss out of bed and he's on his way here. They're probably gonna call someone from legal in to figure out the legality of this whole thing. All I wanted was a quiet, routine night. Now answer this question: did you brandish your weapon while you were inside that bar?"

"Define *brandish.*" Jackson used his fingers to make air quotes for the word 'brandish'.

"Never mind. Don't answer. I don't want to know."

"Do you want to talk to her?" Jackson asked the detective.

"Send her in," the detective said as if he resigned himself to a very unpleasant fate.

Jackson waved at Ashley, who walked the young woman into the detective's office.

"Now, explain to me again why you didn't call the local sheriff, Jackson?"

"Because he was already at the bar," Jackson said.

"The sheriff raped me," the young woman said, joining their conversation, as she sat down across the detective. "Upstairs, in the room. Before that, at that house in the woods. He's not a good guy."

"Shit," the detective said, upset at this turn of events. "Are you sure?"

"Yea. He's not a good guy," she was in shock.

"We need to get this woman to a hospital," the detective said.

"She needs police protection," Ashley noted.

"Oh shit, look who's here. The sheriff from up north. Great. This is about to be a total clusterf..."

The sheriff and two of his deputies walked into the room, interrupting the detective.

"What in the hell is going on? Did you send this asshole to my county, my jurisdiction to enforce a warrant without my knowledge? And this girl, she's coming with us. I have a warrant for her arrest."

"Okay, hang on," the detective said. "Let's slow down here. She just made an allegation about what happened out there. We need to process that first."

"Since whatever she is alleging happened in MY jurisdiction, we can bring her back there, on the warrant we already have, and she can file her complaint after we book her into jail," the sheriff said.

"They're gonna take me to the lake!" the young woman started panicking, "Don't let them take me to the lake. They're gonna kill me!"

Ashley put her arm around her shoulders. "You're gonna stay here in Port City. We'll stay with you to make sure."

"No. She's coming with us. I have a warrant. I can give a rat's ass about her complaint, but we'll let her make it in the county she claims it happened in," the sheriff said. "Now come on. Time to go to jail."

Diana walked into the office and stepped between the young woman and the sheriff. "I'm sorry, sheriff, I will need to see that warrant before we go any further. And I will need evidence of probable cause resulting from your investigation before you take my client anywhere." Diana already knew this meeting would happen. She was dressed for work, in a black skirt with matching heels and jacket, and it was after midnight. Diana held an envelope in her hand.

"Can we fit any more people into this office?" the detective rubbed his temples in frustration.

"And my client has a criminal complaint. As her attorney, I'm going to advise her to make it at this station because her complaint is against your office, sheriff. I'll get a court order in less than an hour if you want to fight about it. I've already called the Assistant District Attorney and the Honorable Judge Gannon. The Texas Ranger Division is about to be involved as well as the FBI. They are all very interested in what's going on in this case."

"I'm gonna get fired," the detective said.

"And why don't you tell me what this complaint is, since you're her attorney all of a sudden," the sheriff said.

"He raped me. He paid the men money so he could have sex with me. So did the other men. They told me that if I didn't do what they said I would have to go to the lake where they would kill me," the young woman said.

"She doesn't have any proof. This is bullshit and you all know it. You gonna arrest me, detective? Or can I take my prisoner back to jail in my jurisdiction where she belongs?"

"Your prisoner is part of a missing person's case, filed right here in Port City. Why didn't you report that when you first picked her up?" Jackson asked.

"Good question, and I still haven't seen your warrant," Diana said. "But I'll show you this: a restraining order. You are ordered to stay away from my client. You have five minutes to comply with this order."

After the sheriff looked at the restraining order and scowled, Diana dropped it on the desk. The detective looked it over. "It's legit. I don't know how you got a restraining order in the middle of the night, though."

"And my client would like to file charges against the sheriff and other conspirators," Diana said, "and you need to leave my client's presence in the next four minutes, sheriff."

"Clock's ticking," Jackson added fuel to the fire.

"Are you going to arrest me?" the sheriff asked the detective.

"If you don't leave, I won't have a choice. And I want to see this warrant you keep talking about. Her family reported her missing here, in our jurisdiction. I'm sure my people are going to need to know why you didn't report finding her."

The sheriff looked at the detective, at Diana, at the young woman, and back at Diana. Diana had one hand on her hip and the other pointing at the door. She stared him down without blinking. Diana Jones wasn't backing down.

He nodded and backed out of the office. "I'm gonna call your mayor first in the morning and get this sorted out. This bullshit won't stand for long. I'll come back with that warrant."

"Two minutes, sheriff," Diana said.

The sheriff turned and, with his two deputies, walked out of the office, cursing under his breath.

***

"Everyone is so on edge right now. My parents are acting like they're preparing for something. It's weird," Angelique told Melinda and Jett at the coffee shop the night after their ill-fated trip to the mall. "They don't talk much, but they keep saying I need to get back on track before it's too late. Something's up."

"What do you think it is?" Melinda asked.

"I don't know. Their racist little clique has had meetings lately. I've had to leave my own house while they met a few times. They tell me to avoid certain places. Like it would be dangerous or something."

"Who's all involved in this?" Jett asked.

“Oh, I’m sure the Kraytons for one. And the other families they associate with. I don’t know for sure though. I can’t be around it anymore. It’s like they belong to a cult and they have something big planned. I get sent away. My sister thinks something huge is going to happen.”

“Like what?” Melinda asked.

“They always talked about social and political change. To them, it’s an ‘upheaval.’ That’s how they describe it. My sister said they are big into some kind of revolution thing, but she says it’s so unlikely. Surely no one is that stupid, right?”

“Don’t ever underestimate the power of collective stupidity,” Melinda said.

“Well, they have talked about this upheaval a lot,” Angelique said, “and they are all in on social change. But what they want sounds so... fascist? I guess that’s the word. They just believe they should control everyone and are resentful that people don’t live the way they think they should. They talk a lot about doing something about it. I just figured they would just vote for people who were assholes like them.”

“My dad said they’re racists. They don’t talk to my parents anymore though. My mom wouldn’t put up with that shit,” Melinda said. “And they are pissed at our family because we’re friends with Jett’s family. It bothers those assholes.”

Angelique looked at Jett. “I don’t know how to tell you this, Jett, but they freaking hate you and your family. You should get out of this town after you graduate. For real. The Kraytons for sure. But it all rolls downhill. They want you gone. Really bad.”

“But I didn’t do anything to them. I’m just doing my best to... I don’t know. To do my best. Their kids started trouble with me.”

“No one ever accused them of being rational, Jett. They’re crazy. Seriously crazy.” Angelique said.

Melinda looked at Angelique. “I appreciate you telling us this stuff. Can you keep an ear out for more information and let us know what you find out? It helps to know what they’re thinking about us.”

“I will, Melinda. I’m scared though. It all seems so... uh... creepy, but I will keep you guys up to date on things I find out. I have to run now. I have to open in the morning.”

“Yea, school is getting intense and we need to get some studying in this weekend.”

“Okay, Later, Jett, Melinda. Be safe,” Angelique said as she left the coffee shop.

As Jett and Melinda opened their books to study, an older, graying man in a polo shirt, pressed jeans and white sneakers approached them. He had been sitting at the other end of the coffee shop while Jett and her friends were talking. He stood over the table, across from Jett, and said, in an exaggerated Texas accent, “Excuse me, ladies. I hate to be rude, but I think I know your father. You’re Jackson’s girl, ain’t ya?”

“Uh, Yes.”

The man was polite, but there was something menacing about his demeanor. It made her nervous. Melinda must have sensed it too, as she gently kicked Jett under the table.

“Yea; me and your daddy go way back. I don’t know if he’d remember me or not. I haven’t seen old Markus Jackson in years. I remember when your mama used to run around this town. Whatever happened to your mama? She was just up and gone one day.”

“She died, six years ago.” Now Jett was nervous because no one knew who her mom was unless they worked for Krayton.

“She was a fine lady. She worked for me at an establishment I managed downtown, many years ago. My name is Eddie. You must be Jetitica.”

Jett swallowed hard. “Yes sir. Nice to meet you.”

“If you would, could you please give your daddy a message from me? Tell him I said he needs to take some time off work so he can spend time with his family. Family is more important than work and you never know what could happen in the future. Someone could be just, be up and gone one day before you know it; and you just end up wishing ya had more time to spend with ‘em. Tell him that, just like I said it. Okay young Jeticia, or Jett, as they call you.”

“Okay,” Jett said cautiously, “I’ll tell him.”

“Thank you and good night ladies. And be careful. Lots of bad people out there looking to do bad things. You should go straight home from here.”

Eddie turned and walked out of the coffee shop without looking back.

Jett turned a lighter shade of brown and her heart was pounding. Melinda was pale too. “Are you going to tell your dad?”

“I don’t know,” Jett said, “that was too messed up.”

Chapter Nineteen: The Port City Pounders

Jett and Melinda were driving around town in Jett's truck on a sunny fall day. It was Saturday and Jett had been teaching at the studio for half the day before lifting weights and sparring with Denise. In the evening she and her friends were planning to meet up at the coffee shop to play board games.

The rest of their junior year went well. The girls had their school routine, and they hung out with their friends. School, karate, homework, and studying took up all of Jett's time. Jett continued to win karate tournaments, winning yet another state title, and Denise hired her to teach the younger kids as a part-time job. Many people within the sport labeled her an up-and-coming elite athlete. She even entertained the idea of competing as a professional athlete after high school.

The girls got together any chance they could. Sometimes they spent time at each other's houses, sometimes they would go to the movies or the coffee shop with the rest of their friends. They went to the mall, out to the country for hiking and other activities. Laser tag and paintball were two of Jett's favorites, as she would use her athleticism to her advantage. Today they were going to a walking track at the park to walk before going back to Melinda's house to get ready for their game night.

While Jett continued to lift weights and run, Melinda had enlisted Jett to help her get in shape. Jett was taller now, up to five foot six inches and she was looking more like an adult. She was lean but muscular. Somehow, she was strong without looking bulky. She continued to avoid wearing makeup, and Ashley had stopped trying to talk her into it. Melinda was changing too. She had grown to five feet seven inches and had her mother's slender build. She wore her long brown hair in layers and supplemented her natural color with blonde highlights.

While neither girl had yet to have a boyfriend, or even a date, they were both starting to get noticed by boys their age. Their geek status in their high school, along with their near-religious focus on academics, kept them both ensconced in the single category.

Jett got on the ramp and sped up as she merged onto the highway. She wore sunglasses; she had pulled her hair back, away from her face with a scarf and she was still wearing her workout clothes from karate. She looked in her rearview mirror and saw the same truck behind her, with two guys in it. Curious, she thought, but she figured it was a coincidence.

Melinda was talking about their senior class. "I love the way our senior class is cliquish. I know that sounds bad, but it's not like anyone has a superiority complex. Everyone just hangs out with their crowd and is cool about it. Even the seniors on the football team are cool to everyone else, even if they don't hang out with them."

"Yea, I think they had enough of Mike's bullying and wanted to be different. Remember last year when Mike got suspended and the football team played better without him? That was so awesome."

"We should go to prom this year. Without dates. We'll go together and just have fun. Get all our friends together. Just one big group. One last time at a dance."

Jett cringed. She hated getting dressed up and Ashley would start with the makeup again. "We should. I don't want to go with a boy, anyway."

"Do you like girls, Jett?" Melinda asked mischievously.

"No," Jett laughed. "Just you. Awkward?"

"You noticed!"

"I wonder if my doing karate intimidates guys."

"Not men. Not real men. They'll appreciate the fact you're undefeated and now a two-time state champion in your karate league. I bet real men would think that was badass. I bet a lot of boys already do. You're beautiful."

"Aww. You're beautiful too Melinda."

"Aw. But I'm not state champion undefeated karate master beautiful like you. You should just ask boys out."

"Nah, I just don't have those feelings. I think boys are cute, but none at this school. It seems all the boys around here are boys that are going to grow up to be gross. To get fat, drink lots of beer, always wear a ball cap and fart and burp like it's funny, like a thirteen-year-old. The other boys are really funny and like stuff I like, but I just don't feel that way about them. They're friends, which is cooler than a boyfriend, anyway."

"I know what you mean. Where are the classy guys? Guys who dress up. Who take pride in how they look. Guys who read and study and can talk about interesting things. Guys who wear nice suits. Guys who make you feel safe without getting in your way. Guys like..."

"You're describing my dad, Melinda. But, you're right. Where are the guys like my dad? Guys who always know what to say, or how to handle a situation."

"Old fashioned classy men are a dying breed Jett. I think your dad may be the last of them. You know what he reminds me of? Those old-fashioned detectives in those old film noir movies. And they always end up sacrificing themselves to save the day, because it's the right thing to do."

"Okay. I don't want my dad to sacrifice himself to save the day. I'm sure he'd figure out how to save the day where everyone gets to go home."

"But you know what I mean. They always end up being the hero that no one knows about because they don't do it for recognition or praise. They do it just because, no matter what they've seen and done, it's just in them to do the right thing."

"You're over-romanticizing this, you know?"

"I know. But I hope we meet men like your dad one day."

Jett took the exit towards downtown and drove along the curve that would take them to the warehouse district. From there she took a side road towards the port and took a right and headed towards the art district. After they drove about a quarter-mile they took a left turn on a street that dead-ended at the north entrance to the walking track. Jett looked in her rearview mirror and noticed the truck was still behind them.

"I'm gonna text my dad. That truck has been behind us since the highway." Another car pulled up behind the truck.

Jett texted her dad. He texted back. He was getting coffee and he would walk to their location; it was quicker to walk than it was to drive.

"Who is it?" Melinda asked.

"I don't know. A couple of guys and some car just pulled up behind them. And they blocked us in. We can't leave."

"Creepy," Melinda said.

Suddenly, someone violently pulled both doors to Jett's truck open.

"Get out of the car, bitches," Jett heard a guy yell as he yanked her out of the car and threw her on the ground.

"Get her before she gets up!" Another guy yelled. Before she could move one guy had grabbed her legs while another guy secured her arms in front of her body. Melinda started recording the assault for evidence, and for a lack of anything helpful she could do.

The two guys who had Jett immobilized conferred with each other to assure she had no way of getting loose.

"What's going on?" Jett demanded, angry and scared.

"Ass whooping, bitch. That's what's going on. Meet the Port City Pounders."

"My dad's coming. I already texted him."

"And I'm live streaming everything for evidence," Melinda said, "So let her go."

“Fuck off, both of you. We’ll be done before either your dad or the police get here. It won’t take long.”

Jett recognized the third guy. It was Mike Krayton Jr.

“Hey, half-breed. You thought you were done with me? Meet a couple of friends of mine. They just moved here, from Indiana. Part of an elite group of street fighters. You’re so fucked. I told them what’s been going on and they felt like it was time to make things right. To put you in your place.”

“Stop it, Mike,” Melinda said.

“Damn, Melinda. I can’t believe you’re friends with this degenerate.”

Jett noticed that Mike had continued to bulk up since graduation. He didn’t look like a teenager anymore. She was trying to figure out how to get free of the men’s grip. These weren’t high school boys; these were grown men, and they seemed to know how to fight.

“So, if you want to intimidate a hostile, first scare the shit out of them. If that doesn’t work, you beat the shit out of them. See Mike, you were approaching this wrong. You don’t square up on a hostile. You ambush em. You pick where and when. You get your intel, then you make your move. Now, it’s your time.”

The guy who was on Jett’s right had her in an impossibly tight grip. He was tall, muscular, and wore a tank top with jeans. His head was shaved bald. The other guy was just as tall but leaner. He wore a gray tee-shirt and jeans. He had red hair and a buzz cut. Between the two guys, Jett felt very small.

Mike smiled and reached into the pocket of his jeans and pulled out a set of brass knuckles. He took off his shirt and threw it on the ground. He put the knuckles on and walked up to Jett, getting in her face. He pressed the knuckles against her cheekbone and smiled at her.

"Just like we talked about. You can inflict maximum pain on the cheekbone. Make sure you hit the bone with the brass," the bald guy said.

"Hey, half-breed," Mike said, "I'm going to cut your face up. Every time you look in the mirror, you're going to think of me. And don't think the police are going to do much. My dad is the mayor, and he's got dirt on the police chief and DA. I'll get a misdemeanor assault at the most. Pretty soon it won't matter anyway, things are going to change. And then I'll come for the real revenge. Remember I said I was going to own you one day. In the meantime, your dad needs to back the hell off. Hopefully, he'll get the message today."

"Stop it, Mike. You're going to hurt her!" Melinda yelled as Mike stepped away and put his fist back to hit Jett. Jett couldn't move.

Mike took his time getting set up to hit Jett. He wanted to draw this out, to make her dread what was coming. He pretended to swing first and touched her face with the brass knuckles. Jett flinched but didn't cry. "Mike, fight me fair if you want to fight."

Mike smiled, took a few steps back, cocked his fist, and started to swing at Jett.

A cup of hot coffee hit Mike square on the cheek. Mike screamed in pain from the hot liquid and fell to the ground holding his face. Markus Jackson had the drop on him and, as Mike tried to get up, punched him on the cheek multiple times, where he had already burned him with the coffee.

“What did I tell you, Mike? When you turn eighteen and you pull this shit? What did I tell you? Never. Mess. With. A. Man’s. Daughter.”

For each word, from ‘never’ to ‘daughter’ he punched Mike hard in the face. Mike fell back to the ground, gasping in pain.

The red-headed Pounder let go of Jett and started towards her dad. Jett worked her way out of the grasp of the other man. He responded by swinging at Jett, however, she moved away from his strike and kicked him hard, at full strength, in the rib cage. He looked at her, shocked, as he bent over for a second before recovering. As he recovered, however, Jett used his momentum to force him to the ground. She turned and did a roundhouse kick to the side of the other guy’s head before he could reach her dad. He weathered the kick and turned around as Jett kicked the other guy in the face. The red-headed guy swung at Jett, but she sidestepped him and kneed him hard in the ribs. As he bent over, she slung him to the ground.

“Did you mean this ass whooping, bitch!” she said to the guys on the ground, bruised and bleeding from the carnage she unleashed on them. “Pounders? What kind of stupid shit is that?”

The police arrived. After Jett and her dad talked to the police, Melinda offered them the video. Ashley pulled up in her car, jumped out, and ran to check on Melinda first.

"You okay kid?" Markus asked as things were winding down.

"Yea. That was close though. I'm glad you showed up."

"Me too. Coffee makes a good weapon."

"That was pretty badass, dad."

"I knew I had one more good fight in me, I guess. Gonna be sore tomorrow, though. Come here." He took his daughter and embraced her. He didn't want to let go. He was shaking too, at the thought of what could have happened to her.

"Thanks, Dad. I love you."

After hugging Melinda, Ashley ran to Jett and put her arms around her, and held her close, without saying a word. Jett put her arms around Ashley, and they just held each other for a long moment as Markus checked on Melinda.

"You okay, kid?" he asked.

"Yes, sir. And I recorded the whole thing for evidence. I already showed it to the police."

"Good job, kid. You know, you got good instincts under pressure."

"Thanks!" Melinda said as she walked over to Jett and put her arm around her.

Markus approached the police officer looking at the video and said, “This guy called himself and his friend a Pounder? Any idea what it means?”

“Some radical group,” the officer said. “They’ve been settling here in Port City, call themselves the Port City Pounders. It’s a nationwide group. These guys came from the Indiana chapter to start a chapter here. Got guys coming from all over the country to join as well as recruiting locals. They claim to be some kind of elite street fighting gang. Claim to be the foot soldiers for some other group or groups who have been coming here. It’s all new and hard to keep track of. Anyway, we can get assault with a deadly weapon on the other guy. He’ll sit in jail for a while. His dad is the mayor. But we’ll book him, put him in jail, put him through the process. You want to press charges on behalf of your minor daughter?”

“I do.”

“Okay. Come on down to the station and swear out a complaint. We’ll get these assholes off the streets. Between the two of you,” the officer continued, “you messed up those guys good. The coffee burned up that boy’s face. But the other two men, she kicked the shit out of them. I’m sure one of those guys has a few broken ribs and the other may have a concussion from her kicking him in the head. Don’t feel sorry for them, attacking a girl, but damn. I don’t think they’ll try that again. She’s a tough girl.”

“That’s my girl. My kid knows how to throw a punch.”

Chapter Twenty: Hippie Aunt Lydia

"Hey kid, I need to talk to you for a second," Markus said.

"Sure dad. What's up?" Jett approached her dad as he walked from behind his desk, out the door of his office, and into the lobby, holding his coffee mug. It was a mug Jett had given him as a gift with "Coolest Dad in the Multiverse" printed in plain black letters. He took a sip of his coffee and looked at his daughter. Markus was cautious. Since her senior year started, every time he asked something of his daughter she got upset. She was spending a lot of time with her friends. She'd say that her senior year was going by too fast and it was stressing her out.

"Well, I have some news for you. First off, I heard from the DA. Mike's got one year in jail plus probation. He got six months off for time served and has to sit in county for the other six months, then six months on probation. The other two guys got probation, but they aren't allowed to be within five hundred feet of you while on paper."

Jett looked at her dad for a long time before speaking. "I'm glad he's being punished, but I actually feel bad for him for having to go to jail and be away from his family. Is that weird? It's not like they would feel bad if I went."

"It's not weird, it's just how you're wired."

"Maybe he'll come out a better person."

"Maybe, but don't get your hopes up, kid. But I like your optimism. There's something else I want to talk to you about."

Jett folded her arms and leaned against the reception desk. "Ok. What?"

"Spring Break. We're going on a little trip. We fly out Friday afternoon and come back on Monday. I know you want to spend time with your friends but give me those three days and the rest of the week, weekend, is yours to do whatever you want. Just let me have those three days. It's very important."

Jett had this pervasive feeling of urgency. She was running out of time to spend with her friends. She felt anxious and depressed anticipating all the changes coming after graduation. Her senior year seemed to be flying by. Time was passing too fast, and she just wanted it to slow down. She regarded her dad coolly and nodded, but her skin became hot and her heart started beating faster.

"You don't look too enthused," he said.

"I'm fine. Where are we going?" She kept her arms folded in front of her to express her discomfort.

"Two places. First, Ashley and I have business in Chicago. We have a meeting Saturday afternoon. It won't take more than a few hours. We thought we'd make it a family trip. The three of us. We're going to see your aunt Lydia. My sister. Whom I haven't seen since before you were born. She wants to meet you and spend time with you. So, while we're doing our business, you're going to spend the day with her."

"I thought you didn't talk to each other. Over something that happened when you were young?"

"We didn't. But when you got here, I got to thinking. She doesn't have kids. You're the only one in your generation in our family. So, I started emailing her. Pictures, stories, anything, so she could know about you. Your aunt has been begging me to send you up there to see her for years. We spoke on the phone last night. She wants to take you for lunch, coffee, to a museum, an art gallery, her studio."

Jett swallowed the lump in her throat. Meeting new people was difficult. She wanted to meet her aunt, but it was a lot of pressure.

"You've never really known her at all," Jett said. She saw the expression on her dad's face. He looked as if he failed. It was only for a moment, then he recovered.

"I know, Jett. I haven't been the best son, or brother, to my family. But I've never been a family kind of guy until the last seven years or so. We haven't been in the same room since I was a few years older than you are now."

Jett stared at her dad for a moment longer. Finally, she unfolded her arms and said, "Ok. I'm fine with going."

"I understand you're not crazy about this kid. But I think it'll be good for you."

"You said two places. What's the second one?"

"Baltimore," he said, looking into her eyes.

Jett's heart sped up again, and she took a deep breath. "Why?"

"Because we'll be in the neighborhood?"

"No, we won't. Why?"

"Because you have unfinished business there."

"What are we going to do there?"

"You're gonna pick out some nice, beautiful flowers and..." he paused. Jett's eyes widened. She knew what was next.

"No. No. It's too much. It's too hard."

"After that," her dad continued, "we are going to visit your mother's grave. So, you can do whatever you feel you need to do."

A tear rolled down Jett's cheek, and she folded her arms again and looked away from her dad.

"Why?" she asked, sniffling.

"Because you need to. So much of your life is going to change soon. You need to deal with some of your anxieties. You don't want to end up like me."

"I'll see a therapist instead?"

"A therapist? I don't know what a therapist is going to do for you that you can't do for yourself."

"Do I have to?" She secretly hoped her dad would pull rank and just tell her she had to go. She wanted to, but if given the choice it would be easier not to go. She felt emotion with such depth that she often had to shut herself down to avoid feeling overwhelmed. But her dad was right. She was hanging on to so much pain about her mom. Tears ran down her cheeks as she stared at the floor, just to the left of her shoes.

"Yes. You have to. Is that better?"

Jett walked over to the couch and plopped down, into the seat, and stared at the carpet. "Is adulthood this hard? This intense?"

"It has its moments."

She shook her head. "I don't want to grow up."

"I'm not crazy about it either, kid. It's all happening too fast."

"Way too fast."

***

On the Friday before Spring Break, the seniors got out of class at noon. Jett went straight home. She had her bags packed and ready for the drive to the airport. She continued to have mixed emotions about this trip.

"So Chica, are you excited to meet your Aunt Lydia?" Ashley asked from the passenger seat.

Jett took her earbuds out. "I'm curious. I don't know what to expect."

"She is excited to meet you. You are your family's legacy."

"No pressure," Jett said.

"I know you're nervous. I also know she will love you so much, just like we do."

"She'll be waiting there for us when we leave baggage claim. I told her we'd rent a car, but she insisted on meeting us at the airport. We'll have to get a cab into town for our meeting," Markus said.

"Or an uber. Get with the times, Dad."

"In my day we got a cab. And cab drivers know things about a town. You can get a lot of good info from a cab driver."

"Oh lord," Jett said. "Okay, Mr. Marlowe."

***

When it was time to board the airplane, her dad paused and gestured for Ashley and Jett to board first. Jett showed her boarding pass to the lady at the desk and walked down the tunnel, following Ashley to the plane. When she crossed the threshold from the tunnel to the plane, she felt the floor give just a little as she walked into the narrow tube that would soon careen through the atmosphere while carrying about one hundred people. Jett followed Ashley to their seats. This time they waited for her dad to go first. He would sit by the window and Jett would sit in the middle. Ashley would take the aisle seat.

As the plane started to taxi towards the runway Jett became nervous. Her dad said she'd be okay once they got in the air. Jett gripped the armrests as the flight attendants talked about what to do in the 'unlikely event of an emergency.' That didn't help.

Jett's heart pounded as the pilot revved the engines on the runway. Jett thought of all the things that could go wrong and her anxiety escalated. Finally, the plane started rolling, slowly at first but gaining speed. The front of the plane started angling upwards. The plane left the ground and climbed into the clouds. After a bank that turned the plane to the north, they were headed for cruising altitude. Jett decided they were okay now and she was ready for her nap. She folded her arms, leaned to her side until her head was on Ashley's shoulder, and closed her eyes. Ashley leaned to her side until her head was nestled against Jett's head and closed her eyes. Within minutes they were both asleep. Markus was annoyed: they turned a perfectly good flight into a slumber party, he thought. He closed the shade to his window, took out a report on Ukrainian Oligarchs, and started reading.

***

Jett's dad nudged her awake as the plane approached Chicago. Jett opened her eyes and tried to focus, but she was still groggy from sleep.

"What?" she said in a drowsy, whiny voice.

"Wake up, kid. We're approaching Chicago. If you need to go to the bathroom now's the time."

"I don't," she said, still whiny and sleepy.

"Okay. Well, look out the window."

Jett leaned over her dad and looked out the window. "Clouds. So, what?"

"Look down."

Jett looked down. "What is all that?"

"It's a huge lake, and then Chicago."

Jett squinted as the plane started to bank. The pilot announced they were approaching Chicago and asked everyone to return to their seats and buckle their seat belts.

"How many people live in Chicago?"

"Millions, I'm sure. It's a huge city."

"And just like that, we're flying over most of them."

"Yep."

"From this far out, everything seems so insignificant. But it's not. That's so strange."

"Yes, but soon we're going to zoom in. And it's all back to normal. Normal life is huge again."

The plane was making a hard bank now, orienting itself towards the tiny cluster of buildings on the shore of the lake. Engines whined as they reduced power and altitude. The plane shook as it leveled out.

"How do they even find the airport and the runway?"

"Well, first they find Chicago. Then they get lower until they see the airport, then they get directed towards the runway. One step at a time. You'll see. Keep watching."

Ashley woke up next to her. "Are we landing already?"

Markus laughed. "You two slept through the entire flight"

"Good. Takeoff and landing are the only interesting parts of flying," Ashley said.

"It's the scariest part of flying," Jett said.

"Nah. This crew makes this route all the time. They take off and land every day, twice a day. Then they go home, sleep, wake up, and do it again. This is their life."

"It's still scary," Jett said.

"I've heard that most of these pilots are retired Air Force Pilots. Many of them have flown combat missions. Taking off and landing on aircraft carriers, avoiding radar, working in teams with other jets, avoiding and fighting enemy craft, avoiding anti-aircraft fire. After all that, this is like driving to the store. These pilots are professionals. You're safe. Look!"

The plane was now flying east of the buildings and approaching the airport. "See? There it is."

"Oh. Just like that. We're zoomed in," Jett said.

"And down there, your aunt Lydia is waiting to meet you. She's so excited," Ashley said.

"I know. I wish I knew what to feel. It's weird."

"Just be yourself, Chica. But let her hug you all she wants. She will probably want to hug you when she first sees you."

"And knowing my sister, she'll probably be crying a lot. She's very sensitive," Markus said.

"Is that where I get it from?"

"Maybe. Your grandmother was like this too. But she was my mom. She had a good reason to cry."

"Grandmother," Jett said wistfully, "I have no idea what it's like to have one of those."

"Well, you're about to have an aunt."

The plane began the final approach. The landing gear made a loud buzz-thump as they engaged and locked into place.

They began reducing speed and altitude at an alarming rate. Jett gripped her dad's arm, feeling anxious.

"Relax kid. This is going right on schedule. Look."

Jett looked out the window again and saw the plane was almost, almost, almost on the ground until the wheels touched down and they were speeding down the runway. She lurched as the brakes screeched and slowed the plane to a gradual, chaotic stop. The pilot came back over the speaker and told everyone they had arrived in Chicago and to remain seated until the plane came to a complete stop at the terminal. The tension on the plane resolved itself almost immediately. Once the plane arrived at the terminal, people started talking and laughing as they gathered their belongings and stood up to leave.

Jett walked with her family from the terminal to the baggage claim with a pit in her stomach over meeting her aunt. She hadn't met a new family member since she was ten. She had no idea what to expect.

After they gathered their bags and walked to the parking area, she saw a petite woman with short, black hair, blue eyes, and light complexion rush towards them, her arms extended. Jett swallowed hard as she approached. She didn't know what to do, and she had no template for this situation. She took a deep breath, smiled, and ...

***

Jett loved Lydia's home. There was so much artwork. Paintings, photography, sculptures; all over the house. Her home was like an art gallery. But Jett was intrigued by a monochrome photograph displayed on a wall in the hallway. Jett went straight to the photograph and stared at it. It was a picture of three people: A young woman, who looked like a young Lydia, with big, frizzy hair, lots of make-up, a big grin on her face and her arm around the boy next to her; a long-haired boy, confident and smiling for the camera, one arm around the girl's waist and the other arm around the shoulders of the third person in the photo. The third boy had shorter hair, with a cigarette hanging out of his mouth and he was holding up a bottle of Jack Daniels as if it were a trophy he earned in a contest. They looked to be in a bar, standing in the back of a crowd of people, with a stage in the background. What got Jett's attention was the long-haired boy's smile, the shape of his face, the look in his eyes; they were all familiar. She looked at the picture and looked at her dad as he maneuvered his suitcase across the living room, past Jett, and to the bedrooms on either side of the hallway. Lydia approached her and put her arm around her shoulders.

"Oh my God. Is that... seriously?"

"It's me, your dad, and a good friend of his when we were young. It was before our parents died. Your dad had already moved out of the house and was living with the other guy in the picture. That's Jerry. He was a good guy. Partied a lot, but he was a good guy. I was in college but any time I was in town I would find out where he was playing, and I'd go to the show. Your dad was quite a musician in his time. We had good times. But that picture is the last picture we took together. I don't know if it was the last time we had fun together, but it's the last picture of us together. I look at it all the time. It makes me happy and sad. So much has changed. We're old now. But I'd like to think that somehow, deep down inside, we're still the fun, cool kids in this picture. Your dad was cute, wasn't he?"

"Not what I expected, that's for sure."

"Come here and look at this picture," Lydia said to Markus.

He came out of the spare bedroom and stopped at the picture and stared. He didn't say anything at first; he just looked at the picture.

"What happened to us?" Lydia said.

"We got old and stubborn. That was probably the last time we all hung out together before mom and dad died."

"Whatever happened to Jerry?" Lydia asked.

"Overdose. He was thirty-nine years old. Just went to sleep and never woke up. I miss that guy. He was one of a few truly close friends I had. He was a great guy."

Lydia grimaced. "Poor Jerry. He would do anything for anyone without hesitation, but he couldn't help himself."

"Jerry had a disease. Drug addiction. I don't blame him. He never meant to hurt anyone. He was one of the most generous and compassionate guys you ever want to meet. We all had substance abuse problems. Part of the problem was the lifestyle. At the time the band was playing all the time, all over the region. We'd sell tapes and tee shirts and made enough money for food and gas to the next gig. We'd sleep in the van or someone at the bars we played would let us shower and crash at their place. When I wasn't on tour, I made money playing in restaurants, teaching guitar classes, sometimes working at the guitar store, or playing sets with other bands. It was grueling. Having so much work probably saved my life. Jerry wasn't in a band. He worked whatever jobs he could find. I crashed at his place when I was in town. We were roommates. It's a damn shame. Jerry was a smart guy in high school. He was good at math and had a twisted sense of humor. And he was a good guy. A damn good friend. You would have liked to have Uncle Jerry around, kid."

"That's so sad. I'm sorry for your friend," Jett said.

"Everything changed all of a sudden. We didn't know when we took this picture that this would be the last picture we ever took together. Everything just changed, overnight."

Everything changed all of a sudden. This sentence stuck with Jett. It rolled around in her head all night and kept her awake.

The next morning Lydia sat on her patio with a cup of tea, a camera, and a sketch pad. She took pictures of Jett as she worked on her kata in the yard. Lydia sipped her tea and started sketching. While she knew of Jett's skill with karate, she saw that she was also graceful and poised. It was almost a dance, Lydia thought; rhythmic and deadly and beautiful. She looked at her sketch pad and considered her work.

Jett focused on controlling her body while working on technique and strength. She moved through several kicks and strikes, holding poses as she went. She balanced on her right foot, as she extended her left leg outwards, at almost a forty-five-degree angle from her body. She held this pose while moving her arms into position, extended from her sides to the space in front of her, in a defensive position. She lowered her leg and did the same with her left foot maintaining her balance. Lydia took more pictures with her camera to use as a reference for another sketch. Jett, she thought to herself, is an athlete and an artist. It was her goal to capture the beauty and strength of her niece on film and canvas.

***

Lydia's passion and enthusiasm for art amazed Jett. At the art galleries they visited, she showed Jett exhibit after exhibit of artwork and talked about each artist. She would get carried away talking about each piece they looked at and what it meant to her. She encouraged Jett to take some time and consider what she was experiencing. Jett appreciated the aesthetics of the work. The colors, the lines, the visual appeal. But she felt some pieces told a story and she would tell Lydia her idea of the story she thought the artist was trying to tell. "There are no wrong answers here," Lydia would say when Jett asked if she got it right. "What you get out of it is what you bring to it."

Some work evoked emotion in Jett. This seemed to make Lydia happy; that Jett could connect with the art. While viewing one-piece, Lydia saw a tear roll down Jett's cheek.

"Jett, are you okay? You're crying," Lydia asked, concerned.

"It's okay, Aunt Lydia, I'm just sensitive sometimes."

"What are you sensitive to?"

"This painting. The woman looks like my mom, but she is old and sick. My mom was sick the last time I saw her, and she looked old and tired," Jett whispered.

"Now, look at the painting next to it. They go together. It's a younger woman, looking to her future with hope and anticipation."

"Is she supposed to be the older woman when she was young or is she the daughter of the older woman?"

"She's whatever you feel she is, Jett. What do you see?"

"What I see is my mom, and me. Because the younger girl is without the older woman. She looks hopeful, but also sad."

"Maybe these pictures touch something that you're struggling with."

"I'm going to Baltimore tomorrow to see my mom's grave. And I'm scared."

"I know. I could tell this has been bothering you. Let's sit down a moment," Lydia said as she took Jett's arm and walked her to a bench. The two of them sat down and Lydia turned to face Jett.

"What is it you're scared of, Jett?"

Jett stared across the room for a moment, and then looked at her aunt. "I'm scared that I'm going to lose control of myself, and just stand there and cry; like I'm a little girl again. I'm afraid it's going to hurt too much."

"What's wrong with crying like a little girl?"

"I don't know. I try to be in control of my emotions. Everything is just so intense all the time. It's overwhelming and I'm not sure I can handle it. I'm not normal. I just... feel too hard I guess."

Lydia smiled and put her arm around Jett's shoulders. "Oh Jett. You're just like the rest of us. Me, your father, our father. We all cope in different ways, but we all feel things with more intensity than most people. I bet other peoples' suffering is hard for you to take, isn't it?"

Jett nodded.

"It's okay to have intense feelings. It's part of what makes you... well, you. You're one of us. We're like this. And it's okay. Even good. You should embrace this part of you. It's part of what makes you special."

"It's hard. I just feel things all the time. How do you deal with this?"

"Me? Art. I paint, I draw, I write, I put my emotions out for the world to see. I let it drive me instead of hiding from it."

"And your dad? What did he do?"

"Oh, sadly enough, he drank a lot. And he was frustrated all the time. He never learned that it was okay to feel. I often wondered if your dad was going down the same path, with his drinking, before you came along."

"My dad drank a lot?"

"Oh, yea. A lot. I don't know if he was ever an alcoholic like our dad, but he tried to suppress his emotions with alcohol. But he took his last drink the night he found out he had a daughter."

"Wow, I didn't know that. He doesn't tell me these things."

"He's not much for the past, your dad."

"Mm... He said something about how I need to do this, so I don't end up like him. Is that what he meant?"

"He wants you to learn to deal with your emotions instead of trying to be in control all the time."

"It's hard, Aunt Lydia. It's so hard. I miss my mom so much."

"That's normal Jett. Maybe it's time to tell her this. It's time to let yourself be that little girl again and just cry and wail and be how you feel instead of trying to be so tough all the time. Don't doubt the healing power of expressing your emotions, especially grief. You are so much like your dad. But you're like me too. You need to just let yourself be you. Because you're beautiful just how you are. You have a beautiful heart."

"I just don't know what to do. I need help."

"There are no wrong answers, Jett. You do what you feel moved to do. May I offer a suggestion?"

"Please."

"Write your mom a letter. Read it to her. Leave it somewhere near her grave. That way you can tell her everything you want her to know."

"Thanks, Aunt Lydia."

"Any time you ever need me, Jett, I am a phone call or a text away. You never have to feel alone. Now give me a hug."

Jett leaned in and hugged her aunt for a moment. "Thank you," she whispered.

"Any time you need me, just let me know. Now, let's go get some lunch. I know of an amazing place I want to share with you."

For lunch, Lydia took Jett to an organic vegan restaurant near Wicker Park called the 'The Chicago Diner.' She explained that Wicker Park was gentrified but some surrounding neighborhoods still had some nice shopping areas run by local merchants looking to make more of a statement than a dollar. Jett realized her aunt was much like her dad. They both struggled to hang on to an ethos that was being swallowed by a society that was becoming disconnected from its own humanity. They were both anti-establishment types in their own way. Their work was their protest.

"You have to try a milkshake here. They are famous for vegan, gluten-free milkshakes," Lydia said.

Jett ordered a milkshake and a Vegan Ruben sandwich.

"There are a lot of young people your age here. Artists, students, musicians. You would make a lot of friends in Chicago. I could see you hanging out with young people your age, having lunch at a place like this before going to the museum, or a club, or to the movies or wherever smart, young people go these days."

Jett smiled. "Are you trying to talk me into living in Chicago after high school?"

Lydia smiled back. "Yes. Well, I want you to know it's an option for you. You could stay at my home for as long as you like. It would be fun. I'd steal you from my brother for a while."

"I haven't made plans for after high school yet. I don't know what I want to do with my life."

"No one really does at your age. They all think they do. I did. But you never know where you'll end up from year to year. It should be an adventure."

"What did you want to do at my age?"

"I wanted to be an artist. But I was taught all my life that I needed to get a 'real' job and art was just a hobby. I was told I'd get bored with it. I was told I needed to find a *'good man' and settle down and start a family*. So, I majored in education. I figured I would teach until I found a *good man and settled down to start a family*; like I was told to do. I minored in art though."

"How did you end up an artist, I mean, for a job?"

"Well, I graduated and started teaching and I was bored with it. It seemed so hypocritical to tell kids they could be anything they want if they tried hard, and here I was not trying to be what I wanted. So, I spent one summer just painting. All the ideas I had pushed aside I put on canvas. I painted my experience. I told my story. Eventually, I showed what I had painted to a friend of mine, the art teacher at the school, and she suggested I show my work. I was able to get studio space at a small studio and took part in some shows. It started small and kept getting bigger. People recognized that I had something to say, and they found the audience. A few years later I was making more money as an artist than as a teacher. I had to give one of them up, so I gave up teaching. And here we are."

"That's awesome, Aunt Lydia."

"Follow your bliss. What do you want to do? Right at this moment, what is your passion?"

Jett thought for a moment. "I want to be a professional athlete. If there is a way to make money competing in professional karate tournaments, I want to do it. I can teach karate on the side, get part-time jobs, but I want to at least have the chance to see if I can compete professionally while I'm still young enough to do it."

"Follow your heart, Jett. Follow your bliss."

Jett smiled and finished her organic shake.

***

"How was today?" Markus asked Lydia while Jett was taking a shower. It was eight in the evening and they were winding down their last night in Chicago. They were leaving for the airport first thing in the morning.

Lydia smiled. "It was wonderful, I really enjoyed spending time with her."

"Do you think she'll want to come to Chicago?"

"I hope. Can you just tell her to come to Chicago?"

"She's my kid. She'll only do it if she wants to. She's too much like me."

“I let her know it was an option, and I showed her things I figured she would enjoy. I hope she makes this choice.”

“I worry about her. I hope she makes this choice too.”

***

The next morning was rushed as they packed their things and got ready to leave. Jett took a long look around Lydia’s home before leaving, but she was drawn back to the picture in the hallway. She looked at it one more time, again feeling the anxiety and sadness the picture evoked.

“C’mon kid, we gotta go!”

***

As they arrived at the airport Jett donned her backpack and grabbed her suitcase to roll it towards check-in. Her dad and Lydia said their goodbyes first. It was hard to read her dad, but she could tell he was sad to leave his sister.

It was now Jett’s turn. “Thank you for everything Aunt Lydia. I promise I’ll come back, and we’ll spend a few weeks together. Okay?” A tear formed in the corner of Jett’s eye and started to roll down her cheek.

“I know you will honey,” Lydia grabbed Jett and hugged her close. She let her go and looked at her tear-streaked face. “I know today will be hard, but I want you to just go with you how you feel and be yourself. There are no wrong answers. Remember that, okay?” She hugged Jett again. “Oh, I love you so much, Jett. Thank you for being you.”

“I love you too Aunt Lydia. Thank you.”

They hugged one more time. "Okay, you have to go. Check your suitcase later. I put a little gift I made for you in it. Look at it when you get home, okay? And call me or text me anytime."

Chapter Twenty-One: Elizabeth Janice

Jett stood in front of her mother's grave. She was starting to cry. She stepped closer and read the inscription on the headstone: "Elizabeth Janice Landry. Mother, Friend, and Christian." She looked at Ashley, who handed her the flowers. Jett carefully placed the flowers on her mother's grave, her cheeks now wet from tears. Ashley stepped forward and put her hand on her back and rubbed it.

"You okay, kid?"

Jett turned her head and nodded and turned back to her mother's grave. "Hi Momma," she whispered and started sobbing. Jett put her arm around Ashley's waist as Ashley put her arm around her shoulders.

"I'm okay," she said to Ashley, "may I please be alone, though?"

"Of course, sweetie. We're right here if you need us." Ashley stepped away, to watch from a distance, with Markus.

Jett sat down on the ground in front of her mother's grave. She put her face in her hands and sobbed for a moment. Ashley started for her, but Markus touched her arm and whispered, "she'll let us know."

Jett reached into her pocket and pulled out the letter she wrote for her mom. Her hands shook as she unfolded the note and read it to herself. Tears streamed down her cheeks and her lip quivered, but she kept reading. She reached into the ground and tore some grass up near the headstone. She used her hand to dig about three inches deep into the ground. When the hole was big enough, she folded the letter again and placed it in the hole. She covered it with dirt and put the grass over it again.

"Momma. I wrote you this letter, and I put it here, so you can read it as much as you want, over and over again. I told you how I feel, what I've been doing, and what life is like with my dad. I want you to know that I'm okay. But I miss you so much. I never stop missing you. But I am okay. I love you momma, and I'll never forget everything you did for me, how hard you worked to take care of me, and what all you sacrificed so I could have a better life. I promise I won't waste it. I miss you momma and I love you. And I'm going to shut up and stop talking and just sit here for a little while and be with you one more time before I have to go."

For fifteen minutes Jett sat at her mom's grave, not saying anything. Finally, she stood up, looked at her mom's grave one more time. "Goodbye momma. I love you."

Ashley saw the look on the girl's tear-drenched face and started crying. She walked over to Jett and embraced her and held her tight for what seemed like forever. Jett sobbed the entire time.

"I love you so much Chica. So much. Forever and always. With all of my heart. I know I can never replace your mother, but I love you so much."

Jett sobbed harder. "I love you too. So much." She started to say, 'forever and always,' but she started sobbing harder and couldn't get the words out. Her dad approached her from the side and put his arm around her and held her close too.

Jett put one of her arms around her dad's waist and he put his other arm around Ashley. The three of them held each other in front of her mother's grave.

Chapter Twenty-Two: Pizza and Gloom

"My aunt Lydia is like an older, white version of me," Jett said. "She was so cool. I love her. We talked about everything. She told me so much about Dad, my grandparents, Chicago, all kinds of stuff."

"How was Chicago?" It was Tuesday night after Jett's trip. Jett and Melinda were waiting on their pizza, at a local pizzeria, for their party.

"Chicago was okay. I got the feeling they were trying to sell it to me though. I heard them quietly talking about me living there and maybe going to school there."

"Do *you* want to go?"

"I don't know. It's so different. I'm going to visit in the fall."

"What's your plan for college?"

"I'm not going to college yet. I'm going to work for Denise teaching karate and compete in a national tournament before I turn eighteen. While there, I'm going to talk to people about competing as a professional. I want to be a professional athlete."

"Like MMA?"

"There are professional karate tournaments with cash prizes. I got a letter from a professional karate organization who has tracked my progress in competition, and they want to meet with me at nationals. You have to belong to an organization to compete and it's invitation only. I want to pursue this while I'm young. I'll work college in later. Have you decided between the Bears and the Bovines yet?"

"I think I'm going to Baylor. It sounds lame, but my parents are pushing it. My mom graduated from Baylor. I think they feel like I won't get in much trouble there."

"That's so far away."

"We're still gonna get together any chance we get, okay Jett?"

"Okay Melinda."

The anxiety of their imminent separation lingered in the background of everything she did. Jett couldn't shake her feeling of dread. The news broadcast on the television in the restaurant didn't help:

"... Moscow warned Washington to withdraw Marines from Berlin, or risk escalating the land war in Europe. Russian Tanks and Armored Personnel Carriers paraded through downtown Warsaw in a show of force to NATO. While rebel forces aligned with Russia hold much of the interior of Poland, the western border is being maintained by Russian forces. NATO Intelligence has reported a buildup of troops on Poland's border with Germany. Russia has expressed solidarity with an enclave of East German partisans who have demanded sovereignty from the German government. In Asia, the Chinese Navy continues its blockade of Taiwan. Japanese and US forces are threatening to intervene."

"I hate the news. It's so depressing." Jett took a sip of her soda. "I wish they wouldn't be playing it like that. It kills the vibe."

"... *On the home front, Texas has seen an alarming increase in hate crimes. According to reports, there has been a call on social media for a mass migration of white nationalists and white supremacists to relocate to Texas and assert their influence in local government, especially in rural areas...*"

"Now they're talking about Texas and hate crimes. Great," Jett said. "Like we need the national news to explain it to us. We live it. Those guys with Mike, who attacked us in the park, were from Indiana; part of some group that came here."

"It's not just outsiders, some people who already live in Texas are jumping on the bandwagon," Melinda pointed out.

"My dad says that some people are like sheep. If enough people start a movement, they just jump on board, whether they really agree with it or not. But he also said that this is Texas, and when push comes to shove, a lot of people will stand up and do the right thing."

"Like us! We're the Renegades of Funk. Normal, everyday people who change the world."

"Yea, right? I don't think two high school girls are going to be able to pull that off."

"I don't know. Sounds good. Or maybe we just ride it out until it's all over."

"'We don't need the DOJ or the federal government to come to Texas and tell us how to conduct our business. It's the oppressive policies of the federal government that started this mess, so we're gonna have to fix it ourselves, even if it means secession... We'll do what we have to do.' The fiery Texas governor frequently refers to secession as the solution to the embattled state's conflict with the DOJ regarding the governor's interpretation of a new voting rights law recently passed by the Texas Legislature..."

Jett, now oblivious to the news report in the background, collected the pizzas while Melinda took care of the bill.

"Explosive allegations of rape and human trafficking against a sheriff in Texas, in a story that keeps getting bigger and stranger, when we return."

The newscast continued as the girls left with their pizza.

When they arrived back at Jett's home, Melinda looked at Jett. "So, are we going to make our big announcement tonight?"

***

Co-Valedictorians, Markus Jackson thought, as he sat in a diner twenty miles north of Port City, sipping coffee. His girl was named valedictorian along with her best friend. He barely graduated when he was her age, but his girl was at the top of her class. Jett's mother was smart. Ashley is smart. They talked about math and science. Ashley taught her Spanish. Markus and Jett, though, talked about good guys and bad guys. Right and wrong. Heroes and villains. That was their thing.

He wasn't a good student when he was her age. He was irresponsible and reckless. He goofed off with his friends too much, drank too much, and smoked too much. He sure as hell never cracked open a book. Not one he was told to read, at least. He was just another kid struggling to hide the pain of a hard family life.

But the night he found out he had a daughter he drank the last glass of whiskey he was ever going to drink. Markus Jackson's daughter deserved the best version of Markus Jackson there is, and he wasn't going to do what his dad did. He vowed to never drink alcohol again.

As an older man, he enjoyed a good book, and often read about psychology, sociology, history, and other topics that helped him get better at his job; but he wasn't smart like his daughter. She learned everything from math to art and never made a grade lower than an A. The kid was just smart, and she worked hard. He once told her that this was the secret to success: hard work and brains. He sipped his coffee and reflected on how, maybe, he managed to be the father his kid needed. Or maybe his kid is perfect on her own. Either way, she was two for two and he was a proud dad.

"Are you Jackson?" the man said, interrupting his musings on parenthood.

"Are you the dolphin?"

"I am the dog." The man looked over his shoulder to see if anyone was paying attention. This was their code to prevent someone else from hijacking their meeting.

The man sat down across from Markus and stared at him. The waitress approached, and Markus held out his coffee cup and gestured at the other man. “Get my friend here coffee too, and a couple of menus.”

“I didn’t come here for a breakfast date,” the man said after the waitress walked back to the counter.

“Look around; see these people here? If we just drink coffee and talk about a conspiracy, they’re gonna think something’s up and start taking notes. Someone here may be involved in the very thing we’re over here talking about. So, order a couple of eggs, bacon, whatever. It’s on me so don’t go crazy. We eat and talk about normal stuff, then we pay the bill, go outside, and talk about the real stuff. Got it?”

The man nodded as the waitress returned with the coffee and menus. They ordered scrambled eggs and bacon and ate while talking about their kids and their imaginary jobs.

After eating, the two men sat in Markus Jackson’s car.

“Before we get started, before I turn this recorder on, I have to ask: you sure you want to do this?”

“Yes. It’s too late to turn back now.”

“You haven’t told me anything yet so you can still back out. I just want to make sure you understand what you’re getting yourself into. Why do you want to do this?”

“Why? Because I can’t be a part of what they’re doing. I thought I could. I thought the cause was more important than the cost. But now that I see the cost up close, I can’t do it. I have daughters, so this trafficking thing, I can’t sleep at night. I’m having panic attacks. I need to make it right, for my daughters' sake. My wife understands. She took our daughters out of town, just like you said. Are we gonna get protection?"

"I can arrange something. And a deal. Our lawyer will represent you if you work with us, okay? She's the best. If you have your own, that's fine, but we're picking up the tab for her if you give us something actionable."

"Okay. How do I get out of here?"

"You're leaving your car behind and I'm bringing you to a safe house while we work out the arrangements. I got a guy that's gonna come get your car later. We can hide you and your family. But first, I have to hit record and see what you got. So, you want to do this? I need you to tell me you do so I can hit 'record.'"

"Do it. I'm all in."

Markus pressed 'record' on his old fashioned, handheld mini-cassette recorder and started driving. "You talk, I drive."

The man took a deep breath and said, "First off, there's a lot more to this than you guys know. It goes really deep..."

Chapter Twenty-Three: Fake News

"Dad!!! What the hell?" Jett yelled while looking at her smartphone. She had been sitting on the couch in the living room but was now on her feet, walking towards her dad.

"What?" her dad replied.

"This internet article. About graduation. It's horrible. They don't even know me, or Melinda, or the situation."

"Let me see." He took the phone from her hand.

It was from an internet publication known as 'The Market' and the headline was 'Texas School Caves to Political Correctness, Socially Promotes Black Student to Valedictorian.' Jett read it aloud to her dad:

"Port City, Texas' local leaders finally got it right; or so they thought. Port City High School is located just west of downtown and is the premier high school in the district. Created by a coalition of government and business leaders, Port City High has consistently outpaced all other schools in the surrounding area in terms of academics and athletics. The student with the highest GPA usually earns the title of Valedictorian at graduation. One student, however, has demanded to be socially promoted to Valedictorian; over the objections of the student who actually EARNED it. Jeticia Landry, the school's only black student, will be co-valedictorian at this year's graduation. According to reports, Landry does not have the highest GPA in the school, and she does not qualify to be Valedictorian. That honor went to the student who worked harder and earned a higher GPA. But, being the only black student in the school, Landry demanded she becomes valedictorian, in the name of diversity. So, Landry will be

socially promoted to co-Valedictorian, robbing the actual winner of what's rightfully hers.

We're sure liberals will rejoice at this decision. All GPA's matter, right? Just because it's the highest doesn't mean it's the best, at least to the liberal way of thinking. Was it white guilt or the threat of being accused of racism that caused the principal to cave? The Superintendent, who is on the record for opposing this act of social promotion, cannot intervene because school policy allows the principal of Port City High to name the Valedictorian. We stand with the student who actually EARNED the title of Valedictorian!"

"Damn." her dad frowned. "That's just some fly-by-night propaganda page, Jett. They specialize in stirring up racial resentment. It sucks that they managed to distribute it locally. It must have hit a nerve."

"I didn't want to hit any nerves. But this article has been re-posted all over social media. It's embarrassing."

"They just make stuff up to suit their agenda and get people all twisted. All they had to go on was the fact that you two are both valedictorians."

"And the comments from a local news page, who shared it, are terrible."

"Don't ever read the comments, kid. It's a descent into the dark abyss."

"Too late." Jett scrolled through the comments and read them to her dad.

"That's reverse racism.

I heard that she went to the principal and demanded this or her mom would sue.

Well, they got to keep that single mom happy, I guess, so she doesn't make a scene at the school.

Oh, it's worse than that. Her dad is actually white, and her mom is part black and part Mexican or something. Probably illegal.

What the hell kind of race do you call this kid then? Blitespanic? LOLOLOL,

That's NOT what happened at all. The girl with the highest GPA only had the highest GPA by less than a quarter of a point and SHE went to the principal and convinced him to make them co-Valedictorians. The other girl is her best friend.

Shut up, bitch. We can figure out what happened. Some feminazi race-baiting bitch demanded an honor she didn't earn, and the principal caved.

I hate that stupid bitch.

Y'all are all wrong. These are good kids.

Good kids? You sure? I heard that the black, Mexican, white, whatever kid starts fights and bullies other kids. Now she bullied the whole school. Nothing but a thug.

No, some of the other kids bullied her. So STFU.

Look at the snowflake, getting her feelings hurt because we already know what we need to know about the little social promotion warrior.

You should all be ashamed. This is a child you're talking about. She did nothing wrong. I know one of her teachers and she said that she is one of the brightest kids she ever taught and is very respectful.

All you racists need to back off. Let the girl be co-valedictorian.

Typical. Always want things they didn't earn.

We're organizing a protest at graduation. We'll do it outside in the parking lot, but we're going to take a stand. PM me for details. We're gonna get in that thug's face.

Way to go!

If you demonstrate, we'll counter demonstrate in support of the girls, and all the kids. I hear the entire class supports this and both girls are well-liked by their classmates. Come on ya'll. Let's support the kids!

Screw off Snowflake.

Is this the same girl that won all those karate tournaments?

Then she can karate chop her way back to the hood. I'm sick of all this social justice bullshit. It's time to make things like they used to be.

I'm the other Valedictorian and I AM THE ONE WHO WENT TO THE PRINCIPAL because Jett is my best friend, she's awesome, and we've studied together through most of high school. Jett tried to turn it down, but I talked her into it because she deserves it as much as I do. Our GPA's are so close that they are within the range of statistical error and, therefore, it's a statistical dead heat. It's only fair to share the honor since we both earned it. Protest all you want, but it's going down and you can't stop it. The good guys always win. #smartkidsrule."

"I said you shouldn't have read the comments, kid."

"Melinda posted. They are going to go after her," Jett said.

"She probably felt bad about them going after you."

"Why are people so awful?"

"I don't know, kid. They just are. And this isn't even the worst of it. The things I see would make your hair turn white."

Jett's phone buzzed. It was Diana.

Before Jett could say anything, Diana started talking. "I'm exploring legal action against that website. We're going to own it. They used your name, you're a minor, and they were inaccurate with the facts and caused all those people to say horrible things about you and damage your reputation. I already have one of my colleagues who specializes in libel working on it. He's a nightmare to anyone he goes up against and this time he's pissed,"

"And you're going to graduate, and you're going to be beautiful and charming and you're going to knock 'em dead with your speech. That's all you have to worry about. I'll take care of everything else."

"Thanks, Diana. You're the best," Jett said.

"Nobody messes with my Jett like that. Nobody. They are going to pay for this. Are you okay?"

"I'm freaked out."

"I understand. Looks like your friend is mixing it up with them for you. She's feisty and rebellious. I like her," Diana said. "And I'm getting screenshots of everything for evidence."

"Thanks. I appreciate your help. And Melinda is very feisty"

"Anything for you, love. Now, you just get ready for graduation, and don't worry about any of this. I got it. Love you girl. Be tough girlfriend."

"Love you too," Jett said as Diana ended the call.

"I have to meet Melinda at the coffee shop. We're gonna work on our speech," Jett told her dad.

"Okay. Be careful. Don't stop anywhere tonight. Go straight there and straight home. And don't look at those comments. Tell Melinda to knock it off. She's getting sucked into a conflict."

"Okay. See you tonight."

***

Three weeks after the article about Jett's graduation status came out, she and her dad were driving north, down a busy highway.

"Hey kid, I want to ask you about some things that have been going on," Markus said while driving. Jett sat in the passenger seat, looking out the window. Her hair fell over her left cheek; she brushed it away as she turned to look at her dad.

"Sure dad, what's up?"

Jett was getting anxious about graduation and needed a distraction, so her dad was taking her to a gun range to work on her shooting. The range in Port City was crowded, so he decided to go to a range in the country instead. They would have more space and more time to practice.

"You've been dealing with a lot of unpleasant things, haven't you? With what happened with Mike, those people at the mall, those assholes at school, those guys at the coffee shop. It worries me."

"It worries me too, Dad, but I can handle myself if I need to."

"But I don't want you to need to."

"I know. Neither do I. But that's how things are."

"Having a kid brings up things you never really think about before you have a kid, you know? Before, I only had to worry about myself, and I never worried about myself. I was reckless, stupid. Now, I keep thinking about what's best for you. Your future. Your safety."

"What were you like before I came along?"

"Less responsible. More impulsive. I just did what I did. Look," he said, getting serious. "I can't pretend to know what it's like for you, with the racism and all. It's not something I've ever had to deal with. It breaks my heart that I don't have the fatherly words of wisdom that puts it all in perspective. I feel helpless about it. You know what I mean? I'm sorry if I haven't been able to teach you how to deal with it like I should. I'm your father and I should know these things."

Jett smiled at her dad. "I don't know. 'Screw those racist assholes' was good advice."

He smiled back. "But it wasn't enough. I worry about your safety and your peace of mind. You deserve to have some peace of mind in life."

"That's sweet, Dad. But you also taught me how to stand up for myself, and when to stand up for myself. I'm gonna be okay."

"What did you think of Chicago? Lydia?"

"Chicago was nice. I love Aunt Lydia. I can't wait to go visit her again. We text each other all the time."

"What do you think about living there after graduation?"

"Are you trying to get rid of me, dad?" Jett laughed.

"No. But I want you to go where you'll get a fair shake. Where you won't have to deal with all this racism and discrimination."

"There's no racism in Chicago?" Jett asked, raising her eyebrows.

"Not like there is here."

"Maybe not. But here, a lot of the racists kind of let you know they're racists. In other places, they act like they aren't racists when they are. I'd rather know at least who the racists are."

"There's more racist people than you realize, kid."

"But dad, racism isn't always people. That's bigotry. Racism is when you walk into a store and the manager watches you because she thinks you're going to steal something. It's not getting the benefit of the doubt when there's a conflict with a white person. It's when people don't even realize they're treating you different because it's so ingrained in them to do it. It's like they're just, I don't know, conditioned to act that way and don't realize it half the time until you point it out. And they still want to argue with you about it. It's when people want to argue about something that happened to you when they weren't even there because they don't want to believe there is racism. Do you think Chicago has found the magic solution to this? Because, as bad as this can be, this is my home now. I like it here and I want to stay. I want to make it a better place instead of running away from it."

"You're right, kid. But things are happening that you don't know about. Something's gonna go down. I want to know you're somewhere safe when it does."

"Where are you going to be?" Jett was concerned for her dad's safety.

"I don't know. I may be caught up in it and have to deal with the fallout, maybe work to make it right. But I want you out of here. I'm afraid you could become a target."

"Me? What the hell do I have to do with any of it?"

"Because it may involve powerful people. They may use you to get to me. I can't live with that."

"You're not making sense, Dad. What's going on?"

"It's all murky, kid. I can't really tell you. I want you out of town and safe because it keeps getting bigger, and your aunt Lydia really wants to spend more time with you."

"Dad, if you make me leave, I'll just turn around and come back. I'm gonna do what I want."

"I know, kid. You're too much like your old man. I wanted to teach you to be independent. I guess that's what I get."

"You think we're a lot alike?"

"Yea. And that's what scares me most," her dad said as he parked the car.

They got out of the car and Jett approached her dad, as he walked around the car. She put her arms around his neck and hugged him. "I love you, Dad, now say it back."

"Why you wanna make me get all sentimental? You know how I feel."

"Say it back. Your daughter needs to hear it."

"I love you, kid. Now let's go inside and start shooting holes in shit. Or, as we call it, family time."

On the way into the gun store/shooting range, he noticed the Texas flag hanging over the door. Not unusual, but he also noticed the American flag was missing. *Clock's ticking*, he thought to himself.

***

Jett took the Glock from her dad and checked the chamber. Her dad taught her to shoot when she was fifteen and she'd enjoyed shooting ever since.

"I've been working on my kinetics and breathing. Now I just need to get the shot right," she said as she pointed the gun at the target.

"Good posture. You look like a pro."

Jett fired off three rounds and squinted to see the target.

"Looks like you hit center mass each time. Good shooting kid."

Jett's shooting had improved since their last trip to the gun range. Her dad wasn't surprised. Jett was an over-achiever and excelled at everything she did. *She's a special kid,* he thought. He hoped that when she's older and looks back on her youth, she'd know he tried his best to be the father she deserved.

Two men walked up and observed them for a moment. When Jett set the gun down, one of the men said, "Good shootin,' young lady."

Jett turned and removed her ear protection. "Thank you, sir."

The man who complimented her was wearing a black tee-shirt with the sleeves cut off and a pair of jeans. The other man wore a pair of canvas shorts and a camouflage tee shirt. He sported a ball cap with a Confederate flag on the front.

"Can I help you gentlemen?" her dad said.

"Yes, sir. I hate to be rude, but I think it's time for you two to pack up and leave," the second man said.

"Excuse me?"

"Oh, it's not like that. See, certain people reserved the range for this time for a private event so we have to clear it so they can begin. Is this your daughter?" he asked.

"Yes. SHE is my daughter," he emphasized the word 'she.'

"Well, she can shoot good. You taught her well. Sorry for the inconvenience."

Markus holstered his Glock as Jett took off her eye protection and put it in her bag. As they left the range, Jett felt a subtle hostility from the men. They had been polite, even complimented her, but she couldn't shake the feeling.

When they got outside, her dad noticed a Confederate flag hanging over the Texas flag in the space where they usually hung the American flag. He made a mental note as two other men approached. The first man looked to be in his mid-twenties and was portly, with a red beard, a trucker cap, a white tank top, and jeans. The other man was older. He wore sunglasses, a camouflage ball cap, and a camouflage shirt with jeans. He sported a longer beard than his companion.

The younger man walked up to Jett and her dad as they stood by the passenger door of her dad's car. Jett started to open the door to get inside when the man pushed the door shut again. Jett flinched and tried to step away, but he almost had her pinned against the car. The man looked at her dad and said, "What the hell are you doing here?"

"I think you need to step back, away from my daughter," Markus said.

"That's your daughter?" the man said, with disdain in his voice.

"Yes. SHE's my daughter. Now back the hell up."

"Just say what you got to say and then walk off brother," the other man said, as he pulled his friend away from Jett. "And don't crowd the girl." Both men spoke with what appeared to be rural midwestern accents. They did not sound like they were from Texas.

"Listen to your friend there, 'brother,' and back away from my daughter," Markus said.

The man, now from a more appropriate distance, pointed at the Confederate flag hanging over the door. "See that flag over there? We're the real thing. This ain't no 'it's heritage, not hate' thing here. We don't do it the way some people preach it. That flag means exactly what it means, and we believe in it; so, you need to git your ass in the car, leave this establishment, and don't never come back. I'll inform the proprietor that you want to revoke your membership. Got it, 'brother?'"

Markus weighed his options. Ten years ago, he would have punched this guy in the mouth on principle and punched his companion for not picking his friends wisely. But he looked at his daughter's face and decided this wasn't the time for recklessness. After a moment's pause, he said, "Get in the car, kid. We're gettin out of here."

Jett opened the door and slipped inside. Markus walked around to the other side of the car and got in the driver's seat.

"Good riddance. Be glad you didn't throw down. I know you thought about it. Now git outta here!"

Jett looked over her shoulder in time to see the man in the tank top gesturing with his middle finger as they left the parking lot and headed south. Her heart pounded, and she took a deep breath and started typing on her phone.

"So... you were saying about racism, dad?"

"What are you doing?" he asked, irritated, as she typed on her phone.

"I'm texting Ashley, telling her what just happened."

"This isn't gonna go well." The phone rang.

He heard Ashley's voice. "Put it on speaker, Chica." She was louder after Jett adjusted her phone. "What are you thinking, bringing her out there? You know the current climate, how it is right now. Are you crazy?"

Ashley's Cuban accent was more obvious when she was angry, and she was angry.

"I figured she's with me so there wouldn't be a problem."

"You need to think about things from her perspective, not yours. People will not treat her the way they treat you. You shouldn't have taken her to a place where people are so openly hostile. Promise me you'll be smarter than this from now on."

He assured her this would never happen again. Jett had never seen Ashley this angry at her dad, or anyone.

Markus looked at Jett after Ashley hung up the phone. "I'm in trouble, aren't I?"

Jett nodded her head as they continued the drive to downtown Port City.

***

"There is something distinctly ideological about what's going on here. These are believers. They've embedded themselves in this community, and in communities like this all over the state. They are extremists and they've sold this idea here and people have bought in," the voice on the recorder said.

Markus, Ashley, Diana, and Doug, who was sitting at the table this time, were huddled around the recorder listening to the man's statement. Doug was an impressive man. Six foot one and muscular; he was a former Navy Seal who currently works as a liaison for counterintelligence between the CIA and the FBI. He was an African American man, with dark skin and short hair.

"He rambles here for a minute, but I reel him back in with a question," Markus said.

"What attracted you to all this in the first place?" he asked on the recording.

"Look, I'm not an extremist, but I have political beliefs, including a belief in a smaller government. I'm a libertarian. That's what they offered at first. But this other stuff? It was a tough sell, but I got to a point where I lost faith in our government and I was willing to go in on it. But the right way.

I didn't want a war. I wanted a peaceful transition. They started out promising that, saying it's what they wanted; but they said they had to compromise a few things to get there. Especially with funding. They don't tell you everything at first. They bring you in and assess what they think you'll accept and then slowly push your boundaries."

"Like a cult?"

"Yea, you could definitely use that term. Like a cult. Eventually, you're in too deep."

"How do they bring you in?"

"It starts as a social thing. They bring up these ideas at parties. Neighborhood block parties; or at the country club; or they get you alone somewhere. They talk about things in the abstract to get a feel for where you're at, ideologically. It's very strategic. Some people never get to the next 'level,' so to speak, because of their attitudes at the start. They target people with money and resources they can use. They've created their own local oligarchy that occupies every political office and organization with any influence at all."

"It's not just here, though, is it?"

"It's a statewide movement. Very carefully planned."

"Dad!! I'm back! Are you here?" Jett yelled from the lobby as she shut the door behind her.

Doug leaned over the table, turned off the tape player, and looked at Markus. "Is that your daughter, the one who outclassed you guys with her internet research skills?" he asked, smiling.

“She’s my kid. Graduating co-valedictorian this year too.”

Jett opened the door to the conference room and started to walk out when she realized she was interrupting a meeting.

“Come on in kid, I want you to meet a friend of ours.” Jett walked back into the room.

“Doug, this is my daughter, Jett,”

Doug rose to shake Jett’s hand. “Hi Jett. It’s nice to meet you. I’ve heard nothing but good things about you from your family here. Are you the same Jett who found all that geological information?”

“Yes sir,” Jett said. “Not that big of a deal though.”

“Well, you found more info than this knucklehead here found,” he said, laughing while gesturing at her dad. “You ought to consider a career in the intelligence community when you graduate from college. You’re the kind of person our country needs to help keep us safe.”

Jett blushed a little. “I was grounded when I did that; for smoking weed at a party.”

“Chica!” Ashley said. “Don’t tell people your personal business.”

“Does that disqualify her from working for the federal government and handling classified material, Doug?” her dad asked, with sarcasm.

“I don’t know. Did you get arrested?”

“No sir,” Jett replied.

“So, there is no actual record of this happening. I didn’t hear a thing. As far as I know, you were grounded for coming in after curfew. What are your college plans, Jett?”

Jett kind of froze for a moment. “I don’t know. I had another idea in mind.”

“Jett,” Ashley interjected, “is a two-time state champion in her karate league. She should qualify for the national tournament this year. She is a very accomplished athlete.”

“Impressive. You could be a field agent with your brain and those skills,” Doug said.

“I’m going to interview for a professional karate league. I think I can compete professionally after I graduate.”

“That sounds exciting,” Doug said. “Good for you. When you do go to college, have your dad get in touch with me and I’ll set you up with some recruiters. If you want to consider that kind of career. You have to make excellent grades and you have to be of the highest moral character. We only take the best of the best.”

“My kid is the best of the best.” Markus was irritated that anyone would even question his daughter’s credentials. “But there are a lot of different things you can do and that’s only one of them. Don’t let Doug talk you into anything you haven’t thought through yet.”

“I’m gonna return phone calls at the front desk. Do you guys need anything?” Jett asked.

“We’re good, kid, thanks,” her dad said.

“It was nice meeting you, sir,” Jett said to Doug.

Diana stood up and walked over to Jett with her arms out.

"What?" Jett asked.

"I just want to hug you. I'm so proud of you. Just hearing it all at once is overwhelming. You're an exceptional girl with such a bright future, and people are already wanting you on their team. You're amazing." Diana wrapped her arms around Jett as Jett hugged her back. "I love you, Jett."

"I love you too, Diana."

After Jett walked out of the room and shut the door, Doug said, "That was a nice family moment. But it brings up something important we need to talk about."

Diana sat back down and focused on Doug again.

"Do you guys have an escape plan in case this goes bad?" he asked.

"Sorta. We have one for the kid. I don't think she's going to like it though," Markus said.

"Does she know how serious this is?"

"We do our best to shelter her from the realities of what we see every day. She's young and should focus on more age-appropriate things," Ashley replied.

"Understandable, but... If this goes bad, she needs to do what she's told to do, for her safety. I understand some of this has crept into her personal life. That's concerning."

"It is. I have people who keep an eye on her though. She doesn't know. She would probably try to dodge them if she knew. But I got people who look out for her all over town."

"As for you two," Doug continued, "take a break. You deserve it. Give your informants a break, everyone needs some time to breathe. Overwork leads to burnout. Burnout leads to mistakes and mistakes, in this field, could lead to tragedy."

"That's so true," Diana said. "You both need to hear this."

"It's the end of the school year and you have a daughter graduating. Take time off and enjoy the moment. You two have accomplished a lot. But all that comes with a price. The closer you get, the easier it is for the bad guys to see you.

"Let people see you doing something else for a while. Our agreement won't change, and you'll still be compensated. Understanding the ebb and flow of this work is part of the job. After graduation, we'll sit down and come up with a plan for the next phase of this operation."

"Thanks, Doug, for the feedback," Markus said. "I think it's good to spend some more time with Jett, but we need to get back on it soon. My gut tells me something is going down. Too much is on the line here."

This case was very important to Markus Jackson. It all started seventeen years ago when he was sitting at that lonely bar on the south side of town and a woman named 'Cassandra,' who would become a woman named 'Elizabeth Janice,' walked in, sat down beside him, and asked him for help. Markus Jackson was always a sucker for a woman with a story, but he fell in love with Cassandra. At the time, he felt she'd be the death of him somehow; but if she lived, he'd die with no regrets. For Markus Jackson, this case was very personal.

Chapter Twenty-Four: Renegades of Funk

"They were having so much fun last night," Melinda's mom said, "laughing about all of their adventures this year. They were supposed to be practicing their speech, but they ended up getting silly and giggling. They told this cute story about how they went to laser tag earlier this year and ended up competing against a bunch of college guys. They said they came up with a series of secret signals and a strategy and ended up winning the game. Those two are something else."

"That sounds like them," Markus said. "They make a good team." It was graduation night and Markus, Ashley, Diana, and Melinda's parents were sitting together in the crowded stadium waiting, anxious to see their daughters graduate. It was dusk and the ceremony was about start. It was a beautiful night for a graduation ceremony.

"I wanted to tell you how much we appreciate and love Melinda. She's the friend Jett needed so much and we're so glad you've always opened your home to her. Their friendship means so much to her; and to us," Ashley said.

"Thank you. We love Jett. She's such a wonderful young lady. We couldn't ask for a better friend for Melinda."

"Anyone heard their speech yet?" Diana asked.

"They've kept it under wraps. I guess it's a need to know kind of thing," Markus replied.

"I'm sure it will be fantastic," Ashley said. "I just don't how to feel. Happy, sad, excited. It's a rollercoaster."

"Ooh, it's starting," Diana said as the music started.

The graduates entered the far end of the stadium, as the guests of honor walked onto the stage. Mr. Preston, the superintendent, select members of the faculty, the school board, and the mayor, Mike Krayton Sr., took their positions in front of their chairs and waited.

"They tacked Krayton on as commencement speaker right after they announced Jett would be co-valedictorian. Coincidence?" Markus said.

"Shh... Stop working. It's your daughter's graduation," Diana replied.

"There they are!" Ashley said as Jett and Melinda stepped onto the dais after Krayton. "They are so beautiful," Ashley said, smiling to herself as Diana took pictures with her new camera.

When everyone was in place, Mr. Preston stepped up to the podium and introduced everyone on the dais.

"Look! You can see her smile from here. She's so happy!" Ashley said.

Mr. Preston delivered a short address. He talked about the honor of working with all the students graduating today, and all the students who have graduated during his tenure. He congratulated Jett and Melinda for their hard work and discipline. Then he announced his retirement. He said he was ready to spend more time with his wife and grandkids.

"Preston's retiring?" Markus whispered. "Allowing this co-valedictorian thing must be like flipping the finger at the Superintendent before he goes."

“And cramming Krayton on the bill to speak must be like flipping the finger back,” Diana said.

Preston ended his speech to a standing ovation. He introduced Krayton next. Krayton gave a disjointed commencement address. His speech was short, unimpressive, and unfocused.

“Okay?” Diana said when he finished.

“That was awful even by Krayton’s standards; but notice he referred to the graduates as the future leaders of Port City, Texas, and the world. He left out the country,” Markus said.

“Not an accident.”

“Stop working. Your daughter is about to speak,” Ashley mumbled.

Preston introduced Melinda and Jett. Both girls stood up, hugged each other, and approached the podium, holding hands. Jett spoke first.

“When I was ten years old, my mother died. I was devastated. We lived in Baltimore and I moved to Texas to live with my dad. My mom and I lived a very private life. I had few friends and no other family. All I can think about today was how proud she would be to see me up here. My mom taught me to read, do math, find answers to questions, and to be curious. She helped me learn to figure things out for myself. She wanted something better for me than what she had. She lives on in me. After my mother died it was really hard. But I wasn’t alone. I’ve had my dad, who took me in and protected me, taught me everything he knows, made me learn to do things for myself, and taught me how to be confident and strong. I've had Ashley, who stepped up and became my mom. She's been so amazing, and I love her so much. She taught me how to let my guard down and let people get close to me again. I've had Diana, who has always been there for me when I needed her. She's loving and fiercely protective. I've had this whole new family that has been there for me in every way. I can't ask for more.

"School was hard at first. There were bullies and racists. But I wasn't alone in school either. Melinda became my best friend. We stood up for each other and we stood up for the other kids. We studied together, played together, and struggled together. My family became her family, and her family became my family. Soon, I was making a lot of friends, and at this point, I've made so many friends in our class that I'm sad to leave. It's been a great year and I will miss every one of you so much." Jett smiled as Melinda stepped up to the podium.

"Hi Mom!" she said and smiled. "And hi Dad! It's been a great year, and a great time at Port City High. I don't know what to say other than my parents, my class, my friends are awesome! We've been through so much and it's amazing that we got here in one piece, right Jett?" Jett laughed as Melinda continued. "I don't know how to thank everyone who has supported me to this point. My mom, my dad, my friends, my friends' parents. I love y'all so much. I want to thank my dad for all the advice and jokes and for making me feel special and important. My mom for all the hugs, late-night talks, and advice. And for getting onto me when I needed her too. And Jett's parents: Mr. Jackson and Ms. Garcia. Thank you for always looking out for us and making sure we're safe. And Jett, for being my best friend. And we are going to save the world somehow. We'll figure it out. We're absolutely determined."

After Melinda's comments, Jett and Melinda stood together in front of the microphone and alternated lines. Jett spoke first.

"Once upon a time, there was a lonely, scared girl."

"and a nervous, angry girl."

"The scared girl learned to stand up for the other kids."

"The angry girl learned to stand up for the scared girl."

"Without one of us, there wouldn't be another."

"We're a team."

"Best friends."

"Sisters."

"Soon we had lots of friends. Greg, Lara, Marsha, and Justin. And many others."

"We all stood up to those who tried to push us down."

"One day we noticed the other kids were lifting us up."

"And the bullies were gone."

"We persevered."

"We survived."

"We thrived."

"Not just the two of us up here."

"But all of us. We learned that by raising each other up."

"Those that would bring us down were destined to fail."

"And that's when we became..."

Together, both girls said, "The Renegades of Funk!"

After their speech, they gave each other another hug and exited the podium to applause from their classmates and the audience.

Mr. Preston approached the podium and said, with a smile, "Well, Mr. Krayton, you're going to have to bring your A-game if you're going to give a speech here. Our kids bring it every day. Now, let's graduate seniors!"

Ashley was an emotional mess after Jett's speech. She cried so hard that Markus had to hold her to help her calm down. He'd never seen her like this.

After the ceremony, Jett and Melinda's families met them on the field. Ashley approached the two girls and held them close, crying again. She didn't want to let them go.

"Good speech kid," her dad said when he finally got a chance to hug his daughter. "You made Ashley cry like a baby with your speech. I'm proud of you, kid. You did good."

"Thanks, Dad," Jett said as they exited the field. Jett and Melinda planned to ride with Melinda's parents, just in case the protestors from the local news' comment section tried to make good on their promise to confront Jett. Her dad and Ashley were decoys while the girls, surrounded by other parents and kids, covertly made their way to the car.

Jett and Melinda fell into the backseat, giggling. Melinda started singing "Renegades of Funk." Jett soon joined in and they sang all the way to the party their parents planned for them at Joey's.

***

Ashley sat in the back of the diner they were using as a meeting place. The owner was one of their contacts and she allowed the use of her diner, and her bar, outside of usual work hours, to meet with their homeless informant. Six weeks had passed since graduation.

"Where's Jackson," her informant was anxious. "I talk to Jackson."

"He's indisposed. You know me. We don't have much time so say what you need to say."

The man looked around to make sure no one else was in the diner. "It's all messed up and I think they're on to me. They may be looking for me."

"There's no way they can follow you here without me knowing. And I'm keeping an eye on the road. If anything goes down, I'll get you out of here. Now, what was so important that it couldn't wait?"

The man eyed Ashley for a moment before talking. "It's getting closer. They're gearing up for some shit. They got these militia people all over the place. These militia people are getting more weapons, more ammo, more trucks; everything. They're getting training. Everyone is getting extra suspicious. I've been sneaking pictures. I'm getting the evidence just like we talked about, but it's gonna take a while because they are watching every freaking thing right now."

"Well, be careful. Don't take unnecessary risks. Now, who is providing all these weapons and ammo and training?"

"Mercenaries. Alpha types or some shit like that. Or foreigners; some of them talk funny. I don't know, but," he leaned in closer. "Shit's about to go down. They're on the edge."

The man was sweating as he spoke. Ashley weighed the man's comments, his mood, and his body language. This is the problem when your informant is already paranoid, she thought. It's hard to trust his judgment; because you don't know where his observations end, and his stream of consciousness begins. Professional mercenaries were very unlikely. But they were investing a lot of resources to protect this trafficking ring. They also knew the trafficking ring supports whatever else it was they were planning, and they were drawing private militia and anti-federal government types from all over the country. Whether the militia members knew they were involved with a human trafficking ring was still unknown. Ashley needed something more concrete than the paranoid ramblings of a frightened conspiracy theorist who lives in the woods.

"What evidence do you have of all this?" She leaned back and folded her arms.

"I got something big. Did Jackson tell you what my warrants are for? Burglary. I used my skills and slipped into the cabin and stole a laptop. When I turned it on, I realized it was the mayor's laptop. Krayton. And they are freaking out over it."

"Whoa. He was there?"

"Yep. Along with the sheriff, the judge, and some other guy with an accent. Some kind of meeting; and I stole his laptop."

"Do you have it with you?" Ashley was interested.

"Okay. This is a good news/bad news thing. I hid it in case they came to our encampment to look for it. The good news is, they didn't find it."

"Aaaand... what's the bad news?"

"Look, I've been working with you guys for a while. I helped you find the girl. I've provided a lot of pictures. But this is huge and if they figure out it was me, I'm dead. So, I'm going to need more compensation before I get it to you. In the meantime, I hid it somewhere safe."

"Can you find it?"

"Yea. I'll get it to you after we talk numbers."

"I can't do anything right now. Gonna have to talk to my people first," Ashley said. "We're going to get you out after this, though. This is too hot a situation, and they will look for anyone that may have taken it."

"I have it hidden away. And I'm staying out of sight too. Okay, I need to go now before someone sees me. I have warrants. Watch my back when I leave. You got that Sig... whatever on your hip there?"

"It's ready to go. I'll watch for you," Ashley puller her blazer back, exposing the gun. "I have a guy on the main road keeping watch. If you see a black car, he's one of us."

“I stay off the main roads,” the man slid out of his seat and rushed out the door. Ashley waited a moment, placed a twenty-dollar bill on the table, and slid out after him. She got in her car and drove down the old Farm to Market road that intersected with the highway a few miles away. At the end of the road sat a car. It was Markus Jackson, keeping watch in case anyone tried to ambush Ashley. Ashley’s cell phone rang.

“Did you get all that?” she asked.

“Yea. I got it. I’m curious about the laptop. It could be a huge break, or it could be some bullshit to get more money.”

“What do you think about the other stuff?”

“Alphas? Mercenaries? Those guys are elite. Why would they be supplying those white supremacist assholes with weapons and equipment? It’s probably some grifter running a scam and selling them crappy weapons. Those assholes are too stupid to know the difference.”

“Do we pull the plug and get him out of there?”

“I’ll ask. It’s not our call though.”

“Okay. See you back at the office.”

Chapter Twenty-Five: The Last Night

Melinda and Jett were lying side by side on a mat on the roof of Jett's building, looking at the stars. The summer went by fast. Jett won her final state karate championship. Melinda and most of their friends spent the summer going to freshman camps and preparing for college. Jett was preparing for the National Karate Championship Tournament and to visit her aunt in Chicago.

But tonight, they were saying goodbye. Earlier in the evening, Jett and Melinda's families had dinner together and visited at Jett's home until ten o'clock. The other kids started arriving later. First Justin, then Greg, Lara, and Marsha arrived. They just sat and talked until two in the morning, when everyone started leaving. Jett and Melinda hugged each one of their friends and promised to get together every time they were home. Jett felt gloomy as each friend left. She could feel the anxiety in the pit of her stomach, and it kept getting worse. She wasn't ready for this. After everyone left, Jett and Melinda went upstairs to the roof to look at the stars one last time before going their separate ways.

Jett exhaled, sighed, and said, "I'm going to miss you. It's going to be hard not having you to hang out with."

"Me too, Jett. Come to Baylor with me! We'll be roommates. Please?"

Jett was quiet for a moment, before saying, "Part of me wants to, but I don't even know what I want to major in. I really want to do this professional karate thing."

"I know, and I want you to be happy. I'm going to miss you though."

"Yea," Jett said, and they both fell silent until Jett spoke up again.

"There was this picture at my aunt's house, the one I sent you, remember?"

"Of how hot your dad was back in the day?" Melinda giggled.

Jett giggled and nudged her best friend. "I didn't tell you everything about the picture. That picture was the last picture my dad, my aunt, and their friend ever took together. It was the last time they had fun together. My dad and my aunt had a falling out when my grandparents died, and the other guy died of an overdose."

"That's so sad."

"Yea. The saddest part is they didn't know it was the last time they would all be together, just having fun. They loved each other. But everything changed, and they couldn't adjust to it. They didn't know it that night. It was just another night of good times and partying. But it was their last night together. I'm so afraid this may be the last time we'll be together. Things are going to change. You'll have lots of new friends, boyfriends. Maybe a special boyfriend. Soon you may not come home as often, or for as long, and you'll bring your boyfriend. And you'll want to spend more time with your family. And we may get together a little, but nothing like now. It's going to be different when we get older. You'll get married, have kids. Then you won't have time. I'll become a memory."

"Jett! You're talking like you're going to be here forever, not doing anything but waiting for me to come back. We're going to be friends, forever. We're going to have more adventures. I'm sad too, you're the best friend I've ever had, the best friend I will ever have. We're sisters. I'm not good at making friends. I'm goofy and awkward. So are you. We're perfect."

"I know," Jett sighed. "I'm just scared and depressed. I hate this. I don't want this to be like my dad and Aunt Lydia."

Melinda smiled at Jett, took out her phone, opened the camera app, and set it to selfie mode. She held the camera up and said, "This is not the last picture we're ever going to take. There will be more."

"Okay, I promise," Jett said, "but I'm sure dad and Aunt Lydia thought that too."

"But we know what happens next. They didn't. So, smile for the camera, Rockstar."

Jett smiled, and Melinda took several pictures. They looked at the pictures together and picked their favorite one. Melinda posted it to her Facebook with the caption 'this is not our last picture, I promise.'

"Thank you," Jett said.

"Thank you, Jett."

Melinda's phone buzzed. "It's my mom. I have to go home now."

Jett reluctantly got up, extended her hand to Melinda, and pulled her up. The two girls hugged each other and went down the stairs, into the maintenance room, and back to the apartment to get Melinda's things. Ashley and Markus were waiting up.

"Well, I gotta go ya'll. Thank you for everything," Melinda said.

Ashley hugged Melinda tight. "We'll miss you so much, Melinda. And we can't wait to see you again. Okay? When you come back, we'll all go out for dinner again, like tonight."

"Thank you. I'll miss you too."

"Come here kid," Markus gave Melinda a quick hug. "Give 'em hell at Baylor. And make good grades and all."

"Yes sir," Melinda chuckled.

"I'm going to walk her down," Jett said. The two girls left for the elevator.

The elevator ride was quiet. When they got to Melinda's car, they faced each other one last time and didn't say a word at first. A tear rolled down Jett's cheek as she told her best friend goodbye. Melinda wiped her tear away as she shed one of her own. The girls embraced. After what seemed like forever, Melinda pulled away. "We need boyfriends for this, you know?" She laughed.

Jett laughed too, but tears stained her cheeks.

"I love you, Jett. I'll text you tomorrow, and I'll call first chance I get, okay?"

"Okay. I love you too, Melinda."

Melinda turned away, opened her car door, and got inside. She flashed her lights and honked before pulling out of the parking lot and onto the road. Jett stood, alone in the parking lot, and watched her best friend drive away.

Chapter Twenty-Six: Everything Changes

Frankie sat in his car, watching the building. He was told to call when he had eyes on them and report their location. In his gut, he knew what was going down, but he didn't like it. It was wrong, and he couldn't settle it with himself. The cause was much bigger than the lives of a few people; they said. The cause paid better, too. His boss didn't mind. This solves his problem and keeps his people happy. All Frankie had to do was wait, follow, make the call, and get out. And he hated himself for it.

***

Jett became depressed after Melinda went to college. It had been three weeks since they said their goodbyes. Melinda had already started classes at Baylor. They still texted back and forth and talked on the phone, but those conversations were often short as Melinda was always busy. A first-year student's life was full of things to do, she said.

Jett spent her time either teaching in the studio or preparing for nationals. Sparring with her teachers, working out on the bag, lifting weights, running, studying new techniques; she tried to stay busy. When she had downtime, she had nothing to do. She had grown accustomed to having homework and friends; now she had neither.

Her parents were busy too. They were working long days and nights, often her dad came home tired and somewhat disturbed. Ashley was also distracted, something about the case they were working affected them.

Jett tried watching television, but all she found was news about the wars in Europe, Asia, and the Middle East, and domestic problems in Texas. It made her nervous. She was already depressed, but now she had a pervasive feeling of impending doom that would not go away.

Jett sighed and turned off the TV. She thought about going to the coffee shop on her own, but she didn't know what she would do when she got there. Finally, she texted Ashley.

Jett: *Hey Mi Madre. I'm lonely. You finished soon?*

After a minute Ashley texted back. Jett was relieved.

Ashley: *Hey, Chica. We're on our way to the office now.*

Jett: *Can we do something tonight?*

Ashley: *Sure. How about dinner? Can your dad come too?*

Jett: *Yes! Joey's?*

Ashley: *Your dad figured you'd say that. Be ready. We'll be there in forty-five minutes.*

***

Ashley tapped send and looked at Markus Jackson very seriously. "So, we're doing this tonight?"

"We tell her tonight, after dinner; then she leaves for Chicago. I bought two tickets though."

"Two?" Ashley was cautious. "Are you going?"

"No. I want you to go. There's nothing for you here, and Jett needs someone to protect her."

"Why not buy three tickets?" Ashley raised her eyebrows.

"Because I need to see this through. I'll join you guys in Chicago later."

"I don't want to leave you here, doing this alone."

"I need to know my daughter is safe. And I need to know you're protecting her. You're the only person I trust."

"Why don't you go, and I'll bring this to Doug? You should be with your daughter."

"No. I started this and I'm going to see it through. I can't ask you to take any more risks."

"You get this done and get your ass to Chicago and be with your daughter. She will be so worried about you." Ashley sniffled, suppressing tears.

"I will. Let's secure this laptop, pick up Jett, have dinner and spend some time together as a family, then we'll give her the news. When you guys head for the airport, I'll deliver the laptop to Doug. We'll be together again in a couple of days. Maybe he can figure out how to use what's on here to stop this thing before it gets going."

"Poor Jett. She's not gonna like this," Ashley looked out the window.

"She'll be angry, but she'll be safe."

"And our informant?"

"He's headed to The Ranch as we speak. He'll be fine."

***

An hour later Frankie followed the car to the parking lot. They were here. He waited for them to get out and make the walk to the door before calling.

"They're at Joey's. Just walked in. Now, keep me out of your phone."

"Relax," the guy on the other end of the call said. "None of it matters after tonight."

"Yea. All the same, I don't want nothing to do with it."

Frankie hung up the phone and drove off, heading straight to the nearest bar for a drink, or twenty.

***

"So how is Melinda doing?" Ashley asked.

"She's having a lot of fun, really busy. Lots of classes, social stuff, homework. She doesn't have much time to talk." Her voice trailed off at the end of the sentence.

"I know you miss your friend, Chica. She misses you too. But be happy for her. Soon you'll be in New York for the tournament, and I have a feeling things will start happening for you too."

"I know. Are you going to be there?"

"Do you need to ask? We'll be there. Got to watch my little girl kick some ass."

"I'm not a little girl anymore, Dad."

"You'll always be a little girl to your dad," Ashley said. "And to me too. And yes, I will be there."

Jett smiled at Ashley. Somehow these two hard-boiled private eyes were her parents, complete with dad jokes and family time. Jett took another bite of her cannoli. "Thanks. I hope it goes well. Denise says my reaction time is phenomenal and I've run out of people to spar with who can compete with me."

"Hey, I'm sorry we've been working so much. But let's do something together tonight. Let's all watch a movie together at home, maybe Star Wars, for old times' sake. Ashley? What do you say?"

"Sure, I don't know much about Star Wars, but I'll enjoy the company."

"We'll talk you through it. What do you say, kid?"

"Yes!!! Ashley, you'll love it. It's about good versus evil. It's the main thing you need to know, like life."

Markus paid the tab in cash and the three of them got up and walked out the front door. Ashley put her arm around Jett's shoulders, and they walked around the corner towards the sidewalk. Three noisy motorcycles passed and took a right. Jett could hear them speed up and take another right.

"Oh, crap," Ashley said. "I left my purse at the table. I'll be back."

"We'll pull the car around to the front," Markus said.

Ashley reached under her beige blazer and felt her sidearm on her hip, relieved it wasn't in her purse. She straightened out her black slacks, turned around, and hurried up the sidewalk, her high heels clicking as she went.

Her dad threw Jett the keys. “You’re driving home kid.” As Jett reached out to catch the keys, a motorcycle raced by and the rider pushed her down as he passed. Markus reacted to the motorcycle by pulling out his gun as another man grabbed Jett, right as she was getting up, and pulled her into the alley. She was caught by surprise and fell to the ground again.

“Jett! Where are you?” her dad yelled.

As Jett struggled to her knees, she heard a click and looked up, in time to see the barrel of a pistol aimed at her forehead. “Don’t fucking move,” she heard a man say. The man yelled, “better get back here Markus Jackson, and rescue your little girl.”

He hurried into the alley where he saw Jett on her knees, with a pistol aimed at her forehead. He aimed his pistol at the man’s head. “Drop the gun, now.”

“Dad?” Jett was near panicked. She didn’t dare move.

“It’s okay, kid. You’re going to be okay. Just stay calm.”

Markus Jackson heard another click from behind him and felt the muzzle of a pistol in the small of his back.

“Why don’t you drop yours,” he heard a man say.

“Okay, what do you want?”

A third man, the man who pushed Jett, approached from the other end of the alley, his gun drawn, aiming at her dad as well. “There are three of us, and there is one of you. And a scared little girl,” he said, looking at Jett.

Tears flowed over Jett’s cheeks as she trembled with fear.

"What do you want?" her dad asked again.

"Guess," the man replied.

Jackson never took his gun off the man's head. He saw the patches on their vests and the tattoos on their arms. They were the Nazi Bikers; white supremacists who engaged in human trafficking. He knew exactly what they wanted. His anxiety spiked for a moment, but he took a deep breath. "You're some kind of gang?"

"Don't be fucking coy. You know exactly who we are, and you know what we do."

"You're gonna have to fill me in guys. I can't read minds."

"You've been fucking with us. Where's that bitch you run with? I was told all three of you were here."

"She took her own car, she's gone," he replied.

"Damn. We'll have to get her later. But now that I see your kid, I got an idea."

"Dad? Please." Jett said.

Markus tried to reassure Jett. "Take a deep breath kid. We're going to get through this."

"Yea don't believe it, little girl. See, your daddy has been messing with us and he's caused us a lot of trouble. All because he couldn't mind his own damn business. We have to make him pay. I think we're gonna let him live though. Is that good?"

"Yes. . . y... y... yes, sir."

There was a tense silence until the man spoke again. "He's gotta pay. We have to make him pay. We swore an oath. But we're gonna let your dad live. That's the good news. But there's bad news too."

***

Ashley had texted both Markus and Jett but didn't get an answer. Something was wrong. They should have either responded or pulled around by now. She opened the phone finder app where she had Jett's phone logged, activated the finder, and started following the beacon on the app. It took her halfway down the sidewalk to an alley. She heard voices in the alley. She stopped to listen.

"Sorry, little girl. Blame your dad. We're gonna put a bullet in your head and make him watch. People here are gonna learn not to mess with us ever again. We're not monsters though; we'll make it quick."

Ashley ducked behind the wall and pulled out her sidearm. Her heart was pounding, and her breathing was out of control. Suddenly she was soaked with sweat, and her hands shook as adrenaline and terror had its way with her body and mind. She peeked back into the alley. Three men, each with guns. One was aiming a gun at Jett's forehead. The other stood behind her dad with a gun in the small of his back. The third did the talking. In her mind she calculated all the moves, as if it were a game of chess, to determine who would live and who would die when she acted. She thought through several scenarios. She only had one chance to get it right and all three of their lives depended on her making the right decision.

“Okay. Leave the kid out of this,” Markus Jackson sounded scared now. He wasn’t used to feeling vulnerable, but this was his daughter they were talking about. “Do what you want to me, but let her go. She’s just a kid.” He heard a slight buzz from Jett’s backpack. Ashley was using her phone finder to find Jett. The frequency of the buzzing meant Ashely was within a few feet of them, likely hiding, trying to figure out what to do.

“Sorry man. Girl’s dying tonight. Imagine if we killed you and took her, what she would go through. It’s better this way.”

“Dad? I don’t want to die.” Jett was crying now.

“You’re not going to die, kid.” To the guy with the gun to her head, he said, “Could you take the gun off her head for a moment? So, we can work this out?” This was a message to Ashley. He was trying to tell her that if she could do something to get the gun off Jett’s forehead, he could get a shot off and take the guy out. Ashley would have a chance to get the other two guys. He didn’t see a way out of this for himself. He swallowed hard and gave Jett a hard look. She looked back; her eyes huge, even more scared.

“Don’t take the gun off that girl’s head,” the other man said. “As soon as you do, he’ll blow your brains out.”

“You kill her, I kill your friend here. There’s no way around it.”

“Yea? Then the guy behind you takes your ass out. You both die.”

Markus looked at his daughter with grief in his eyes. This was their goodbye. Jett saw it and started shaking.

"No, dad. No. No. No."

"Jett, I love you, kid, but you know that. Always have. I hope I did right preparing you for this world because it's your time now. I'm sorry I won't be here for Nationals. But you will. When you hear shots, drop to the ground, cover your head with your arms, and don't come up until it's quiet, okay?"

Tears streamed down Jett's cheeks. A single tear rolled down her dad's cheek. An overwhelming sense of despair enveloped her. This was the only time she'd ever seen her dad cry. "No, Please?" Jett begged her dad.

He looked back at her and winked. "Screw these racist assholes, right, kid?"

"I hate to interrupt your little Lifetime Movie moment here, but... What the hell you talkin' bout? You can't save her. If you shoot him, then I shoot her. Then my brother shoots you. What do you think is gonna happen?" the third Biker said.

Markus Jackson sighed in resignation and said, in a loud voice, "You're right. It would be great if there was another person with a gun who could create a distraction, but, you know, it's just us..."

Ashley was still shaking with terror as she stood behind the wall. Her heart was broken. Markus knew he wasn't going to make it. She couldn't see a way for her to make it. But she could save Jett. She pumped herself up by telling herself they were messing with her cub and they were about to meet one pissed off mama bear. "Not today, motherfuckers," she whispered. Her terror started turning into rage.

She waited for a signal and when she heard Markus say it would be great if someone else had a gun she took a deep breath, reminded herself where everyone was, chambered a round, and …

Jett heard the click first. This caused the man with the gun to her head to aim in the direction of the click. Her dad took the shot. Jett dropped to the ground and covered her head. She heard another shot from beside her. Continuous shots blasted from behind and in front of her. She heard Ashley yelling in pain amidst the continuous gunfire.

Jett closed her eyes tight and tried to tell herself that when she opened them her dad and Ashley would be okay, and they'd be together and would go home to watch Star Wars as a family. She imagined herself cuddled up with Ashley under a blanket, dozing off, like when she was a girl, trying to get through a Disney movie together. But all she heard were gunshots and Ashley screaming in pain and fury as she fired. She heard nothing from her dad.

Ashley aimed at the man with the gun on Markus. The man holding the gun to Jett's head pointed it at her when she emerged from behind the wall. Markus Jackson took him out first. She pulled the trigger as the man behind Markus opened fire. Markus dropped, dead, as the man she shot dropped. The third man started firing at Ashley, grazing her rib cage and hitting her left shoulder. He tried to aim at Jett, but Ashley kept firing as she approached, howling in a violent rage; using anger to block the pain. He shot Ashley multiple times, but she wouldn't go down. She should have been dead, but she kept relentlessly firing at the man. Her focus on saving Jett never wavered, no matter how much fire she took. She was fueled by pure ferocity now.

She shot the man several times. He succumbed to multiple gunshot wounds and collapsed but not before getting one last shot off, hitting Ashley in her left thigh. Ashley dropped to her knees but held herself up and continued pulling the trigger until all she heard were clicks. When she out of ammunition, she collapsed in a heap of blood and agony.

It was eerie and quiet. Jett uncovered her head and looked around. First, she saw her dad lying lifeless to her left. For a moment she forgot to breathe. Tears blurred her vision and soaked her cheeks as she shrieked in anguish. When she looked behind her, she saw Ashley lying on the ground in a pool of blood. Ashley was still breathing.

"Ashley!!!" Jett wailed. The third biker had shot Ashley several times, but the worst wound was on her left thigh. It looked like the bullet hit an artery. Jett sucked up her grief and went about saving her. She ripped off her shirt and put it over Ashley's wound and put pressure on it, but she couldn't stop the bleeding. Ashley was slipping away. Jett looked around to find something she could use for a tourniquet. She grabbed the scarf from her hair and grabbed Ashley's gun. After releasing the empty magazine, she wrapped the scarf around Ashley's upper thigh and used the gun as a lever to pull it tight enough to cut off circulation to her leg. Jett maneuvered herself behind Ashley, so she could prop her up, to prevent her from asphyxiating, while wrapping her arms around Ashley's waist to hang on to the tourniquet. She yelled desperately for help.

Joey and a couple of guys entered the alley and saw the carnage.

"Oh shit!" Joey said. "No!! Not him. Not him!"

"Shit Joey, the kid! Garcia!" Vinnie yelled, running towards Jett.

Joey rushed to Jett's side. "Oh, kid. I'm sorry kid. I'm so sorry. We got help coming. They're on the way. Did you get hit? No? She's gonna be just fine kid. She's gonna be fine. Vinnie, go get the boys out here to look out." Joey didn't know what to say to comfort Jett, who was still holding Ashley from behind, supporting her head on her shoulder, with her arms wrapped around her waist, desperately holding the tourniquet in place and sobbing uncontrollably.

***

Frankie was at that bar on the South Side of town. He was putting down one rum and coke after another, but he couldn't get drunk fast enough. The bar was empty as everyone was preoccupied with the big news. Frankie didn't care anymore. He sold his soul tonight.

He never liked Markus Jackson or Ashley Garcia. They were always meddling in shit he was trying to cover up. If he was the villain, and he was a villain, they were the good guys. He didn't like them. But he respected them. They didn't deserve this. And the kid. He hated himself for what this would do to her. She's just a kid. For a moment Frankie thought he'd hunt those assholes down and make them pay for hurting the kid. Not for Markus Jackson or Ashley Garcia, but for the kid. A job's a job though, he kept telling himself, but it wasn't working. His stomach was burning and his head ached. He lit another cigarette and asked for another drink. His phone rang, and against his better judgment, he answered.

"It's done. We made our point. Cost us all three guys though," the voice on the other end said.

"I have no idea what that means," Frankie responded. He knew.

"You know what it means Frankie. They took Jackson out. Not before he took one of their guys out. But he won't be a problem for us anymore. That Mexican bitch put up a hell of a fight, but she got shot up really bad. She fought like a fucking demon, got shot up from the start but kept shooting until she took the other two guys out. She's in surgery right now. Not sure if she's gonna make it. She's almost dead."

"Afro-Cuban."

"What?"

"She's not Mexican, she's Afro-Cuban. Get your shit right."

"Whatever, Frankie."

Frankie took a deep breath, took a drag from his cigarette. "What about the kid?"

"The kid? I don't know how, but somehow, she survived. The plan was to kill her and make the other two watch. They killed Markus, damn near killed Garcia, got all three of themselves killed and the kid survived without a scratch. Not even sure how. Don't matter. We made our point."

Frankie hung up the phone, downed his entire drink in one gulp, and smiled to himself as he contemplated the significance of the kid. *That kid's a survivor. There's something special about her. I could always tell. Good kid, but she'd been through a lot. She's smart, and she can fight, with all her kung fu shit. And she's Jackson's kid. He's a clever guy, and the kid is smarter than he was. I don't think they realized what they just did. That kid is gonna go off and they're not gonna be able to stop her. They just lit a short fuse to a big ass bomb. And I'm gonna have a front-row seat to the show.*

Frankie sat back, took a deep drag of his cigarette, and said out loud, "I hope she gets every one of those motherfuckers."

Epilogue: The Fuse

One Year Later

Jett went to the coffee shop every Tuesday. She sipped her latte with no enthusiasm. At night, she didn't sleep. She didn't eat much. She didn't care anymore.

Everything changed. Diana became Jett's guardian after her parents died. Michael Krayton Sr. was the Regional Director of a five-county region. Diana was on The Regional Board that managed the region. This felt like a betrayal, but everyone has secrets.

Melinda was still at Baylor. Traveling through rural areas was dangerous now, because human trafficking had exploded, and no government entity would do anything about it. Gang leaders were warlords and the Sheriffs, who were now appointed by the Regional Directors, either played along or looked the other way. Melinda's parents had urged her to stay in Waco and found a family to host her when school was out.

Her aunt Lydia couldn't visit because there was a prohibition on anyone entering or leaving the New Republic. Diana called her often, but she didn't answer. She left messages telling Jett that one day everything would be okay. But for Jett, nothing would ever be okay again.

She relived the events of that night in her head all the time. She blamed herself. With her martial arts training, her intellect, and her special ability, she still couldn't save her parents. Maybe if she used her special skill, she could have stopped the bad guys from shooting. Instead, she froze, cried, and waited for everything to go wrong. What good was it? What good was any of it if she couldn't use it when she needed it the most? She thought of these things often.

That night haunted her. The look in her dad's eyes. The sound of Ashley yelling as she was repeatedly shot. Her final goodbye to Ashley in the hospital. After it was all over, she shut everyone out. She wanted to be alone. But she still went to the coffee shop in downtown Port City every Tuesday because it reminded her of her dad. It was his favorite coffee shop.

But now Jett sat in that coffee shop staring at a half-empty cup of latte. Life seemed meaningless and empty. She wasn't sure if it was worth it anymore.

The tables inside were full, but there were two tables outside. At the counter, Jett saw two men wearing biker jackets with patches and tattoos on their wrists. They were with two women and three kids. Jett's heart sped up, but she looked at her cup and tried to ignore them.

"I can't find where to sit," one of the women said. "Y'all want to go outside?"

"It's too damn cold outside," one of the guys said. Jett saw 'Team Lead' on the front of his jacket.

"We'll sit here," the other guy said, standing over Jett's table. Jett looked up at two very large men; white supremacists with Texas Republic patches who signified their gang affiliation on their jackets. They were part of a very dangerous Neo-Nazi gang. The same gang who killed her parents. They operated on pure intimidation. Jett looked down at her latte again.

"That girl is sitting there already. Can you get her to move so we can sit?" one of the women said.

"She'll move," the Team Leader stared at Jett. She still hadn't looked up from her coffee. Jett felt the anger building up inside of her.

The other guy chuckled and said, "Hey you, stupid bitch. Get out. We want this table. You sit outside."

"I'm already sitting here."

"Well, you can already leave. Get up."

"No," Jett was calm. "I'm not moving. I'll leave when I'm finished. You sit outside."

"My kids have ice cream. You want them to sit outside and get cold eating ice cream?"

"At least it won't melt."

"You're a smartass? You know who we are?"

"I don't care who you are. I'm trying to drink my coffee." The anger was rising to the surface. She felt her face getting hot.

"Look, you're lucky I don't drag your ass back to the hood. Get out. We're taking this table," Team Leader said.

Jett looked up at the man. The anger was spilling over and she was becoming defiant. She felt a fire burning inside of her. She recalled a memory of her dad when she was just a girl, and a talk they had about bullies. It seemed like something from another lifetime.

"Screw you, you racist asshole," she said.

The room was getting quiet as people were paying attention to the confrontation. A large man, wearing a cowboy hat, approached, intending to resolve the situation. "Look, sir," he said to the Team Leader in a thick, calm drawl, "we're leaving. You can have our table."

"We want this table," Team Leader said, staring at Jett.

"I'm not moving." Jett took a sip of her coffee.

"All I'm saying is, no one wants any trouble and we're leaving, anyway. Come on now, just take our table. Besides, she's just a kid. Give her a break."

"Oh yea," he said, "I know this kid. Her parents killed three of our guys. And you, Bubba, mind your own business." He pulled his vest open to reveal a large knife.

The woman who had been sitting with the Cowboy walked up, took his arm, and said, "Come on honey, let's just go."

The Cowboy looked at Jett and said, "I'm sorry."

"It's okay," Jett said, "but thank you."

"Get your ass up and leave, NOW!" Team Leader raised his voice, shaking in anger.

Jett took a deep breath. "I'm not scared of you."

"What are you talking about?"

"I'm not scared of you. You're stupid and weak. You thrive on fear. I'm not scared of you."

"You will be when I'm finished with you." He was getting louder.

"You're already out of control, just because I'm not scared of you. You're not for me to fear."

"I bet your parents would disagree." He was trying to rattle Jett.

"I know what happened to my parents. I was there. You should be scared of me."

"Shut up and get out of here."

"I'm not scared of you," Jett looked at him without flinching.

"GET OUT OF HERE!"

"I'm not scared of you."

"Ok. That's it. I didn't want to do this, but I'm gonna drag your ass out of here myself."

"I'm not scared of you."

Team Leader grabbed Jett's arm and pulled her to her feet. Jett stood up as he pulled her, which put him off balance. He stepped close to her. "I'm going to enjoy beating your ass."

There was tension in the room as everyone feared what they were about to do to Jett. These guys were vicious, and the sheriff didn't intervene.

Jett looked him in the eyes. "You have until the count of three to let go of my arm."

"Or what?" The other man moved to the right side of Jett, a few feet away.

Jett looked at the second guy out of the corner of her eye and said, "One," as she unleashed a kick straight to the second guy's head, busting his lip and knocking a tooth loose. Jett threw a hard punch to the throat of Team Leader. He let go of her arm and fell to the ground, clutching his throat and trying to breathe. She punched the other guy hard in the mouth, where she had just kicked him. She followed this with a kick to the groin, doubling the man over, and slinging him to the ground next to his friend. The first man tried to get up and Jett kicked him, hard, in the face.

Jett then yelled at the men:

"I told you I wasn't leaving until I was finished. But you always keep pushing. You killed my parents. But you're not going to mess with me. Not today, not ever. I'm not going to leave for you. I'm not getting up for you. I'm not doing anything for you. And one day everyone is going to rise up, and there are more of us than there are of you, and we are going to kick your asses out of our city. Remember my name: I am Jett fucking Landry and I will never take your shit again! Do you fucking understand me?"

Jett stared at the men with an intensity and power she had never felt before. She took a deep breath before turning around and looking at the rest of the people in the coffee shop.

She regarded the faces of the shocked patrons and baristas. They were people, like her, who were tired of being pushed around and intimidated.

She walked to the counter, pulled a twenty-dollar bill out of her pocket, dropped it in the tip jar, and said, “Sorry for the mess.”

The shocked silence gave way to applause and cheers as she walked out the door and hurried down the sidewalk.

The fire inside of her blazed out of control and The Fuse was lit.

The Beginning.

Made in the USA
Coppell, TX
03 August 2024

35541219R00215